I0765591

The Unbroken

David Lee Corley

Copyright © 2025 David Lee Corley
All rights reserved.

Table of Contents

Quote

"Some must fight the darkness so others may live in the light."

\- Anonymous

Occam's Razor

The convoy rolled through Baghdad's dark streets. Frank rode shotgun in the lead Humvee, eyes scanning rooftops, doorways, windows. The night vision goggles painted everything in greenish shades and eerie flares of bright lights.

Sorenson drove, young hands gripping the wheel too tight. "Quiet night, Sarge."

Frank said nothing. Quiet was never good. Quiet hid things.

"My girl sent another letter," Sorenson said. "Says she's already picking out bridesmaid dresses. Guess my goose is cooked the second I step off the plane. " He laughed, the sound hollow against the armored walls.

Frank grunted, eyes never leaving the street. Focus absolute. Movement in the third-floor window. Just a curtain. Nothing.

The intersection loomed ahead. The convoy slowed. Protocol demanded they check for IEDs. Frank raised his fist, signaling halt. The radio crackled with confirmation.

"Holding at Checkpoint Delta," Schooler called from the trailing vehicle.

Then movement. A teenage girl stepped into the road. Black abaya covering everything but her eyes. In her arms, she cradled something wrapped in pale cloth, holding it close against her chest.

"Stop," Frank ordered. He opened his door, using it as a shield. His rifle found its way to his shoulder without conscious thought.

"Miss! Stand where you are!" Sorenson called through the loudspeaker.

The girl kept coming. Her eyes showed no fear, only purpose.

"Something ain't right," muttered Jenkins from the backseat. "She shouldn't be out after curfew."

Frank saw it then—the wire trailing from beneath her garment. The slight bulge at her waist. The wrongness of her approach.

"Back up," he barked at Sorenson. "Now."

"I can't. Petersen's Humvee is right behind me and the street's too narrow."

"Then go around her," said Frank.

Sorenson cranked the wheel and pressed the accelerator. Frank climbed back in and closed the door. The Humvee lurched with impatience, rolling forward. Then, the breeze kicked up and Sorenson and Frank saw it – the pale cloth fluttered revealing an American mortar shell underneath.

"Oh, shit," said Sorenson.

"Keep going," said Frank as he opened the door once again and took aim with his rifle.

"Don't kill her, Sarge. She's just a kid," said Sorenson.

His finger on the trigger, Frank hesitated.

As they drove past her, Frank saw her eyes. Young. Determined. Empty of hatred, full of something worse. Resignation.

Too late.

The explosion tore through the night. A bright flash that burned away darkness. The Humvee lifted, flipped, tumbled. Metal screamed. Glass shattered. The concussive force hit Frank like a giant's hammer, driving broken fragments from the door panel into his face and neck. Something hot sliced through his throat. His left arm caught by the door snapped as the vehicle rolled, pinning him against twisted metal.

The world spun. Sky. Road. Sky. Road. Until it settled with a final crunch of metal.

Frank came back to consciousness upside down. Blood ran into his eyes from a gash in his throat. His forehead burned where shrapnel had torn the flesh to the bone. Something sharp pinned his left arm to the vehicle's frame. The smell of fuel and burning rubber filled his lungs.

"Sorenson," he called. His voice emerged as a rasp in the smoke-filled cabin.

No answer.

Frank turned his head. Sorenson hung limp in his harness, neck bent at an angle no living person could achieve. Eyes open but seeing nothing. A piece of the windshield had peeled away in the blast, slicing through his chest. Jenkins lay crumpled in the back, half his skull missing.

Behind them, the second Humvee had stopped. Soldiers poured out, rushing toward the wreckage, some forming defensive positions. Frank heard them shouting but couldn't make out words. His ears rang from the blast.

"Jesus Christ," someone yelled, face appearing in the shattered window. "Sarge is still alive! Get the medic!"

Frank felt hands pulling at him, metal shrieking as they cut through the frame to free his arm. Blood poured from wounds he couldn't even feel yet. His skin burned where it had been flayed open by glass and superheated metal.

"Stay with us, Sarge," a voice urged. "Medevac's coming."

Frank's eyes found the road where the girl had stood. Nothing remained. Not even pieces. Just a blackened crater in the middle of the street.

He looked back at Sorenson's lifeless face. Twenty-two years old. From Minnesota. A future now erased.

Because Frank had hesitated. Because he'd seen a child instead of a weapon. Because he'd ordered Sorenson to try driving around the threat instead of eliminating it. Because he'd let his humanity override his training.

As darkness closed around him, Frank made a silent promise to the dead men. Never again. No hesitation. No mercy. No weakness. The world was filled with evil, and he'd treat it accordingly.

The darkness took him then, carried him away from Baghdad's broken streets. But the lesson remained, etched into his soul as permanently as the scars would be etched into his flesh.

Frank woke with a gasp, skin slick with sweat despite the lighthouse's chill. Wind howled around the stone tower, finding every crack, every seam.

The cat raised its head from the foot of the narrow cot, yellow eyes narrowed with feline contempt. It yawned, showing teeth and pink tongue. Then it turned away, it's ass pointed toward Frank's face, tail twitching with clear disapproval.

Frank sat up, feet finding the cold floor. His watch showed 3:17 AM. He couldn't remember when he'd fallen asleep. Couldn't remember the last time he'd slept without his past visiting him.

The cat stretched, claws extending into the thin blanket. It jumped to the floor and padded to the door, waiting expectantly.

Frank rose and moved to the window, pulled back the curtain. Outside, the ocean heaved, black waves tipped with white, breaking against the rocks below. The beam from the lighthouse swept across the water in steady rhythm, pushing back the darkness for moments at a time.

The cat meowed, impatient. Unconcerned with human matters like dreams or conscience or oceans churning in eternal disquiet.

Frank let the curtain fall. He reached for his boots, pulled them on with mechanical precision. No sense trying for more sleep. The ghosts were awake now, restless, demanding.

The cat meowed again, louder this time. Demanding.

"Fuck off," Frank growled.

The cat ignored him. Its tail twitched faster, yellow eyes fixed on the door that led outside, to a world where breakfast might be found if the useless human would just open it.

Frank reached for the lantern on the small table. Dawn was still hours away. He'd use the time to continue the restoration. Stone and mortar waited. The sea would still be there.

And the ghosts would still whisper, no matter how many stones he laid between himself and memory.

The Mexican American Border

Darkness concealed the desert's truth, a blackness deeper than the absence of light where human desperation and righteous anger waited to collide.

The blowtorch burned blue against the steel wall. Sparks cascaded down into the dirt where they hissed and died. The man worked methodically, his welding mask reflecting the harsh glow of his torch. No insignia. No markings. Just black clothes and purpose.

The cut formed a rough doorway through the newly built border wall. Five feet high. Three feet wide. The barrier that had stood as both symbol and division yielded to heat and pressure.

The steel plate fell inward with a hollow sound that echoed across the empty desert. Dust rose and settled in the beam of a single flashlight. A water bottle splashed the red-hot metal cooling it to the touch.

Silence stretched as eyes watched the horizon for any sign of border guard vehicles.

"Apúrate," the cutter whispered, the word carrying across the silent desert. Hurry.

Then movement. A hand appeared at the edge of the cut. Then another. A face peered through, eyes scanning the darkness beyond the wall. A man gestured behind him and stepped through the opening onto American soil.

A woman followed, pulling a child by the hand. Then more came through. They moved quickly but cautiously, helping each other through the jagged opening. No sounds beyond labored breathing and the occasional scrape of fabric against steel. Their footprints formed a chaotic pattern in the dust of a new country. The last was an old man who stumbled and fell to his knees in the dirt of a new country. The immigrants gathered in a tight cluster, whispering about which direction to head. Their water bottles clinked together. A baby whimpered and was quickly hushed.

A drone approached silently, rotors barely disturbing the night air. Its infrared camera captured heat signatures gathered near the wall, huddled masses waiting in the darkness for orders of where and when to go.

Miles away, a technician sat upright in his chair. His eyes fixed on the monitor where thermal images bloomed like strange flowers.

"Sir. Sector seven breach in progress."

The watch commander leaned over the console, coffee breath mixing with the recycled air. The screen showed red-orange figures pouring through a gap in the wall's otherwise unbroken line.

"How many?"

"Twenty-three. No, twenty-five. Our guys need to get to them before they scatter."

The immigrants gathered in a tight circle. A young mother clutched her son against her leg. The old man wiped sweat from his forehead despite the night chill. Their whispers in Spanish created a soft hum beneath the desert wind. Their water bottles sloshed.

Movement stirred the darkness beyond the mesquite. Shadows separated from shadow. The immigrants fell silent.

Armed figures emerged from three directions, boots crunching on hard-packed earth. AR-15 rifle barrels caught the moonlight. Crooked American flag patches adorned camouflage vests. Others had American flag bandanas tied around their necks or arms. Well-armed, self-appointed amateurs.

"No muevas," a bearded man called out, his voice flat and hard as the desert floor.

"On the ground," a man with a hunter's cap called. "Face down. Hands where we can see them."

Flashlight beams caught the immigrants in harsh white glare. The immigrants looked to each other in confusion and fear. One of the younger immigrants broke from the group, desperate flight triggering in his mind. He made it eight steps before being tackled from behind. His body hit dirt. Grunts of pain. A plastic zip-tie cinched tight around his wrists. Roughly pulled to his feet and shoved back toward the group.

The bearded man stepped forward, rifle held across his chest. "This is American soil," he said in broken Spanish, voice carrying in the desert night. "You have no right to be here. Now get on the goddamned ground before I shoot one of you as an example."

Slowly, the entire group lowered themselves to the ground. Milita men moved in with their plastic ties, securing each immigrant's hands behind their backs.

In the border command center the watch commander and the technician studied the drone video feed. "Who the hell are they?" the technician asked, fingers hovering over the keyboard.

"Homegrown militia," the watch commander said, reaching for his radio. He pressed the transmit button. "All units in sector seven. Code three response to mile marker eighty-three. Multiple civilians intervening in border crossing. Possible armed encounter."

He watched the screen a moment longer, the clustered heat signatures pulsing with tension.

"Get me another drone," he ordered. "And call Tucson for backup."

Half a mile away from the intrusion on the ridgeline, three figures lay prone against the rocks, their jackets displaying logos for "Helix Behavioral Analytics." Their equipment hummed softly—long-range, parabolic microphone, thermal imaging camera with a telephoto lens, biometric monitors, satellite uplink. Olivia Chen, the team leader, adjusted a dial, fine-tuning the audio feed.

The sound of engines grew louder from the eastern approach road. Headlights swept across the desert floor—three pickup trucks, two passenger vans, and a flatbed loaded with workers. They formed a wide circle around the armed militiamen and the prone immigrants.

Doors slammed in quick succession. More than thirty figures emerged. Workers in dirt-stained clothes. Men with callused hands and sun-darkened faces. Among them, three stood apart: a man in a button-up shirt with rolled sleeves who carried a clipboard, a woman in work boots and a flannel shirt, and a younger man with a worn baseball cap.

Several of the new arrivals carried shotguns or hunting rifles, keeping them pointed at the ground. Others gripped lengths of pipe or baseball bats, shifting their weight from foot to foot.

The woman stepped forward, her voice clear in the desert air. "Let these people go. They're here to work, not to cause trouble."

The bearded militia leader laughed. "They're here illegally. Breaking our laws. We're taking them in."

"To whom? You're not Border Patrol." The woman gestured to her companions. "We've got 3,000 acres of crops that need harvesting. These people have jobs waiting."

The man with the clipboard stepped forward. "I've got contracts for every one of them. Legal work permits pending."

"Pending isn't approved," the militia leader countered. "And we all know those permits are rubber-stamped anyway."

One of the workers from the flatbed called out in accented English. "We paid to come here. Paid good money for jobs."

"You paid smugglers," a militia member said. "Criminals."

The clipboard man took another step toward the militia. "My tomatoes are rotting on the vine. My lettuce is wilting in the field. I've got contracts to fulfill."

"Then hire Americans," the militia leader said.

Several of the farmers laughed bitterly.

"I advertised for six weeks," the clipboard man said. "Offered twelve dollars an hour. Nobody showed. Nobody."

"Your profits aren't our problem," the militia leader said. "These people undercut every real worker in this country. Drive down wages. Take benefits."

The young man in the baseball cap stepped forward. His hands were empty, but tension radiated from his stance. "These workers deserve protection just like anyone else. Fair wages. Safe conditions. Instead, they get exploited because they're afraid to speak up."

Some of the immigrants had slowly raised their heads to watch the confrontation swirling around them.

"These people are criminals," the militia leader insisted. "And we're making a citizen's arrest."

"You're not the law," the farmer woman said, her hand tightening on her shotgun. "And you're outnumbered."

The militia members shifted, spreading out, fingers moving toward triggers.

The baseball cap man moved closer. "Back away from them. Now."

"Or what?" The bearded militia leader stepped directly into his face.

The first shove came suddenly. The baseball cap man stumbled back. Someone grabbed a rifle barrel and pushed it skyward. A shotgun discharged into the air.

Chaos erupted. The farmers and workers surged forward. The militia members formed a tight circle. The immigrants scattered, some crawling away from the confrontation, others running for the darkness beyond the vehicles.

Fists connected with jaws. A pipe clanged against a truck door. The bearded leader and the clipboard man grappled and fell into the dust. A worker swung a bat that connected with a militia member's shoulder, drawing a loud crack and a howl of pain.

Two militia members cornered three workers against a truck. A shotgun blast shattered a headlight. The immigrants who hadn't escaped huddled together behind a pickup, a human knot of fear.

A worker with a pipe rushed a militia member who raised his rifle defensively. The pipe connected with the rifle, sending it flying. The militia member drew a handgun from his waistband.

Three shots in rapid succession.

The worker with the pipe stood still for a moment, looking down at his chest in confusion. Then he crumpled to the ground.

Time stopped. Sound vanished from the desert. Every face turned toward the fallen man. Everybody froze mid-motion as if the air had solidified.

The militia member who fired stood wide-eyed, his finger still on the trigger, surprised by his own action.

For five long seconds, no one moved. Men on both sides backed away from each other. Workers dropped their makeshift weapons. Militia members lowered their rifles. Some crouched instinctively, making themselves smaller targets. Others raised their hands, palms out, as if to say this had gone too far.

The woman farmer's face drained of color. The clipboard man stared at the fallen worker.

In that suspended moment, the choice hung in the air. Walk away. End it now.

Then someone knelt beside the fallen worker. Touched his neck. Looked up with eyes full of grief transformed to rage.

"He killed Miguel!"

The words broke the spell. A worker who had been backing away suddenly charged forward with a scream that held no words, only animal fury. Others followed, fear now burned away by something hotter and more dangerous.

The violence that followed was no longer a fight but a frenzy. Gunshots punctuated the night. Bodies collided with blind rage. Blood darkened the desert sand.

Lights swept across the chaos. Border Patrol vehicles approached from the south, sirens wailing. A dozen agents emerged with weapons drawn and face shields lowered.

"Federal agents! Stand down immediately!"

Few heard over the roar of combat. Fewer listened.

The lead agent fired a warning shot. The sound echoed off the wall.

"Stand down! Everyone on the ground now!"

But it was too late. The conflict had ignited fully. Two agents waded into the mass and were immediately swallowed by the violence. Another was struck by a thrown rock and fell to one knee.

"Call for backup!" an agent shouted before disappearing under a tangle of bodies.

Someone grabbed a fallen agent's weapon. More shots followed.

The immigrants who'd hidden tried to flee again. A truck engine roared to life, its driver attempting to escape. It collided with a Border Patrol vehicle.

On the ridge, equipment hummed softly in the darkness. Recording. Documenting. Olivia's fingers moved across dials with practiced precision, never hurried, never still. Her colleagues remained silent, one tracking movement through high-powered optics, the other monitoring biometric screens filled with scrolling numbers and pulsing waveforms.

They made no gestures of shock when the first shots rang out. No expressions of horror as bodies fell. The violence spreading below registered only as subtle adjustments to their equipment. As sirens wailed in the distance and the chaos intensified, they continued their work with the calm of those who have seen such things before. Perhaps expected them. Olivia checked her watch, made a single notation in a leather-bound journal.

In the valley below, America tore at itself under the cold desert stars, each side believing absolutely in the righteousness of their cause, none of them seeing how perfectly they fulfilled someone else's purpose.

Georgetown, Washington D.C.

The brownstone had stood since the Civil War, though few knew what happened inside now. A desk of dark oak occupied the center, stacked with intelligence reports and analysis papers. Nothing digital where it mattered.

Sitting behind the desk, Culper tapped the television remote. Stations cycled past. Each showing variations of the same scene. Protesters with signs. Police standing in loose lines. Faces shouting across the divide.

He settled on the national broadcast. The anchor wore a pressed blue suit. Hair perfectly arranged. Voice carrying practiced concern.

"Demonstrations continue in Atlanta following yesterday's controversial city council vote. Police maintain distance from protesters gathered outside city hall."

The screen showed crowds behind metal barriers. Signs waving. Nothing burning yet. Just anger building.

"School board meetings in Fairfax County ended in shouting matches for the third consecutive week. Parents divided over curriculum reviews. Officials called recess after threats were exchanged."

Culper wrote in his leather notebook. Recording each incident without comment. Raw data without conclusions.

"Michigan factory workers enter second week of strikes as automation negotiations stall. Union representatives describe atmosphere as 'increasingly hostile' after company security doubled at plant entrances."

"Endless feedback loop," Culper muttered to the empty room.

"Economic analysts warn of market uncertainty if labor disputes spread to neighboring states. Supply delays already reported in automotive and electronics sectors."

His secure phone buzzed on the desk. He answered without looking.

"Are you watching the news?" Slattery asked.

"I am."

"The President is concerned about the tone. These demonstrations feel different from the usual protest cycles. The number of them. All over the nation. No regional focus."

Culper watched silently as the anchor described university campuses across three states with opposing student groups holding simultaneous rallies. Campus police establishing buffer zones between them.

"Something unusual in the frequency," Culper said.

"The President doesn't need theories. He needs assessment. Is this headed somewhere we should worry about?"

Culper made another note in his book. Question mark beside it.

"Any ideas?"

"Too early for conclusions," Culper said.

"That's not what he wants to hear. The President meets with social media executives tomorrow. They're reporting unprecedented surges in threatening content."

"I need more data."

"You've seen the intelligence briefs. Community level tensions spiking in unusual patterns. Not just the usual urban centers. Rural counties too. Everywhere simultaneously."

"Yeah. I see."

The television showed county election officials receiving angry phone calls after voting machine issues delayed primary results.

"I'm on it. I'll be in touch," Culper said and ended the call.

He unmuted the television. The anchor continued with practiced gravity.

"In Washington today lawmakers from both parties accused each other of inflammatory rhetoric following heated exchanges on the House floor. Capitol police increased presence after staff reported threatening messages."

Culper watched the footage of representatives shouting across the chamber. Nothing new in congressional discord. Yet something felt different. The intensity. The absolutism in each face.

"Consumer confidence numbers fell for the third straight month as ongoing disputes affect retail spending. Analysts point to widening urban-rural divides influencing buying patterns and brand loyalties."

He closed his notebook. Poured himself two fingers of bourbon. Drank it standing by the window looking out at a Washington evening still normal. Traffic flowing. People walking home from work.

The anchor's voice continued behind him.

"Social media companies report struggling with increased flagged content as users engage in divisive debates. Content moderators describe heightened tensions across multiple platforms."

Something in the pattern tugged at Culper's instincts. Not enough data yet. Just disconnected incidents. But the frequency felt wrong. The simultaneity across different regions.

He would watch. Wait. Gather what others missed in their distraction. That was his function. His purpose.

The anchor signed off as the broadcast switched to local coverage. Weather report. Sports scores. The ordinary rhythm of American life continuing despite the hairline fractures spreading beneath its surface.

New England Coastline

Frank stood in the lighthouse cupola, calloused hand running over the brass fittings he'd polished to a mirror finish. Three years of mortar and stone dust under his nails. Three years of climbing the spiral stairs each dawn and dusk. Three years of solitude broken only by the occasional whine of the feral cat that had claimed the place alongside him.

The massive beacon sat silent now, the ancient clockwork mechanism he'd rebuilt piece by piece awaiting removal. Tomorrow it would be replaced with cold electronics and computer chips that needed no winding, no oil, no human touch. Progress they called it.

Through the glass he watched a boat approach, cutting white across harbor swells. Four technicians in matching windbreakers, their aluminum cases catching sunlight. The automated system that would render him obsolete.

Frank descended the newly rebuilt stairs, each step solid beneath his weight. His own handiwork. The treads no longer creaked with rust and age. The mortar between stones fresh where he'd repaired century-old damage. He'd given the lighthouse another hundred years of life, only to be pushed aside by technology.

The keeper's quarters echoed with emptiness. His narrow cot gone, the hot plate where he'd boiled coffee each morning packed away. Just the footlocker and toolbox remained, sitting by the door like sentinels.

He knelt, unlocking the footlocker. The twin Ruger Super Redhawks nestled in custom-cut foam alongside the KA-BAR knife and derringer. He ran his fingers over each weapon, checking mechanisms from habit. Everything in order. Always in order.

The faded picture tucked in the lid caught his eye. His niece's school portrait sent six months ago. The handwritten note on the back: "Cookies still work. Thanks. Miss you, Gracie." He slipped it back beneath the foam padding.

Frank closed the lid, locked it. The footlocker held more than weapons. It held a path back to violence if needed.

Outside, the boat bumped against the dock. Voices carried across water. The technicians unloading equipment, already discussing measurements and voltage requirements.

Frank lifted the footlocker, its weight familiar against his scarred hands. The wooden toolbox his father had given him followed. Everything that mattered fit in two containers.

The technicians nodded as they passed on the weathered boards. Frank didn't nod back. Just stood aside, letting them claim what had been his sanctuary.

At the dock, he placed his belongings in the small boat he'd restored alongside the lighthouse. The wooden hull gleamed with fresh varnish, oars resting in polished oarlocks.

He turned, looking up at the white tower against pewter sky. The beacon that had drawn him here when he needed healing. The walls that had held his nightmares and let him rebuild more than mortar and stone.

The matted gray cat watched from behind a weathered piling, yellow eyes narrowed in permanent suspicion.

"You coming?"

The cat hissed, back arched in familiar distrust. Then without warning, it leapt into the boat, landing silently in the bow like it had been planning this departure all along.

Frank rowed with powerful strokes, each pull widening the distance between himself and the lighthouse. His massive frame made the boat sit low in the water. Salt spray caught in his five-day-old beard partially covering his mangled throat and face.

At the shore, the Imperial waited on its trailer, gleaming with new chrome and paint. His brother Richard's money had brought the metal beast back to life once again. The restoration too perfect, too pristine. It would draw attention. Frank frowned at the shine, knowing time and weather would dull it soon enough.

Pulling the trailer his old pickup, battered but reliable. The opposite of the Imperial's flashy presence.

He loaded the footlocker and toolbox in the truck bed. The feral cat jumped through the open window onto the passenger seat, claiming territory as it had done three years ago at the lighthouse. It didn't like Frank, but the wretched human did feed him. That was enough to continue the uneasy partnership.

Frank cranked the truck's ignition. The engine caught with a familiar rumble. The road ahead disappeared into stands of pine. Behind him stood the lighthouse, white against darkening sky, the technicians already at work installing the automatic system.

He didn't look back again. The headlights cut through gathering dusk as he drove away, leaving the light that had harbored him to its new, soulless keeper.

Arlington, Virginia

The Helix Behavioral Analytics headquarters dominated a glass-and-steel complex in Arlington's Ballston corridor. The lobby featured polished marble floors reflecting subdued lighting. Original artwork—abstracts worth more than most employees' annual salaries—adorned walls between curved displays showing data visualizations no visitor could understand.

In the main conference room, Marshall Reed, Helix's director of development, stood at the window, hands clasped behind his back. His posture betrayed his military past—straight spine, feet precisely shoulder-width apart.

Elaine Voss, Helix CEO, sat at the head of the polished table, reviewing data on her tablet. She wore her authority like a lab coat—practical, purposeful.

Olivia Chen fidgeted with her ID badge, her youth apparent next to the others. Her field gear still carried dust from the border.

Reed, still looking outward through the window, pontificated, "Key personalities. That's what we're looking for. Every conflict needs its catalyst—someone who strikes the match that burns it all down. It's never the masses who decide to erupt. It's the individual with enough anger and charisma to convert private rage into public violence. Find these personalities early enough, and you can predict where the fault lines will crack."

"Walk us through what happened, Olivia," Voss said without looking up.

"The militia arrived first," Olivia began. "Led by James Heller. Former Marine, dishonorably discharged after Afghanistan. Runs a contracting business that hires mostly veterans."

Reed turned from the window. "I recognize the type. Trained to respond to threats but no longer bound by rules of engagement."

"Exactly," Olivia continued. "When the immigrants approached the wall, he was already positioning his people in tactical formation."

Voss swiped through images on the screen. "The immigrants?"

"Mostly agricultural workers. Their leader was Eduardo Méndez. Father of four. Two previous attempts to cross."

"And the activists?" Reed asked.

"Graduate students and local organizers. Led by Maria Delgado from Berkeley. She's writing her dissertation on border politics."

Reed nodded. "Perfect storm of opposing ideologies."

"Show us the data," Voss directed.

Olivia projected biometric readings onto the wall screen. Human figures illuminated in colored outlines indicating emotional states. Pulse rates, blood pressure, cortisol levels scrolled beside each person.

"The micro-expressions tell us more than words," Olivia said. "Heller's jaw muscles tensed seventeen times before any confrontation began. His hand moved to his holster unconsciously whenever Delgado raised her voice."

Reed approached the screen. "Look at his positioning. Classic triangle formation—power stance. I've seen it in interrogations. He was preparing for conflict before it started."

"The immigrants' biometrics?" Voss asked.

"Elevated stress markers but consistent with their situation," Olivia replied. "Méndez showed protective behaviors toward the younger members."

Voss pointed to Delgado's image. "Her biometrics seem unusual."

"Yes," Olivia hesitated. "Her vocal patterns indicated outrage, but her body language showed preparedness. Almost like..."

"Like she was performing," Reed finished. "She wanted the confrontation."

"The border patrol's response time?" Voss asked.

"Twelve minutes," Olivia said. "Faster than average."

Reed's eyes narrowed. "Someone may have called them in advance. Look at their approach vector—they arrived from two directions simultaneously. That's not standard protocol for a spontaneous response."

"Three groups converging," Voss murmured. "Each believing they acted independently."

"The shot was fired ninety-seven seconds after Heller grabbed Delgado's arm," Olivia added. "Our thermal imaging captured the shooter's physiological changes—increased hand temperature, pupil dilation, respiratory shift."

Reed studied the data. "At the agency, we called this 'predictable chaos.' Groups with opposing ideologies placed in proximity will generate conflict along reliable patterns."

"Which Fulcrum predicted within a two-minute window," Voss said.

Olivia looked between them. "Isn't that what we want? To predict conflict before it happens?"

Voss stood, walking to the display. "Yes, but we're not there yet. We need more variables. Different environments."

"Urban settings," Reed suggested. "The Detroit auto plant presents ideal conditions—labor versus automation, economic insecurity, community tensions."

"Prepare a research team," she continued. "I want deployment within seventy-two hours."

"They'll be ready," Reed said.

Olivia gathered her notes. "I'll brief the field team."

After she left, Reed turned to Voss. "She doesn't understand what we're really building. The lives it can save."

"She doesn't need to." Voss closed her tablet. "Not yet."

Georgetown, Washington D.C.

Afternoon sunlight fell through the leaded windows of Culper's Georgetown office. Sitting at his desk with his feet up, Culper turned a page on a report, making a notation in the margin. The clock on the mantle ticked, its brass pendulum catching light. The phone rang once.

He let it ring twice more before answering. "Yes?"

"Richard Mercer. It's been a while."

Culper straightened. "Seven years. Tehran conference."

"Good memory."

"Did you expect otherwise?"

A slight pause. "No. I suppose not."

Culper waited, saying nothing more. The silence stretched between them, a technique he'd perfected decades ago.

Mercer broke first. "I need to meet. Today if possible."

"Problem at Homeland?"

"Not on the phone."

Culper studied the window, noting a cardinal that had landed on the sill. "The data's that sensitive?"

"It's not just data. It's patterns. Trends. Things that shouldn't connect but do."

The cardinal flew away. "Martin's. Six o'clock."

"Too public."

"You're being paranoid, Richard."

"Maybe." Another pause. "The canal. Near the old mill. Seven."

Culper considered this. Mercer had always been cautious, but this bordered on theatrical. Still, something in his voice carried genuine concern.

"Seven, then."

He hung up without waiting for a response. The office returned to silence save for the ticking clock.

Culper opened his desk drawer, removed a weathered leather notebook. Names filled its pages, connections mapped in his precise handwriting. He added Mercer's name, drawing a line to Homeland Security, then another to the word "patterns." Lastly, he added the date and time.

Whatever Mercer had found, it was significant enough to frighten a man who had spent thirty years analyzing threats. Culper closed the notebook, returned it to the drawer.

The clock continued its measured count of seconds. Culper returned to his reading, but his mind had already shifted to the coming meeting and what it might reveal.

The canal path stretched empty in both directions. Mist rose from the water, curling around the stone foundations of the old mill. Culper arrived early, as he always did, positioning himself against the wall where shadow met stone.

Richard Mercer approached from the east, his government-issue trench coat buttoned despite the mild evening. His eyes scanned the surroundings with the practiced efficiency of a career intelligence officer.

"You weren't followed," Culper said.

Mercer flinched. "Jesus. I didn't see you there."

"That was the point."

Mercer joined him in the shadows. His face had aged since Tehran. New lines around his eyes. Hair gone fully gray.

"This better be worth the melodrama, Richard."

Mercer glanced over his shoulder. "I discovered something at Homeland. Something that doesn't make sense."

"Elaborate."

"We've been tracking civil disturbances across the country. The data shows a forty-seven percent increase in violent confrontations over the last six months."

Culper shrugged. "Election year."

"No." Mercer shook his head. "This isn't following any normal pattern. Red states, blue states, urban centers, rural communities—the uptick is everywhere."

"Economic factors?"

"We considered that. Unemployment's stable. Markets are up. No significant policy changes that would trigger this kind of response."

A jogger passed on the opposite bank. Mercer fell silent until the footsteps faded.

"The violence is spreading across all demographic groups," he continued. "Border incidents, factory walkouts, university protests, suburban conflicts—none of it aligns with traditional social tension models."

Culper studied the water. "What's Homeland's assessment?"

"That's the problem. There isn't one. Leadership keeps shifting analysts away from the data before anyone can establish a comprehensive view."

"Bureaucratic blindness."

"Or something worse." Mercer pulled a thumb drive from his pocket. "Three months of raw incident reports.

I compiled them myself before they could be buried in separate classification systems."

Culper took the drive, pocketing it without looking down.

"The geographical distribution defies every model we've developed since 9/11," Mercer said. "It's like someone scattered matches across a drought-stricken forest."

"And you suspect?"

"I don't know what to suspect. That's why I'm here."

The wind shifted. Culper caught the scent of the river, of ancient stone.

"What does your director make of this pattern?"

Mercer's laugh held no humor. "I haven't shared it. Not officially."

"Why not?"

"Because two days after I began compiling the data, my security clearance was audited. My home computer was remotely accessed. Someone intercepted a personal email to my daughter."

"You're being surveilled."

"By someone with reach inside our systems." Mercer's voice dropped lower. "I've spent my life analyzing threats, Culper. This isn't random noise. Something's happening."

Culper studied his old colleague. The tremor in his left hand. The darting eyes. But also the analytical mind that had never failed in thirty years of intelligence work.

"These conflicts—what's the common element?" Culper asked.

"That's what's strangest. There isn't one. It's almost as if the violence itself is the point, not the underlying causes."

A boat passed on the canal. Its wake lapped against stone foundations.

"I'll look into it," Culper said.

"I should go." Mercer straightened his coat.

"I'll be in touch."

Mercer nodded once, then walked away along the canal path, his posture slightly straighter than when he'd arrived. The burden shared, if not lifted.

Culper remained in the shadows, turning the thumb drive over in his pocket. It had been months since he'd felt the familiar tension at the base of his skull—the sensation that always preceded something significant.

The mist continued to rise from the canal, obscuring the places where light met darkness.

Midnight crawled through Culper's Georgetown apartment. No lights except the desk lamp illuminating stacks of paper. The thumb drive's contents printed and spread across the hardwood surface in an ordered tangle.

Culper hadn't moved in hours. His tie hung loose around his neck. Coffee gone cold in a mug bearing no institutional logo. He preferred anonymity even in his kitchenware.

The data told a disjointed story. Police reports from twelve states. Security assessments from seven federal agencies. Media coverage cross-referenced with emergency service deployments. None should have connected.

Yet they did.

Culper pressed his fingers against his temples. Patterns emerged from randomness when viewed correctly. Incident after incident. Protests turning violent. Community meetings erupting into fistfights. School board meetings requiring police intervention.

The curve on his hand-drawn graph climbed steadily upward. Six months of escalation with no discernible cause.

He reached for another report. Border confrontation between militia, immigrants, and activists. A perfectly constructed tinderbox with all the elements necessary for combustion.

Something caught his eye. A footnote in small print at the bottom of the analysis page. "Data collection: Helix Behavioral Analytics."

He flipped to another report.

Same footnote. Same organization.

Culper began pulling reports systematically now.

Helix again and again.

One by one, he checked each document. The pattern solidified. Twenty-seven major incidents. Twenty-three had the Helix connection.

Culper pulled his laptop forward, typed in the name. The website appeared professional, unremarkable. "Data-driven solutions for a complex world." Board members with impressive credentials. Government contracts. Private funding. Nothing suspicious on the surface.

He dug deeper. Corporate filings. Tax documents. Grant applications.

Founded eight years ago. Rapid expansion. Current director: Dr. Elaine Voss. Behavioral scientist with two PhDs. Published papers on predictive social modeling.

And below her name: Director of Development. Marshall Reed.

Culper sat motionless. Although he had never met Reed, he remembered the name. Something about an intelligence operation gone wrong in Syria. People died. Too many people.

Culper opened his most secure browser. Accessed databases not meant for civilian use. Typed in Mashall Reed's name. Reed's file was sparse. Fourteen years in Marine Corps Intelligence. Suddenly, resigned his commission and was immediately recruited by the CIA. Reed became the Director of Analytic Methodology. A prestigious position. When he retired from the CIA, Reed was recruited by Helix. The only other info was about a brother that died during a special ops mission in Afghanistan.

Frustrated by the lack of information, Culper moved on. He typed in a search inquiry into Helix Behavioral Analytics.

Helix's funding primarily came from Homeland Security and the Justice Department. Documents appeared, most heavily redacted.

And something called "Project Fulcrum."

The reference appeared three times in procurement documents. No explanation. No details. Just a code name and dollar amounts with too many zeros.

Culper leaned back. The light from his desk lamp cast his shadow long against the wall. Outside, the capital slept, unaware of the currents moving beneath its surface.

Morning light filtered through blinds Culper hadn't closed. The same lamp still burned, its bulb now unnecessary. Coffee rings marked reports scattered across his desk.

Culper hadn't moved except to refill his mug. His shirt collar had lost its starch, tie still hanging loose. He glanced at his watch. 9:07 A.M.

His computer displayed Helix's contact page. Corporate blue backdrop, sterile font. He studied the phone number, then reached for his secure line. Dialed.

"Helix Behavioral Analytics, how may I direct your call?" A woman's voice, professionally modulated.

"Marshall Reed, please."

"May I ask who's calling?"

"Culper."

"Is that your first name or last name?"

"Just Culper."

"One moment, sir."

A secretary entered Reed's office without knocking, a breach of protocol she only permitted herself for urgent matters.

Reed looked up from his monitor, expression neutral but eyes alert.

"Sir, I have a call on line two. The man identified himself only as 'Culper.' He's requesting to speak with you directly."

Something flickered across Reed's face. Recognition. Not of the man, but of the title. He straightened his posture minutely.

"I'll take it." He waited until the door closed before lifting the receiver. "This is Reed."

"Marshall Reed." Culper's voice carried no particular inflection. "Former Director of Analytic Methodology for the CIA?"

There was a long pause. Culper knew better than to jump back into the conversation. Better to let Reed stew.

"Impressive," said Reed as his fingers tapped once against his desk. "You have me at a disadvantage. I know your title, but I don't know you."

"We've never met."

"We should correct that faux pas."

"Maybe."

"Very well. What can I do for you, Culper?"

"I'm researching patterns in civil disturbances. Your organization's name keeps appearing as the source of data."

"I would expect as much. We're a data analytics firm. Our research teams document social behaviors."

"Interesting coincidence. Your teams document conflicts just as they occur."

Reed leaned back in his chair. "We follow indicators. Deploy where the data suggests events might unfold. Nothing more sinister than good predictive modeling."

"Your teams were present at twenty-three major incidents in the past six months."

A pause. Reed's eyes flicked to his closed door. "If you're suggesting causation rather than correlation, I'd recommend reviewing basic statistical principles."

"I understand statistics quite well. The odds of that level of prediction are astronomical. You must be a prophet."

"I am… of sorts."

Culper's voice remained even. "I'd like access to your data sets. For comparative analysis."

"Our data is proprietary. Corporate policy prevents sharing without proper authorization."

"Whose authorization would that be?"

Reed smiled without humor. "Above both our pay grades, I suspect."

"I'm particularly interested in Project Fulcrum."

The line went silent for three full seconds.

"I'm not familiar with that designation." Reed's voice had cooled several degrees. "And I'm afraid I can't help you with access to our systems. We maintain strict security protocols."

"Former Company man concerned with security. Admirable."

"We all serve in our own ways. Some more visibly than others."

"Indeed."

"If there's nothing else, I have a meeting to attend."

"Your border research team—the incident with Heller and Delgado. Their biometric data showed elevated stress markers before any confrontation occurred. How did your team know to monitor them specifically?"

Reed's knuckles whitened slightly around the receiver. "How did you get that data?"

"Oh, you know… spy stuff."

"I see. Well, I don't discuss operational details with unauthorized personnel."

"Of course."

"Good day, Culper. I wouldn't recommend calling again without proper clearance."

Reed hung up and mumbled to himself, "Fuck."

In his office, Culper replaced the receiver. Made a note in his leather-bound notebook.

He'd learned more from what Reed hadn't said than what he had. The mention of Fulcrum had triggered a response—momentary but clear. The border question had confirmed another suspicion.

Helix wasn't just studying the conflicts. They were anticipating them with precision no predictive model could achieve.

Culper stood, moving to the window. The morning light painted Georgetown in gentle hues that belied the machinery turning beneath its surface.

He needed to see Helix's operation firsthand. He needed someone inside. Getting the right man into position wouldn't be easy. He considered Reed for a moment. What type of operative would appeal to Reed? Someone loyal that could keep their mouth shut. Someone that knew when to apply pressure to a situation and when to avoid it.

Culper's reflection stared back at him from the glass— he needed a man who had spent decades in shadows suddenly finding himself needed in the light. He needed Frank Kane.

Northeastern Coastline

Culper parked his rental car in the parking lot next to two vans both bearing coastal authority logos. There was no sign of Frank's truck or the Imperial. The lighthouse stood against the afternoon sky, pristine white as if freshly painted, its restoration complete. Beautiful.

The small boat was tied up at the dock in front of the parking lot. A larger cargo boat was tied up to the dock at the lighthouse. Culper piloted the small boat to the island. The waves lapped gently against the wooden hull as he drifted toward the island's weathered dock.

The door to the lighthouse stood open. Inside, Culper found three technicians in blue coveralls working in the main room. Tools lay scattered across a tarp. Extension cords snaked up the spiral staircase toward the cupola above.

"Excuse me," Culper said. "I'm looking for Frank Kane."

The youngest technician looked up from a circuit board. "Who?"

"The keeper. Big man. Doesn't talk much."

"Nobody here when we arrived," the technician said. "Place was empty. Clean as a whistle."

Culper climbed the stairs. In the cupola, a fourth technician mounted the new automated light assembly. The ancient clockwork mechanism that Frank had restored lay dismantled in a wooden crate, tagged for some museum collection.

"Already gone," the head technician said, not looking up from his installation. "Lighthouse service said he finished the restoration contract early. Left two days ago."

"Did he say where he was headed?"

The man shrugged. "Keeper types come and go. This place doesn't need a human anymore." He patted the automated system. "This beauty runs on solar power. Maintenance check twice a year."

Culper stood at the railing, looking out at the water stretching to the horizon. The restoration was perfect. Every cracked stone replaced. Every fitting polished. The work of a man who fixed broken things, then disappeared.

"He leave anything behind? A forwarding address?"

"Are you Culper?"

"Yeah."

"Just this." The technician handed him a folded note from his pocket, creased from being handled.

Culper's name was on the back of the folded paper. He opened it. In Frank's blocky handwriting: FUCK OFF. –FRANK.

No location. No contact information. Nothing.

Culper descended the stairs. Outside, he paused on the stone steps, scanning the island once more. He walked back to the dock. The one man he needed had vanished.

"Shit," he said to the empty air.

Redeployment

New England Coastline

The Imperial sat on the trailer behind the pickup's cab as Frank drove north along coastal roads. Two days since he'd left the old lighthouse. Two days of silent travel, the cat curled on the passenger seat, occasionally stretching to look through the window at passing shoreline. The cat didn't know where they were going. It didn't care. If it didn't like where they finally settled, the forest was never far away. It knew how to survive on mice and small birds. The human could fend for itself.

Road signs thinned as they crossed into Maine. Pavement narrowed, cracked where winter frost had heaved it upward. Towns grew smaller, farther apart. Just the way he preferred.

The folder on the dash held photographs and the deed. ABANDONED SINCE 1978, the listing had read. UNSAFE STRUCTURE. NO UTILITIES. He'd wired the money the same day.

Near sunset Frank turned onto a gravel track barely visible between encroaching pines. The pickup's suspension groaned as it absorbed ruts and exposed roots. Half a mile in, the trees opened to reveal gray water and sky divided by horizon.

The lighthouse stood on a rocky point, silhouetted black against fading light. Shorter than his previous project. Squatter. A single-story keeper's quarters attached to its base, windows boarded with weathered plywood. The tower itself leaned two degrees north, its once-white surface stained with rust bleeding from the metal cupola.

Frank stopped the truck and stepped out. Wind carried salt and decay. Waves crashed against the point, sending spray thirty feet upward where gnarled trees clung to stone, shaped by decades of identical storms.

The cat leapt from the truck and disappeared into tall grass. Exploring new territory without pause for permission.

Frank circled the structure once, assessing damage. Mortar crumbled at his touch. Rust had eaten through the cupola's supports. The entry door hung from a single hinge, revealing darkness beyond. Gulls had nested in the beacon room, leaving years of waste to corrode metal and glass.

Perfect.

He retrieved his toolbox from the truck bed and approached the listing door. Inside air sat undisturbed for years, heavy with mold and rat droppings. Floorboards had rotted through in places where rain found entry. The spiral staircase missing several treads where metal had succumbed to salt and oxygen.

Frank set the toolbox down and pulled a flashlight from his belt. The beam cut through shadows, revealing graffiti on plaster walls. Beer cans and needles from kids who'd broken in to drink and drug away from parents' eyes. A mattress stained with things he wouldn't consider.

The keeper's quarters held a rust-frozen sink, a woodstove with a hole burned through its back. Mouse nests in cabinets. The bathroom toilet cracked in half from a freeze, pipes burst and spilling from walls like metal intestines.

His boots left prints in dust as he climbed what remained of the staircase, testing each tread before putting his full weight down. The lantern room at top housed only ghosts of equipment. The Fresnel lens long since stolen or salvaged. Iron fittings remained, brown with corrosion. Glass panels broken where storms or vandals had reached.

Frank stood at the railing, looking out at a twilight sea. No neighbors visible in any direction. Just water and stone and sky. He inhaled deeply, tasting salt and decay and possibility.

The cat appeared at his feet, rubbing against his boot once before sitting to wash its face with methodical strokes. Making itself at home already.

Below, the keeper's quarters would need complete rebuilding. The tower required repointing, maybe restructuring if the lean worsened. The lantern room needed everything - glass, metal, mechanism. Nothing simple. Nothing quick.

Frank descended as darkness swallowed the point. He unloaded the truck by flashlight beam - cot, supplies, propane stove. The weapon footlocker came last, placed beside the door where it could be reached quickly if needed.

He swept a corner clear of debris, set up the cot, unrolled his sleeping bag. Hung the battery lantern from a nail. The cat found a perch on the single intact windowsill, watching his movements with measured disinterest.

Frank sat on the cot and pulled a notepad from his pocket. He began listing materials needed, tasks prioritized by weather and season. The walls might not hold through winter storms. The roof would fail with heavy snow. Elements to be battled while rebuilding.

The cat leapt down and approached, sniffing at his boots before curling beside the cot. Not touching. Not asking. Just claiming space nearby, independent yet present.

Outside, waves continued their assault on stone, the rhythm unchanged for centuries. Wind found its way through broken windows and missing boards, carrying whispers of what had been and what might be.

Frank wrote until the notepad was filled, then set it aside. Tomorrow would bring the first of many days of labor. Of purpose. Of rebuilding something abandoned back to function.

He understood such projects well. He had once been such a project. Rebuilt. Repurposed. Useful.

Helix Headquarters – Arlington, Virginia

The fluorescent lights hummed overhead, the only sound in Helix's executive floor at 2 AM. Voss rubbed her eyes, the blue glow of her monitor burning spots in her vision after hours of staring at spreadsheets. The accounting department had flagged several discrepancies for her review, each one sorted and resolved as she worked through the stack.

She opened another file. Invoice #A7729 from Arcturus Holdings. Her eyes narrowed at the amount: $187,000 monthly. A property lease for a facility in Fairbanks, Alaska. She scrolled through the attached documentation. Fifty thousand square feet. Dedicated power station. Reinforced construction.

Voss checked the authorization signature. Reed's name, dated three months prior. She searched previous quarters. Similar payments stretched back eight months, the amounts growing steadily.

She opened the company's asset management database. No listing for an Alaska facility. She tried operations reports. Nothing. The property existed only in these invoices, authorized solely by Reed.

Voss leaned back in her chair. A data facility costing nearly $4,000,000 annually, and she'd never heard of it. She closed the file and checked the time. Questions would keep until morning.

Reed stood in Voss's doorway the next morning. His tailored suit showed no wrinkles despite the early hour.

"You wanted to see me?" he asked.

Voss gestured to the chair across from her desk. "I was reviewing invoices last night. Found something interesting." She slid the printout across her desk. "Arcturus Holdings. Fairbanks."

Reed's expression didn't change. "The backup data facility."

"I don't recall approving a backup facility."

"Board gave preliminary approval last year." Reed sat, straightening his cuffs. "I handled the details. Didn't want to burden you with minutiae."

"Nearly $2.2 million annually isn't minutiae, Marshall."

Reed nodded once, acknowledging the point. "Elaine, we are victims of our own success. Fulcrum and the data used to create it have become too valuable. The intellectual property is worth billions. We needed secure offsite storage."

"And you chose Fairbanks, Alaska?" Voss leaned forward. "Most companies use existing cloud services with multiple redundancies."

"Most companies aren't developing what we are." Reed's voice dropped lower. "Hackers are targeting us daily. And not just hackers. We've had three former employees attempt to access restricted data in the past month. One tried to download the entire Fulcrum architecture."

Voss's face remained neutral. "You never mentioned security breaches."

"Didn't want to worry you."

"I'm the CEO, Marshall. Worrying is my job."

Reed stood, buttoning his jacket. "And I'm your director of development, Elaine. A position you entrusted me with. Data security falls within my wheelhouse. You need to let me do this. You need to trust me. The facility is isolated, secure, and cold. Cooling costs for servers drop nearly sixty percent. It's practical and necessary."

"Why wasn't I informed before now?"

Reed met her eyes. "Compartmentalization. The fewer people who know about our contingency plans, the better." He moved toward the door. "Sometimes protection requires secrecy, even from friends."

Voss watched him leave, the invoice still on her desk. Protection required secrecy. The words settled in her stomach like cold stones. The question remained: protection from what? And for whom?

She had known Reed for years and he never gave her a reason to doubt him. He always had an answer for anything he did. But that was what bothered her. He was too perfect. Like he had thought through everything he did and came up with answers to any objections before they arose.

She reached for her phone, then stopped. Something in Reed's tone, the careful precision of his answers. This wasn't just about data storage.

Voss turned to her computer and began searching through project files, looking for connections to Fairbanks that Reed hadn't meant for her to find.

New England Coastline

Two days of work had emptied his supplies. Frank tucked the materials list into his jacket and left the lighthouse at dawn. The cat watched from a freshly cleared windowsill, tail twitching as the pickup disappeared around the bend. A mouse scampered across the room. The cat ignored it as if it was beneath him to hunt such things. A long nap in the sunlight was far more important.

Seven miles of coastal road brought Frank to Stoneport. Population 837 according to the weathered sign. Main Street ran straight through town, most buildings dating back to when ships carried cargo instead of tourists.

Frank parked in front of the hardware store. PETERSON'S SINCE 1892, the faded lettering proclaimed above windows clouded with salt haze. A bell jangled as he entered. Wooden floors worn smooth by generations creaked beneath his boots. Frank liked hardware stores almost as much as a good dive bar. He felt at home like something he understood and something that understood him.

An old man looked up from behind the counter. "Help you?"

Frank handed over his list without speaking.

The man adjusted his glasses, scanning the page. His eyebrows lifted. "Lighthouse project, eh? Haven't seen anyone out there in twenty years." He studied Frank's face. "Gonna take more than one man to fix that wreck."

Frank stared back.

"Right." The old man cleared his throat. "Mortar I've got. Lumber's in back. Glass'll need ordering." His finger tracked down the list. "Roofing tin, got that too. The specialized fittings though..." He looked up. "I'll make some calls. Might know a fellow in Portland who restores historical buildings."

Frank nodded once.

The old man set about gathering what he could from the list. "Town used to depend on that light," he said as he moved between shelves. "Before GPS and satellites. Saved plenty of fishermen from the rocks." He placed bags of mortar on the counter. "You military?"

Frank neither confirmed nor denied.

"Figured." The old man nodded to himself. "Way you stand. Way you don't talk much. Fine by me." He pulled coils of rope from a back shelf. "My son did two tours in Afghanistan. Came back different."

Frank moved toward windows that needed cleaning, watching the street outside where a woman pushed a stroller past the post office.

"Quarry's still running," the old man continued, unbothered by Frank's silence. "Three miles south of town, follow the gravel trucks. Tell Grayson that Peterson sent you. He'll give a fair price."

Frank paid for the supplies he could get, loaded them in the pickup. The old man wrote down his number on the back of the receipt. "Call when you need the rest. Might take a week to get everything."

Main Street curved where it met the harbor. Half the storefronts stood empty, victims of big-box stores in larger towns. The survivors clustered near the water – bait shop, post office, a small grocery with faded awnings.

Inside the grocery, Frank moved methodically through narrow aisles. Canned goods. Coffee. Dry pasta. Nothing that required refrigeration in his powerless quarters. The teenage clerk eyed his scars when she thought he wasn't looking, then found something fascinating about her fingernails when he turned her way.

The harbor held a dozen fishing boats, most showing the wear of daily use. Commercial trawlers alongside smaller craft for hauling traps. Gulls circled masts, fighting for scraps as men in rubber overalls hosed down decks.

Frank followed his nose to a diner perched on wooden pilings over the water. HARBOR LIGHT CAFE, its neon sign unlit in daylight. Inside smelled of bacon grease and coffee, the windows streaked with salt. Five locals occupied stools at the counter, all turning to inspect Frank as he entered.

He took a booth facing the door, back to the wall. The menu wedged between napkin holder and window offered basic fare – eggs any style, burgers, fish caught that morning.

A waitress approached, gray hair pulled into a tight bun, wry sense of humor, order pad already in hand. "Aren't you a handsome one."

Frank grunted.

"Scars are better than tattoos of tweedy bird. So, what'll it be, honey?"

"Double meatloaf," Frank said.

"Sides?"

"Fries and coleslaw."

"Drink?"

"Coffee and Coke. No ice."

She nodded, appreciating efficiency, and disappeared toward the kitchen. Frank's eyes tracked each person in the diner. The fishermen at the counter. The elderly couple sharing pie by the window. The cook visible through the service window, tattoos covering his arms.

His coffee arrived black and strong, steam rising to meet his face as he inhaled. The conversations around him resumed, no longer focused on the stranger.

"...storm coming in Thursday..." "...wouldn't take less than four dollars a pound..." "...said the lighthouse had a new keeper..."

Frank sipped his coffee, letting the chatter wash over him without response. The waitress returned with the iceless Coke and a plate – double meatloaf covered in brown gravy, fries piled alongside, green beans steamed and buttered. A lump of coleslaw. Simple food. Honest.

He ate methodically, each bite the same size as the last. When the plate was clean, he left cash on the table. Enough for the meal plus twenty percent tip.

The quarry dust hung in the air before he saw the operation – a gouge torn from hillside, revealing gray stone beneath. Trucks lined up for loading where massive blocks were cut free from earth that had held them for millennia.

A bearded man in a hard hat directed operations from a battered pickup. Frank approached, materials list in hand.

"You Peterson's lighthouse man?" the foreman asked over the scream of saws cutting through stone.

Frank nodded.

"Thought you'd be bigger," the man said with a wry smile, taking the list. "Fixing that old wreck'll take an army. Or twenty years." He examined the paper. "I've got what you need. Delivery'll cost extra though. Road out there's barely passable."

Frank's silence was acceptance.

"Payment up front." The foreman named his price, watching for reaction.

Frank counted bills from his wallet. No haggling. No complaint.

"First load Thursday," the foreman said. "Weather permitting."

Frank drove back through town as shadows lengthened. A woman swept the sidewalk in front of the hardware store. The old man appeared in the doorway, raised his hand in greeting.

Frank didn't wave back, but he slowed the truck and nodded. Acknowledgment enough.

The road to the lighthouse darkened beneath pine canopy. Frank's purchases shifted in the truck bed. Enough to start rebuilding. Enough to create shelter before winter tightened its grip.

The cat waited on the porch steps, yellow eyes tracking his approach. It had stayed. Again.

Frank unloaded supplies into the keeper's quarters as night fell. New work waiting. New purpose unfolding one stone at a time.

Behind him, lights from Stoneport appeared as tiny stars on the horizon. Close enough for necessities. Far enough for solitude.

The balance felt right.

Frank stood beneath the leaning lighthouse, assessing its tilt with tools more precise than human eyes. The plumb line hung from the cupola showed three degrees off vertical. Bad enough to threaten collapse in winter storms. Bad enough to demand correction.

He'd spent four days digging beneath the eastern foundation, exposing the original granite blocks that had settled over decades. The soil under them had washed away through a crack in the foundation unseen until now. The lighthouse slowly tipping toward the sea that would eventually claim it.

Frank unloaded four hydraulic jacks from the pickup's bed. Each rated for twenty tons. He'd found them at a salvage yard three towns over, paid cash, loaded them himself while the yard owner watched with suspicion that turned to respect when Frank lifted the heaviest one-handed.

The cat observed from safe distance, tail switching when Frank dragged the first jack into the excavation beneath the foundation. The iron scent of disturbed earth mixed with salt air. Gulls screamed overhead as if warning the structure of coming violation.

Frank positioned the jacks at precise intervals along the eastern foundation. Each placement calculated after measuring the structure's weight distribution. He worked systematically, checking alignment twice before moving to the next placement. No room for error with a hundred tons of stone suspended above him.

Four railroad ties served as cribbing, creating a platform on undisturbed soil beside the jacks. If the foundation shifted suddenly, the cribbing would catch it, preventing collapse.

With jacks positioned, Frank connected them to the manual hydraulic pump with high-pressure hoses. The system would allow all four jacks to raise simultaneously, distributing the force evenly across the foundation. He tested each connection, tightening fittings until his knuckles bled.

The cat ventured closer, sniffing at the equipment before retreating to higher ground. It recognized something dangerous in the steel machinery and compressed force.

Frank placed his palms against the lighthouse stone, feeling its weight pressing back against his hands. Generations of keepers had touched these same blocks, dedicated their lives to maintaining the light that saved others. A purpose worth serving. Worth saving.

He began working the pump handle. Slow, steady strokes that built pressure within the hydraulic system. The gauge needle climbed. Nothing visibly changed for the first hundred strokes, just resistance growing against his movements.

Then a sound emerged from beneath the foundation. A groan of stone that had remained unmoved for a century. The noise traveled through the ground into Frank's boots, up his legs, settled in his chest like distant thunder.

The lighthouse didn't move. Not yet. Frank continued pumping, sweat forming on his forehead despite the cool morning. Every tenth stroke, he checked the plumb line hanging from above, watching for the slightest change.

Two hundred strokes. Three hundred. His shoulders burned from the repetitive motion, but he maintained the same measured pace. Rushing invited disaster.

The first movement came as a shudder through the entire structure. Dust rained from mortar joints. A window creaked in its frame. The lighthouse shifted a quarter-inch upward on its eastern side, reluctant as a stubborn child.

Frank paused, inspecting for new cracks or failures. Finding none, he resumed pumping. The gauge showed eight tons of pressure now, distributed across the four jacks. The noise from beneath grew louder, stone grinding against stone as century-old inertia yielded to mechanical advantage.

The plumb line swung, settling into a new position. Two-and-a-half degrees off vertical now. Progress measured in fractions, but progress nonetheless.

Frank worked through midday, sweat soaking his shirt as pressure built. The gauge climbed past twelve tons. Past fifteen. The lighthouse continued its grudging rise, ancient joints protesting each millimeter of change.

A crack appeared in the northwestern corner. Frank froze, watching to see if it would lengthen. When it stabilized, he shifted one of the jacks two inches inward, redistributing force away from the weakness.

The cat had disappeared entirely, instinct carrying it to safer ground in the nearby woods while man wrestled with stone and gravity.

Stone dust coated Frank's arms, turned sweat to mud that traced the topography of scars across his skin. The work demanded hours of uncomfortable crouching, back bent beneath unforgiving stone. Frank felt nothing beyond the task. Pain existed but held no importance.

At eighteen tons, the plumb line showed one degree off vertical. Frank studied it for ten full minutes, confirming the measurement from different angles. Close enough now to finish the permanent correction.

When the reinforced foundation reached halfway up the jacks, Frank retrieved the granite blocks he'd selected at the quarry. Each stone unique, chosen specifically for this purpose. Not cement blocks or concrete – those were temporary solutions, modern shortcuts. The lighthouse deserved permanence.

Frank placed each stone on the workbench, studying it like a sculptor before the chisel. He measured twice, marking cut lines with soapstone that left pale blue traces on gray granite. The sledgehammer and carbide-tipped chisel waited, tools unchanged since Roman times.

The first strike echoed across the point. Stone dust rose as Frank's measured blows followed the marked line. Not smashing – cutting. Each impact precise, positioned to let the stone's natural grain guide the split. He worked without hurry, letting the material speak through his hands.

The cat appeared, drawn by the rhythm of metal on stone. It watched from a distance as Frank shaped each block to fit the exact space beneath the foundation. Some required a single clean break, others more intricate shaping. The waste pieces piled nearby, saved for smaller repairs elsewhere in the structure.

When a block was shaped to satisfaction, Frank carried it to the excavation. He tested each placement dry before applying mortar, ensuring perfect fit. Stone met stone with seams thin as a dime. The new blocks interlocked with the original foundation, creating a bond that would strengthen over decades as lime in the mortar slowly turned back to stone.

Frank worked through afternoon shadows, the lighthouse's weight suspended above him as he fit each custom-cut block into its place. Granite joined granite, the new indistinguishable from the old except for the sharpness of its edges. When complete, the foundation would stand another century, perhaps two.

No concrete. No shortcuts. Only stone speaking to stone through a man who understood their language.

Afternoon stretched toward evening. Shadows lengthened across the point. Frank continued without pause, eating nothing, drinking only when thirst became distracting. The work spoke its own language through his hands, telling him what came next, what needed correction, what would hold and what would not.

The cat returned as sunset painted the sky copper. It found a perch on a nearby rock, watching Frank's methodical movements with detached curiosity.

With the final cut stone in place, Frank checked the plumb line once more. The lighthouse stood just half a degree off perfect vertical. Better than when originally built, according to the county records he'd found.

He removed the jacks one by one, transferring the structure's weight gradually to its new foundation. As each jack came free, he inspected the mortar for signs of stress. The lighthouse settled millimeters onto its reinforcement, finding stability it had lacked for decades.

When the last jack pulled clear, Frank stood beneath the tower, hand pressed against cold stone. The transfer was complete. The lighthouse stood straight against advancing night, plumb line hanging true against restored stone.

Stars appeared above the cupola, framing the space where light would eventually return. Frank gathered his tools in darkness, muscles trembling with exhaustion. Tomorrow would bring more repairs. Different challenges. The tower saved from its lean but far from restored.

He turned toward the keeper's quarters where no lamps yet burned. The cat followed at a careful distance, their separate paths converging at the damaged door.

Inside, Frank placed the bloodied trowel beside others on his workbench. His hands looked like they belonged to another person, crusted with mortar and grime. The lighthouse stood straighter than it had in forty years, but no one would notice except him. No commendation would come. No acknowledgment beyond his own.

This was enough. Had always been enough.

Labor Relations

Detroit, Michigan

Night pressed against the factory windows, turning the glass into mirrors that reflected steel and fluorescent lights.

Outside, something hovered in darkness—a shadow against shadows, propellers whirring at frequencies designed to evade human hearing. The Helix drone maintained position, its thermal imaging penetrating glass to capture the human heat signatures within the factory.

James McKenzie watched from the elevated supervisor platform, counting workers. Third shift ran with less than a quarter of the manpower of twenty years ago. One hundred and seventeen people overseeing machines that had replaced 500 of their colleagues. By dawn, there would be fewer.

"They're really doing it tonight?" Anna Kowalski asked, joining him at the railing. Thirty years on the line had left her with hearing loss in one ear and shoulders permanently set against invisible weight.

"Two a.m. installation. New automated line." McKenzie nodded toward the empty space at Station Seven where crates bearing Autotech logos waited. "Management moved up the timeline. Didn't want to risk a scene during day shift."

"Cowards," Kowalski spat. "Promised us six more weeks. Families to feed, mortgages due."

Two kilometers away, Evan Morris adjusted recording levels in the back of a nondescript van, capturing each bitter syllable with clinical precision. The Helix Behavioral Analytics logo adorned his jacket. His partner Rodriguez monitored the second drone circling the factory's perimeter.

Beyond the van, three more Helix researchers monitored the factory from different vantage points. Dr. Olivia Chen, the team leader, crouched on a nearby ridge with long-range audio equipment, capturing conversations from factory windows left open in the summer heat. Technician Foster maintained a mobile sensor array from the tree line, mapping heat signatures through the building's eastern wall. The newest member, Wilson, swept the perimeter with electromagnetic sensors, documenting energy fluctuations from machinery inside. Each fed data to the central algorithm, providing different perspectives of the same human drama. Chen's voice crackled through their earpieces: "Stay focused. This is precisely the behavioral pattern we need to document."

On the factory floor, Miller stopped his forklift beside Diaz's station. Heads bent close, voices kept below machine noise. McKenzie had seen this before—

whispers traveling station to station, hands forming fists when supervisors passed.

The security team positioned themselves near entryways while technicians began unpacking crates. Eight men from Centaur Protection Services, a subsidiary of a private military company. Not the usual rent-a-cops.

"Nothing about tonight is in our contract," Kowalski said, watching workers gather around Miller. "Union wasn't notified of the schedule change."

"When did that ever matter?" McKenzie replied, eyes tracking the installation team—six men in matching blue coveralls, moving with the confidence of those who had done this many times before. Ending livelihoods was just another day's work.

The bell signaled midnight break. Workers moved toward the cafeteria while machines shut down. McKenzie watched Miller gather a group near the fire exit instead of heading for coffee.

"Something's happening," he told Kowalski.

"Always does when you back people into corners."

The audio drone repositioned, gliding along the building's western face to track the gathering. Its microphone captured fragments—"...taking our dignity..."—"...time to stand..."—"...let them see what happens..."

When workers returned to the floor fifteen minutes later, McKenzie felt the shift. Something electric in the air. Workers moved between stations with new purpose.

At 2:17, the first crate opened at Station Seven. Workers gathered to watch as technicians extracted components gleaming with factory-fresh metal. The replacement for human hands rose from its packaging— a robotic arm capable of performing the work of eight people without need of a coffee break.

"Gather round, people," called the installation team leader, his voice carrying professional enthusiasm. "Those assigned to this station need to observe the calibration process. You'll be training on this system until six a.m."

The workers moved forward with leaden steps. McKenzie saw their faces—masks of controlled rage beneath forced neutrality.

"Where's the bathroom?" a technician asked, looking around.

"I'll show you," Miller offered, setting down his clipboard.

The video drone tracked them through the factory floor, capturing the moment Miller led the technician not toward the restrooms but to a side corridor where four workers waited. The thermal imaging showed the technician's body temperature spike with fear as he realized his mistake.

At Station Seven, the remaining technicians continued assembly, unaware of their colleague's situation. The first robotic arm rose on its mounting, cables snaking to control panels where diagnostic lights blinked green.

"We need people from stations eight through twelve to observe," the lead technician called, checking his tablet. "This unit will handle all operations previously requiring manual processing."

No one moved. The technician looked up, finding himself surrounded by silent workers. "Is there a problem?"

Miller returned, alone, wiping his hands on a shop rag. "No problem," he said, voice dangerously calm. "Just wondering if you've got a family to feed."

The lead technician glanced toward the security team positioned by the doors. They had already noticed the tension, four of them moving toward the gathering.

"Look, I just install the equipment," the technician said. "Take it up with management."

"Management's not here," Miller replied. "Three in the morning, they're home in bed while we're being replaced by your machines."

The security team's leader approached, hand resting casually near his hip. "Everything okay here?"

"We're fine," Miller told the guard. "Just discussing our future unemployment."

"I need you all to return to your stations," the guard said, eyes scanning the group. "Installation proceeds as scheduled."

Miller stepped closer. "That schedule changed without union approval. We had six more weeks."

"Not my department," the guard replied. "Move along now."

The workers stayed rooted. The security team leader touched his radio, calling for backup. Three more guards approached from the western entrance.

In the Helix van, Morris watched the thermal signatures pulse with growing agitation. He leaned toward the microphone. "Primary feeds showing pre-conflict indicators. Heightened body temperatures, compressed grouping patterns."

"Noted," Rodriguez replied, eyes on the drone telemetry. "Maintaining optimal distance for data capture."

The security leader spoke quietly into his radio. The installation team huddled closer to their equipment, sensing the shift in atmosphere.

"Last chance to disperse," the security leader announced, hand now resting openly on his baton. "Return to assigned stations or face disciplinary action."

The first wrench struck the robotic arm's exposed hydraulic line. Fluid sprayed across polished steel, painting workers and security in industrial blood. For one suspended moment, no one moved.

Then everything happened at once.

A security guard lunged for Miller, baton raised. A pipe wrench caught him in the ribs before he could connect. Another guard advanced, pepper spray appearing in his hand. Diaz tackled him from the side, both men crashing into crates of automation components.

Kowalski appeared with a red gasoline can from the maintenance shed. She doused the nearest automation equipment, fuel splashing across shining metal and exposed wiring. The scent of gasoline cut through machine oil and sweat.

"Twenty-nine years," she said to no one in particular. "This is my severance." The match flared between her fingers. She dropped it without ceremony. Fire bloomed like a toxic flower, catching hungrily on fuel-soaked cables. Flames raced along wiring, claiming the robotic arm that would have replaced her station.

Miller saw what she'd done. He nodded once, then grabbed another gas can. Workers passed it hand to hand, soaking control panels and automation crates still waiting to be unpacked. Fire spread with methodical vengeance, each station claimed by the workers before it could claim them.

"Stop them!" the installation leader shouted, but his team had already retreated, abandoning million-dollar equipment to workers with nothing left to lose. The security team tried forming a barrier between fire and remaining equipment. Batons rose and fell. Blood mixed with gasoline on concrete. A fire axe found a central control unit, splitting it open like kindling for the growing flames.

In the van, Morris leaned forward, gripping the edge of his monitoring station. "We've got physical escalation. Conflict parameters matching Kenosha timeline."

His screen flickered. The drone's telemetry readings fluctuated, altitude dropping ten feet in three seconds.

"Signal interference on primary drone," Rodriguez called out. "Switching to backup frequencies."

The feed pixelated, then stabilized for five seconds before cutting completely to black.

"We've lost primary," Morris said, fingers flying across the keyboard. "No response to override commands."

"Secondary drone maintaining position," Rodriguez replied. "But we're losing visual fidelity from the northeast quadrant."

Morris checked the tracking data. "Primary is still airborne but descending rapidly. Location approximately two hundred meters northeast of the main facility."

"Protocol states we maintain position," Rodriguez said, not looking away from the secondary feeds. "Field recovery team will retrieve the equipment tomorrow."

Morris stared at the empty screen where violence continued unseen. His hand moved to the van door. "That drone contains proprietary Helix technology. Recovery protocols are clear."

"Not during an active conflict scenario," Rodriguez countered.

Morris grabbed a handheld tracker. "I'll be back in ten minutes. Keep the secondary on station."

"Morris, don't—"

But he was already out the door, tracker in hand, moving through darkness toward the blinking dot on his screen. The night swallowed him within seconds.

The tracker led Morris across an empty parking lot, past chain-link fence with razor wire. The factory loomed ahead, its upper windows now flickering with internal flames. He smelled burning plastic and oil.

Sirens wailed in the distance, still minutes away. Workers shouted. Security guards barked orders through megaphones. Morris kept to the shadows, following the tracker's signal toward a stand of scrub trees beyond the northeast loading bay.

The drone lay on its side, one propeller still spinning weakly. No visible damage. Morris knelt beside it, flipping open the access panel. The battery showed full charge, but the transmission module blinked amber instead of green. A clean electronics failure, not physical damage.

He detached the data storage module, tucked it into his jacket pocket. The drone itself would fit in his backpack. He reached to disconnect the remaining propellers.

"Hey! What you doing there?"

Morris looked up. Two men approached from the loading bay, their coveralls stained with hydraulic fluid and what might have been blood. One carried a pipe wrench, the other a metal bracket ripped from some larger assembly.

"Nothing to worry about," Morris said, keeping his voice neutral. "Just equipment maintenance."

The men moved closer. The Helix logo on Morris's jacket caught the emergency lighting from the factory. One man nudged the other. "Look at that. Another company man."

"I'm not security," Morris said, slowly standing. "I'm not with the factory at all."

"Bullshit," the first man said. "Another suit sent to watch us get replaced."

"You're mistaken," Morris backed away, one hand raised. "I'm just a researcher."

"Researching what? How to fuck us out of our jobs?" The second man raised his bracket. "Just another company stooge in a different uniform."

"I don't work for Autotech," Morris said. "I have nothing to do with—"

The first blow caught Morris across the shoulder, driving him to his knees. Pain exploded through his body. The pipe wrench rose and fell again, connecting with his ribs. Something cracked inside him.

"Stop," he gasped, curling to protect himself. "I'm not who you think—"

The bracket caught him across the back of the skull. Morris sprawled face-down in dirt. Boots connected with his kidneys, his spine, his already-broken ribs. Each impact sent fresh agony through his nervous system.

The men worked methodically, their violence cold and precise. No wasted motion. No hesitation. Just the systematic destruction of what they believed represented their suffering.

"That's enough," one finally said. "He's done."

"One more for the road," the other replied, delivering a final kick to Morris's temple.

Darkness claimed him.

Inside the factory, McKenzie found himself moving against the tide, toward Anna Kowalski who stood before the burning automation equipment. The fire had spread through the rafters now, consuming decades-old wiring and insulation never meant to withstand such heat.

"We have to go," he shouted above the alarms.

She turned to him, eyes reflecting inferno she had created. "My entire adult career at this station," she said. "Where am I supposed to go now?"

Outside, firefighters prepared to battle a losing war while police established a perimeter. Workers gathered across the street, some bleeding, others supporting colleagues with broken bones.

Two hours later, as dawn stained the sky above the smoldering factory, a Helix recovery team found Morris. He lay half-conscious beside the recovered drone, his face swollen beyond recognition, internal bleeding gradually claiming organs vital for survival.

"Subject located," the team leader reported into his radio. "Severe physical trauma. Requesting immediate medical evacuation."

Morris's fingers still clutched the data storage module, refusing to surrender the evidence of human predictability even as his own body betrayed him.

His last conscious thought before darkness reclaimed him was that the data would be worth it. The algorithm would grow stronger from tonight's inputs. Violence, after all, followed patterns. Patterns that could be predicted, manipulated, controlled.

In the growing light, the factory's skeleton stood as testament to humanity's resistance to such control. Its ribcage of steel blackened but unbroken. A dragon slain in desperation by those it had come to devour.

Helix Headquarters – Arlington, Virginia

Morning light sliced through vertical blinds, cutting the conference room into bars of shadow and brightness. Voss sat at the head of the table, her coffee untouched. The Detroit factory footage played on the wall screen— flames consuming automated equipment, workers' faces illuminated by their own destruction.

Chen stood beside the screen, her presentation finished. Dark circles hung beneath her eyes. She hadn't slept since Detroit.

"Morris dies, our team falls apart," Chen said. "Four researchers submitted resignation letters this morning."

Voss set down her pen. "Which four?"

"Wilson, Foster, Rodriguez, and Takahashi." Chen's voice remained clinical despite the subject. "All cited safety concerns."

"Safety concerns." Voss repeated the words like tasting something bitter. "They knew the parameters of field research when they signed their contracts."

"They didn't sign up to be beaten half to death with pipe wrenches." Chen glanced at Morris's medical report on the table. "Traumatic brain injury. Ruptured spleen. Five broken bones."

Reed stood by the window, back to the room, hands clasped behind him. His reflection fragmented across glass and steel. "Morris violated protocol," he said without turning. "The equipment wasn't worth his life."

"Tell that to his wife," Chen said.

Reed faced them now. "Your job is documentation, not intervention. Morris forgot that distinction."

Voss tapped her fingernail against the table surface. "The data loss is what concerns me. Four resignations means four gaps in our observation network. We can't afford gaps, not with the timeline we're working under."

"Detroit was just one data point," Reed said.

"A critical one." Voss pushed Morris's tablet across the table toward him. "The factory violence pattern matched our predictive models within two percent. The workers reacted exactly as the algorithm anticipated."

Chen remained standing, arms folded across her chest. "My team won't deploy again without protection. They're scientists, not casualties."

Reed's jaw tightened. "You think I don't understand the risk? I spent decades in conflict zones before this."

"Then you should recognize an unsafe operating environment," Chen countered.

The room fell silent. Voss studied them both, calculating variables beyond the immediate conversation.

"We need the data," she said finally. "And we need the researchers to collect it. If security teams are what it takes to keep them in the field, then security teams they shall have."

Reed nodded once. "I know people. Former military. Discreet. They can deploy with the research teams without affecting data integrity."

"Cost?" Voss asked.

"Less than the cost of compromised research."

Voss considered this, then turned to Chen. "Will security personnel satisfy your team's concerns?"

"It's a start," Chen said. "But I want veto power over team deployments. If I assess a situation as too volatile, we pull out. No questions asked."

Reed started to object, but Voss raised her hand to silence him. "Granted. But your assessment must be data-driven, not emotional. We're not in the business of coddling sensitivities."

"Tell that to Morris," Chen said.

"Morris made a choice," Reed said. "The wrong one."

Voss tapped a command into her tablet. The screen image changed from burning factory to a map dotted with red indicators. "These are our next observation sites. Twelve potential conflict zones identified by the algorithm."

"Twelve?" Chen said. "With four researchers gone?"

"Fill the gaps," Voss ordered. "Recruit from the analytics division if you have to. The timeline doesn't change because we're short-staffed."

"And the security teams?" Chen pressed.

Reed moved toward the door. "I'll make the calls today. You'll have protection for your people by tomorrow night."

"Not just any protection," Chen said. "People who know what they're doing. People who won't escalate situations."

"I said I'll handle it," Reed's voice carried an edge that neither woman missed.

Voss ended the meeting with a gesture. "We've lost enough time already. Chen, keep your remaining researchers from quitting. Reed, get those security teams in place." Her eyes moved between them. "This project is too important for personal grievances."

After they left, Voss remained at the table. She replayed the Detroit footage, watching flames consume machinery that would have replaced human hands. The workers' faces reflected in the screen, their rage a mirror of something ancient and predictable. Something the algorithm understood better than they did themselves.

She touched the screen, freezing on an image of Kowalski standing before the burning automation equipment. The woman's expression held no regret, only grim satisfaction.

Voss recognized that look. She'd seen it before. The face of someone with nothing left to lose.

The most dangerous variable in any equation.

Georgetown, Washington D.C.

Culper sat in his Georgetown study, evening light falling through leaded glass. The leather-bound notebook lay open on his desk, its pages filled with his meticulous script. Names connected to names. Dates to events. Patterns forming before his trained eye.

He picked up his secure phone, dialed a number from memory. Three rings before a voice answered.

"NSA, Bishop speaking."

"John, it's Culper."

A pause. Then, "Well I'll be damned." The formal tone vanished, replaced by warmth. "How long has it been? Eight years?"

"Nine. That business in Bucharest."

"Christ, was it that long ago?" Bishop's laugh carried across the line. "Still wearing those ridiculous tweed jackets?"

"Some things don't change."

"Some things should."

The conversation drifted into comfortable territory. Memories of operations long classified. Names of colleagues now retired or dead. The easy shorthand of men who had once trusted each other with their lives.

"So what's this about, Culper?" Bishop finally asked. "You didn't call to discuss the good old days of Cold War espionage."

Culper's fingers traced the pattern in his notebook. "I need a favor, John."

"I figured. What kind?"

"Electronic surveillance. Domestic target."

The silence stretched long enough for Culper to wonder if the line had gone dead.

"That's a tall order these days," Bishop said at last. "Rules have changed since our time."

"I'm aware."

"Who's the target?"

"Helix Behavioral Analytics. Two individuals specifically. Elaine Voss, CEO. Marshall Reed, Director of Development."

Bishop's voice lowered. "What's your interest?"

"They're developing something called Fulcrum. I need to know what it is."

"Surveillance authorization?"

"Don't have one."

Bishop exhaled slowly. The sound of a desk drawer opening came through the line. "You know what you're asking?"

"I do."

"And if I said no?"

Culper gazed out the window at the streetlights coming on across Georgetown. "Then I'd thank you for your time and figure out another way."

Another long pause. "Keyword search parameters?"

"Fulcrum. Alaska. Fairbanks. Project Catalyst."

The scratch of a pen against paper. "That's it?"

"For now."

"I have some latitude in my position. Discretionary surveillance for national security concerns." Bishop's voice turned formal again. "But I'll need something concrete within seventy-two hours or it goes into the system properly."

"Understood."

"If this blows back on me—"

"It won't."

Bishop sighed. "The things I do for old friends."

"I appreciate it, John."

"Don't thank me yet. You don't know what I'll find."

Culper set down the phone, returned to his notebook. In the margin he wrote HELIX: NSA SURVEILLANCE INITIATED. Beside it, the date and time.

Outside, a car passed slowly down the street. Culper watched it from the window, his mind already moving to the next step.

The game board was expanding, pieces moving into position. Soon the true pattern would emerge from chaos.

Data Center - Fairbanks, Alaska

The three technicians gripped the dashboard as the van fishtailed on black ice. Their Helix jackets, identical down to the embroidered logo, provided little warmth against the Alaskan cold that seeped through metal and glass. Beyond the headlights, nothing existed but darkness and the occasional reflective pole marking the road's edge.

"Some data center location," Braddock muttered, hands on the wheel. The wipers fought a losing battle against falling snow.

"Price of isolation." Torres checked her tablet. "Forty minutes out."

The road narrowed as they climbed. Mountains rose on either side, their peaks lost in low clouds. The van's tires found purchase then lost it, the chains rattling underneath like angry bones.

They crested a final hill and the facility appeared below—floodlights stabbing upward against the darkness, a concrete perimeter wall rising twelve feet high, topped with cameras tracking their approach.

"Jesus," Lawson whispered. "It's a fortress."

Braddock guided the van toward the single entrance gate. Steel barriers capable of stopping a truck rose from the frozen ground. He punched a ten-digit code into the mounted keypad, his breath forming ghosts that vanished against bulletproof glass.

The gate retracted. Red lights turned green.

Braddock drove through. The gate closed behind them with mechanical finality.

The building squatted in the compound's center—windowless concrete, its flat roof bristling with satellite dishes and air conditioning units that hummed despite the bitter cold. Steam escaped from massive vents, forming clouds that drifted upward into falling snow.

They parked at the loading dock. Nobody spoke as they unloaded their gear. The bags were heavy with tools and electronics. Equipment to birth something significant. Something secret.

A guard met them at the entrance, his face blank as he checked IDs against his clipboard. The security door hissed open, releasing a blast of climate-controlled air that smelled of new electronics and fresh paint.

Inside, the building revealed its purpose. Stacked shipping containers lined the walls, their branded logos suggesting contents from a dozen technology manufacturers. The main floor stretched football-field long, raised eighteen inches above bare concrete to accommodate cooling conduits and wiring underneath.

Empty server racks stood in precise rows, waiting for the machines that would give them purpose.

"Five days to bring phase one online," Torres said, checking her watch. "Clock's running."

They moved to their assigned stations. Opened tool cases. Pulled on ESD-safe gloves.

Torres approached the first shipping container. Broke the seal. Inside, rack-mounted servers gleamed like new organs waiting for transplant.

Lawson studied the blueprints projected on his tablet. "Power draw is massive. They've built their own substation."

Braddock wheeled the first server toward its destination. "You know what they're storing out here?"

Torres's expression closed like a vault. "Not our department."

They worked methodically. Each server required precise installation—power connections, network cables, cooling lines. The machines slid into racks with satisfying clicks. Status lights blinked awake, green and amber and occasionally red.

By midnight, the first row stood complete. The room hummed with newborn electronic life. Cooling fans whirred. Hard drives spun up. The concrete floor vibrated with potential.

"Why Alaska?" Lawson asked, tightening a final connection. "Why not some basement at Langley?"

"Heat and bandwidth," Torres answered too quickly. A practiced response. "Cooling costs drop when ambient temperature is below freezing nine months a year. And the satellite uplinks need clear sky access."

Braddock said nothing. He'd seen the backup generators outside. The redundant connections. The security that exceeded even government standards. Whatever they were building here wasn't meant to be found. Wasn't meant to be stopped.

They continued their work under flickering LED panels. Installing future history in a place where no one would think to look.

Helix Headquarters – Arlington, Virginia

The papers spread across Elaine Voss's desk in neat columns. Outside, rain tapped against the window. She squinted at the budget report, circling numbers with a red pen. A pattern emerged. Discrepancies hidden in standard line items. Security upgrades that never appeared in operations meetings. Data storage costs tripled from last quarter.

She pressed the intercom. "Get me Reed."

"He's in the field today."

"Then find him."

Voss returned to the numbers. One entry stood out: "Personnel - Fairbanks." Costs had soared far beyond what she had expected. Five million dollars allocated to a place they had no official presence.

Twenty minutes passed. Reed knocked once and entered without waiting for permission. His suit jacket was unbuttoned, his tie loosened at the throat.

"You found me." He smiled. The smile didn't reach his eyes.

Voss tapped the budget with her pen. "What's this?"

Reed glanced at the circled items. "Security upgrades. Like you requested."

"I requested better security for our research teams. Not whatever this is."

He shrugged. "Security takes many forms."

Voss sorted through the papers, pulled out another sheet. "Three new programming contracts. Specialized AI architecture work. That's not for data backup."

"The system needs customization to run properly in the new environment."

"Three specialists at $300,000 each for a backup system?"

Reed turned from the window. His face gave away nothing. "You want Fulcrum protected. I'm protecting it."

"From what?"

"From whom." Reed straightened his tie. "There are people who would take what we're building and use it differently than we intend."

"People inside the company?"

"People everywhere. They want what we have and they will try to take it if we don't protect ourselves."

Voss leaned back in her chair. Studied him. "You report to me, Marshall. Not the other way around."

"Of course."

"Then keep me informed. No more surprises in budget reports."

Reed nodded. "Anything else?"

"That's all for now."

He left without another word. Voss listened to his footsteps fade down the hallway. Something wasn't right. The numbers didn't add up. Not just the dollar amounts—the reasoning behind them.

She opened her desk drawer, filed the budget report in a folder marked "Reed." It was getting thicker by the week.

Intruder

The pickup's engine died with a final shudder. Frank sat motionless behind the wheel, sunset fading to gray through the salt-streaked windshield. The lighthouse stood against twilight sky, its grey tower catching last light while shadows gathered at its base.

He stepped out, muscles aching from hauling stone all day. As always, he ignored the pain. The cat appeared from behind a stack of lumber, back arched, teeth bared. It hissed at his approach, yellow eyes narrowed to slits.

Just another evening greeting… or maybe something else.

Then he saw them. Boot prints crossing the yard where only his should be. Fresh. Deep-set. Military tread. They led directly to the keeper's quarters, no attempt at concealment.

Frank crouched, studying the impression. Size eleven. Goodyear welt. Combat boots, not work boots. His hand found the KA-BAR at his belt, the worn handle settling into his palm.

The cat hissed again, then padded after him, curious despite its displeasure.

Frank circled the lighthouse, keeping to shadow. The boot prints showed no companion tracks, no sign of a team. One man. Confident enough to approach alone. Dangerous or foolish.

The keeper's quarters stood silent, windows dark against the lighthouse's stone. Frank spotted muddy marks on the step. The intruder hadn't bothered wiping his feet. Arrogant. Or a message.

He moved to the single window on the structure's blind side, pressed his back against cool stone. Listened. Nothing but waves breaking against rock below and the distant cry of a gull.

Frank lowered himself to peer through the corner of the glass. The interior lay in half-darkness. A shape moved across his limited field of vision—a shoulder, the back of a head. Someone sitting at his table, waiting.

He eased back, circled to the rear where the outhouse stood twenty paces from the main structure. From this angle, he could see the kitchen door was closed but not fully latched. The intruder had entered, then tried to reset the door to its original position.

Frank moved like water around stone, each step carefully placed. No sound betrayed his approach. The cat followed at a distance, belly low to the ground, sharing his caution.

At the kitchen door, he paused. Placed his ear against weathered wood. Silence from within, but silence could lie. He tested the handle with feather-light pressure. It gave without resistance.

Frank pushed the door inward with his boot, KA-BAR held low and ready for an upward thrust if necessary. The hinges betrayed him with a single soft creak.

"Door needs oil," a voice called from the main room.

Frank entered in a crouch, blade extended. The kitchen lay in the deepening twilight, square patches of fading light falling through windows. The air carried a scent that didn't belong—aftershave, leather polish, gun oil.

He moved along the wall where shadow lay thickest, eyes adjusting to the gloom. The main room opened before him, separated from the kitchen by a counter he'd built from salvaged pine.

A figure sat at his table, back to the wall, facing both entrances. Professional positioning. The intruder had chosen the optimal defensive spot—able to monitor approaches while maintaining clear sight lines to all exits.

"You've lost a step," the voice said. "You've made enough noise to wake the dead."

Frank shifted his weight, preparing to cross the open space between kitchen and main room. The blade caught a sliver of dying light.

"You gonna stick me with that thing?" the voice continued.

The intruder stepped into the light. Culper's face appeared.

Frank relaxed. The KA-BAR slipped back into its sheath.

"Find my note?" said Frank.

"Yeah, I found it. Rude, but to the point."

Frank grunted.

"You moved without telling me," Culper said. "Left no forwarding address. Some might take offense."

"How'd you find me?" croaked Frank.

"It's my job to find people. In your case it wasn't so hard. There are only so many lighthouses that need restoration."

Culper gestured to the Imperial, visible through the window. "I see you got the Imperial fixed. I was sure it was a goner. Must have cost a pretty penny."

"Brother."

"Ah. Richard always did have more money than sense."

"Wasting your time. I'm done."

"There is no done in what we do, Frank. We took an oath. Our country still needs us."

Frank's grunt carried dismissal.

Culper nodded toward a six-pack on the table. "Brought beer."

Frank crossed to the woodstove, struck a match. Light bloomed as the oil lamp caught flame, casting long shadows across the walls. The cat jumped onto the table, sniffed at the beer bottles, then settled into a tight ball, watching.

Frank opened the first bottle without permission, drank it in three swallows, then opened the second.

"You gonna save one for me?" said Culper.

"No."

Culper walked to the table, opened a beer in defiance.

"What do you want?" said Frank unimpressed.

"Have you read the newspaper lately? America's tearing itself apart."

"Not my problem."

"Maybe it should be."

Frank grunted.

"What do you know about Helix Behavioral Analytics?"

"Nothing."

Culper pulled a thin folder from his jacket. "It's a think tank. Government contracts mostly. They track social behaviors, predict patterns."

Frank drank, unimpressed.

"They've been present at twenty-three major incidents in the past six months," Culper continued. "Always there before things get violent. Always in position to document."

"Coincidence."

"You know better."

Frank stood and walked to the window. Darkness now complete. His reflection stared back—scarred face, eyes hard as stone.

"They're obviously ahead of the curve. I need their data," Culper said. "Need to know how they're predicting these conflicts."

"Why?"

"If we understand their methods, we might prevent the next riot. The next border shootout. The next factory burning. Stop the madness that's seizing our nation."

Frank turned away. Culper set more photos on the table.

"These are from Detroit last week. Auto workers against automation. Two dead."

Frank didn't look. He poured the rest of his beer into a bowl for the cat. The animal sniffed once then turned away. Even the cat wasn't buying it.

"You need an analyst," Frank said, "Not me."

"What do you know about Marshall Reed? Former CIA guy."

"Nothing."

"He's Helix's director of development. He's building security around their data. Tight. Military-grade. Why? If it's just data—"

"Still. Not me."

Culper sighed. "Look, this isn't just curiosity. Something called Project Fulcrum keeps appearing in their communications. Highly classified. Big money. And they've moved key operations to Alaska."

"Cold there."

"It's remote. It's defensible. It's where you hide things you don't want found."

Frank sat at the table. Began reassembling his tools from the day's work, cleaning mortar from the joints. His callused hands worked methodically in the lamplight.

"This place needs me."

"It's stood a hundred years. It can wait a few more weeks."

Frank sorted bent nails into a tin can. "Storms coming. Weather won't wait."

Culper's patience wore thin. "Since when does Frank Kane worry about a little rain?"

"Not your business."

"I made it my business when I tracked you to this godforsaken rock."

Frank rose suddenly, chair scraping floor. His huge frame filled the small room, hands clenched into fists. Culper didn't move.

"You're hiding," Culper said quietly. "Running from what you are."

"Changed."

"Men like us don't change. We just find different battles."

Frank turned away, disgust written across his scarred face. The cat had disappeared, sensing the tension.

"I'm too old for your games," Culper continued. "Too tired. But something's happening—something that could break the country apart. To get to the bottom of it I need to know how Helix is predicting these conflicts."

"Use someone else."

Frank moved to his cot in the corner. Began unlacing his boots as if Culper didn't exist.

"They had these research teams at every hotspot," Culper said, refusing to be ignored. "Border clashes, factory disputes, community divisions. Always there at the right moment."

Frank lay down. Stared at the ceiling.

"If we could access their data, their predictions—imagine the lives we could save. The violence we could prevent."

Frank closed his eyes. "Not. My. Problem." Each word distinct, final.

Culper stood by the door, hand on the latch. He turned back to look at Frank lying there, eyes closed, shutting out the world.

"You know, Frank, you can build all the walls you want, patch all the stone, fix every crack—but you're not an island. None of us are. The same tide that crashes against your rocks is washing away the country's foundations. And when enough of those foundations crumble, even this place won't be far enough away."

Frank grunted.

"I'm not asking you to save the world," Culper said. "Just get into their facility. Access their data. Find out how they're predicting these conflicts. Then I'll never bother you again."

Frank's laugh was a broken sound. Hard and hollow. "Lies."

"Fine. Probably lies. But this matters, Frank. America matters."

"Does it?"

Culper was shocked by the question. He didn't answer right away, then…

"When I was young, I'd have said yes without hesitation." He touched one of the photographs. "Now I look at what we've become. The hatred. The division. Americans killing Americans. Sometimes I wonder. It's not the country I grew up in. It's become something else."

Frank nodded once. The truth acknowledged.

"I remember a hospital in Kandahar. Doctor there—American volunteer. She'd stitch up anyone who came through the door. Taliban. Civilian. Didn't matter. I asked her why. Why risk everything for people who'd kill her given the chance." Culper's voice quieted. "She said, 'Because the idea of being American matters, even when we fail it.'"

Frank sat up on the cot and turned. Met Culper's gaze.

"That's why America's worth saving, Frank. Not for what it is, but for what it should be. The idea of it."

Frank stood and walked to his toolbox. Carefully secured each tool in its proper place. Closed the lid and latched it. The deliberate movements of a man weighing choices.

"Last time," he said finally.

Culper nodded. "Last time."

"When?"

"Flight leaves tomorrow at noon."

"No. I'll drive."

"Okay. Helix's address is in the folder. I got you a room at a nearby motel. It ain't pretty, but it's good cover."

Frank nodded once.

"I knew I could count on you, Frank," Culper said, opening the door to leave.

Frank didn't reply. He was already mentally cataloging what to pack, what tools might be needed for a different kind of reconstruction job.

The cat reappeared as Culper's footsteps faded outside. It jumped onto Frank's cot and settled on the pillow, claiming the space in his absence.

Frank looked at the lighthouse that would have to wait. The stones that had stood a century might never see his hands complete their work. That was the risk.

The cat yawned, unconcerned with larger problems. It had already decided to stay, lighthouse or not. There were mice to catch. Birds to stalk. The human would either return or wouldn't.

Frank opened his footlocker. The twin Ruger Super Redhawks gleamed in the lamplight, nestled in their foam cutouts. The tools of his former trade. He had hoped never to need them again.

He closed the lid. Some jobs couldn't be refused, no matter how much he wanted to.

Outside, waves crashed against the point. The tide going out, drawing everything back to deeper water.

Helix Headquarters – Arlington, Virginia

Reed sat at his desk reviewing security applications, the overhead light harsh against the white paper. Each candidate reduced to bullet points and service records. Men who'd survived war zones. Men who'd killed. Men who followed orders. Most of them not good enough.

He tossed another application into the trash. The stack on his desk diminished by the hour.

Then he paused. Frank Kane. The name meant nothing, but the service record caught his eye. Afghanistan. Peck River Valley. The same hellscape that had claimed his brother's life. Reed stared at the dates, the citations, the black-marked redactions that said more than words.

He opened the bottom drawer of his desk. Pulled out a leather address book worn thin by years. Found the number written in his precise hand. Dialed.

"Colonel Brader." The voice on the other end was gravel and whiskey.

"Sir. Marshall Reed."

A pause. "Reed. Been a while."

"Yes, sir. I'm calling about a man who served in your area of operation. Peck River Valley. Frank Kane."

The colonel went silent. When he spoke again, his voice had changed. "Why are you asking about Kane?"

"He's applied for security work. I need to know if he's reliable."

A short, sharp laugh came through the line. "Yeah, I know him. Special Operations guy. Mean son of a bitch. But he had his shit wired tight. Nobody better in a firefight. Crazy brave. He was a pretty good sniper too."

Reed leaned back in his chair. Studied the photo attached to Kane's application. The hard eyes. The scars. "Would you trust him?"

"Depends on what with. Your secrets? Your life? Yes. Your humanity?" Brader went quiet. "Kane had a darkness in him. The kind you need sometimes. The kind that keeps you alive when everything goes to hell."

"Like it did for my brother."

The colonel's voice softened. "Your brother was a good man, Reed. Different kind than Kane."

Reed traced his finger over the list of operations in Kane's file. Names of places where blood had soaked into sand. "Kane's record ends abruptly."

"They usually do for men like him. They burn out. Or find something worth dying for." A hesitation. "Or they become something else entirely."

Reed considered this. The applications in the trash had contained no such mysteries. No such potential. "Thank you, Colonel."

"Reed?"

"Sir?"

"Be careful with Kane. Some men, once you point them at a target, you can't call them back."

Reed hung up the phone. Placed Frank Kane's application in the small pile of those worth considering. Darkness recognized darkness.

Reed sat motionless behind his desk as Frank Kane filled the doorway. The man's massive frame seemed to compress the air in the office. Reed noted the way Kane's eyes swept the room—exits first, potential weapons second, only then settling on Reed himself.

"Sit." Reed gestured to the chair opposite his desk.

Frank lowered himself into the too-small seat. It creaked beneath his weight. His scarred hands rested on his knees, perfectly still.

Reed studied the face across from him. The scars told their own story—a roadmap of violence survived. The eyes revealed nothing. They were the eyes of a man who had seen too much and said too little.

"Your file is interesting reading." Reed tapped the folder before him. "Extensive redactions."

Frank stared back. Silent.

"Not much of a talker?"

"No." The single word rasped from damaged vocal cords.

Reed leaned forward. "The position requires someone who can handle... pressure. Employees under your protection might be in hostile environments. Collecting sensitive data."

Frank nodded once.

"Why security work?" Reed asked.

Frank's eyes drifted to the window, then back. "Bills."

Reed almost smiled. "I know about Peck River Valley. Made some calls."

Something flickered across Frank's face. Recognition, perhaps. Or warning.

"The word is you're effective... and dangerous." Reed paused. "My brother died there. Trevor Reed. Did you know him?"

Frank shook his head.

"He was different than me. Than us." Reed's fingers drummed once against the desk. "The researchers you'd protect aren't soldiers. They're scientists. Civilians. They'll be scared sometimes. You'd need to keep them safe without... excessive force."

Frank's gaze remained steady.

"Have you killed men, Mr. Kane?"

"Yes."

"Why?"

Frank's jaw tightened. "Orders."

"And if I ordered you to?"

"Depends."

Reed tilted his head. "On what?"

"Reason."

Reed nodded, understanding.

"Do you know what we are offering in the way of salary and benefits?"

Frank nodded.

Reed opened the desk drawer, removed a security badge with Frank's photo already printed on it. Slid it across the polished surface.

"The Helix security team provides protection for our field researchers. You'll be assigned to a team studying community conflicts. Your job is to observe, protect our people, and stay unnoticed."

Frank picked up the badge. Considered it.

"When can you start?"

"Tomorrow."

Reed studied the scarred giant across from him. Recognized what sat beneath the stillness—the capacity for decisive violence held in careful check. A weapon waiting for direction.

"One thing, Kane." Reed stood. "Our work is classified. You report only to me. Not to the researchers. Not to my boss. To me."

Frank rose, dwarfing the desk between them. Nodded once.

"Welcome to Helix."

Frank followed Reed through the glass hallway of Helix headquarters. Each office they passed had walls of clear glass. No place to hide. No shadows to disappear into. Frank's shoulders nearly brushed both sides of the corridor. The badge Reed had given him dangled from his neck, too small against his massive chest.

They rounded a corner and came face to face with Voss in a tailored pantsuit, her blond hair pulled back tight enough to stretch the skin at her temples. She stopped mid-stride, a tablet clutched to her chest. Her eyes moved from Reed to Frank, then widened as she took in his full measure—the scarred forearms, the twisted tissue that had once been a normal throat, the face that had been broken and mended by someone who cared more for function than appearance.

"Dr. Voss," Reed said. "This is Frank Kane. Our new security specialist."

Voss studied Frank like a specimen under glass. "Not exactly subtle, is he?"

Reed's smile didn't reach his eyes. "Subtlety isn't what I hired him for."

Frank remained motionless, eyes fixed on a point past both of them. Expression blank as stone.

"And what exactly did you hire him for, Marshall?" Her voice carried the edge of someone used to being consulted first.

"Protection." Reed's hand touched Frank's shoulder in a gesture that seemed almost proprietary. "Frank will be accompanying our research teams in the field."

Voss lowered her voice. "The teams need professionals, not—"

"Frank is a professional." Reed cut her off. "Over a decade in special operations. Combat experience in seven countries. He knows how to keep people alive in hostile territory."

Voss's eyes narrowed. She stepped closer to Frank, close enough that most men would have backed away. Frank didn't move. Didn't blink.

"Do you speak, Mr. Kane?"

Frank met her gaze. "Yes."

The single word scraped between them like stone on concrete.

"Our researchers are civilians. Scientists. They'll look to you when things get tense." She searched his face for any sign of understanding. "Can you handle that responsibility without escalating situations?"

Frank nodded once.

Voss turned to Reed. "My office. Ten minutes." She walked away without waiting for his response, heels clicking sharp against polished floors.

"She'll come around," Reed said. "Once she sees what you can do."

Frank grunted.

"Let's get you fitted for equipment," Reed continued as they walked. "The researchers deploy tomorrow. Six a.m. sharp."

Frank followed, shoulders hunched slightly against the endless glass, the constant visibility. Nothing about this place felt right. Like a trap built of transparency and light.

But he'd been in worse places. Done worse things.

As they walked deeper into Helix's heart, Frank cataloged every exit, every stairwell, every potential weapon within reach. The mission had begun.

Data Point

The Puget Sound – Seattle, Washington

Gray mist clung to the waters of Puget Sound, obscuring the Seattle skyline in the distance. The Helix research vessel, a forty-foot craft named *Data Point*, bobbed in the chop, its metal hull cold against the morning air.

Olivia Chen adjusted the parabolic microphone, aiming it toward the fishing fleet that had gathered near the restricted salmon spawning grounds. Through her headphones came the rough voices of men who had fished these waters for generations.

"Recording levels optimal," Rodriguez said, checking his equipment. "Satellite uplink stable."

Foster leaned against the cabin, shooting sidelong glances at Frank who stood motionless at the bow. The security specialist's massive frame remained still despite the rocking boat, his eyes tracking the Coast Guard cutter that patrolled the boundary line.

"Think our new bodyguard knows which end of a boat is which?" Foster whispered to Thompson.

"Heard he killed a man with his thumbs once," Thompson replied, voice low. "Built like a damned refrigerator."

Chen silenced them with a look. "Focus on the task. We're here to collect data, not gossip."

The Coast Guard cutter carved through the water a half-mile ahead, sleek and white against the dark Sound. Mounted on its forward deck sat a Vulcan cannon, six barrels capable of firing twenty-millimeter rounds at rates that turned solid objects into vapor.

"Military-grade weapons deployed against civilian fishing vessels," Chen noted into her recorder. "Unprecedented escalation in enforcement tactics."

Frank watched the cannon, noting its traverse range, its capability. He'd seen what those rounds did to armored vehicles in Afghanistan. A fishing boat would offer little resistance.

Through binoculars, Chen observed Captain Roy Blackwood's vessel leading a scattered formation of crab and salmon boats toward the restricted zone. Blackwood's family had fished these waters since before Washington was a state.

"Primary subject group approaching exclusion boundary," she reported. "Conflict probability rising."

The Coast Guard commander's voice carried across the water: "Attention fishing vessels. You are entering restricted waters. Turn back immediately or face seizure under Federal Maritime Order 392."

The fishing fleet maintained course. Morrison's *Northern Star*, a sixty-foot crabber with rust-streaked hull, pushed ahead of the others. Chen zoomed in on Morrison's weathered face, capturing his expression of grim determination.

"His son's college tuition is due," Chen said. "His boat is mortgaged to the limit. Economic desperation driving non-compliance."

New vessels appeared on the horizon—sleek fiberglass hulls with "Salmon Forever" emblazoned on their sides. Environmental activists arriving to enforce what they saw as necessary protection for dwindling fish stocks.

"Introducing tertiary conflict element," Chen noted, excitement leaking into her professional tone. "Model projection accuracy holding at ninety-four percent."

Frank moved from the bow, crossing to Chen at the starboard rail. "Move boat back," he said, the words grating like metal on stone.

"We maintain this position," Chen replied without looking at him. "Optimal data collection range."

The first warning shot cracked across the water. Instead of turning back, the fishing fleet spread into a wider formation. The environmental boats deployed water cannons, striking the fishing vessels with high-pressure streams.

Morrison's voice came through Chen's directional mic: "These waters belonged to my grandfather! I'll be damned if some college kid with a clipboard tells me I can't feed my family!"

The activists' leader responded through her bullhorn: "These salmon populations are on the brink of extinction! Your 'right to fish' doesn't trump their right to exist!"

Frank's hand touched the throttle. Chen pushed it away.

"We stay," she insisted. "This is exactly the conflict pattern we're documenting."

The Coast Guard commander's voice cut through the chaos: "This is your final warning. Reverse course immediately."

Morrison's reply came in the form of his vessel pushing directly into the restricted zone. Two other fishing boats followed his lead. Someone on Morrison's deck raised a rifle.

The Coast Guard cutter's Vulcan cannon swiveled toward Morrison's boat.

"They wouldn't dare," Thompson whispered.

The cannon erupted, its roar echoing across the water. The six barrels spun, spitting a stream of twenty-millimeter rounds toward Morrison's vessel. Wood and metal exploded into deadly shrapnel as the rounds tore through the wheelhouse.

But something went wrong. The cannon continued to fire as the cutter pitched in a sudden swell. The stream of bullets walked across the water, stitching a line of geysers that marched toward the *Data Point*.

"DOWN!" Frank bellowed.

Everyone dropped except Chen, still fixated on recording the destruction of Morrison's vessel. Frank tackled her as the first rounds struck their boat. Bullets punched through the hull like it was paper, shredding equipment and splintering wood.

Thompson screamed as a round grazed his arm taking a chunk of flesh. Foster curled into a ball beneath the console. Rodriguez pressed himself flat against the deck, eyes squeezed shut.

Frank remained hunched over Chen, his body between her and the incoming fire. The rounds could easily penetrate his flesh, but instinct had overridden logic. The firing stopped after three eternal seconds.

"Jesus Christ," Foster gasped as they all looked up. The cabin was riddled with holes. Daylight streamed through the punctured hull. Seawater bubbled in through a dozen places below the waterline.

"Everyone intact?" Frank asked, already moving to check Thompson's wound.

"They shot us," Thompson said, shock making his voice childlike. "They actually shot us."

Through the shattered windows, they could see Morrison's vessel burning, listing hard to port. The Coast Guard appeared to be rescuing survivors from the water. The environmental boats had scattered, recording the carnage from a safe distance.

"The bilge pump's keeping up," Rodriguez reported after checking below. "But we should head back to shore."

Frank nodded, moving toward the helm. Then a new threat appeared off their port side—a fishing trawler barreling toward them at full speed, its captain blinded by panic as he fled the Coast Guard.

"Incoming!" Frank shouted.

The impact threw them all across the deck. Metal shrieked against metal as the trawler's bow sliced into their hull. The *Data Point* heeled violently to starboard, water pouring through the fresh gash torn in its side.

"We're going down," Rodriguez called, clinging to the rail as the deck tilted beneath them.

Frank moved with mechanical precision, checking each researcher for injuries. "Life raft," he ordered, pointing to the emergency equipment stowed aft.

As Foster and Thompson deployed the raft, Chen turned to Frank. "The data," she said. "Voss will have my head if I lose it."

"You. Raft," said Frank already moving, descending into the half-flooded cabin. Cold water rose past his waist as he waded to the rack-mounted server. Using his KA-BAR knife, he pried open the casing, extracting the hard drive from its housing. He wrapped it in his waterproof jacket, securing it against his chest.

By the time he emerged, the *Data Point* had settled deeper, its deck nearly awash. The researchers huddled in the life raft, Rodriguez cradling a broken wrist.

"The equipment—" Chen began.

"Got what matters," Frank said, holding up the bundled hard drive as he climbed into the raft.

The *Data Point* slipped beneath the surface with a final gurgle as they pushed away from the sinking vessel. Around them, chaos reigned. Morrison's boat had vanished, leaving only floating debris. The Coast Guard cutter collected survivors, its Vulcan cannon now silent.

"They fired on civilians," Thompson said, still stunned. "On us."

"Accident," Frank corrected. "Aim walked with the swell."

"Does it matter?" Foster snapped. "They turned a cannon on fishermen!"

Frank said nothing, his eyes on the Coast Guard vessel now turning toward their raft. His hand rested near the flare gun in the survival kit.

"The hard drive," Chen said, reaching for the bundle in Frank's jacket. "Is it intact?"

Frank nodded and handed her his jacket with the drive.

"Good." Chen clutched it to her chest. "Every data point captured. The escalation pattern, the multi-faction response dynamics, the application of military hardware against civilian targets. It's all there."

Frank watched her face, seeing something beneath her scientific detachment—a hunger, an anticipation he recognized from men who called in airstrikes and watched targets disintegrate.

As the Coast Guard cutter approached to rescue them, Frank looked back at the space where the *Data Point* had been. The researchers had gotten their data. The hard drive rested against Chen's chest like something precious. Data drawn from human conflict.

Helix Headquarters – Arlington, Virginia

Sunlight cut through Reed's office blinds, striping his desk where the Puget Sound incident report lay open. Photos of the sunken *Data Point*. Medical forms for the injured researchers. Equipment loss tallies.

Voss entered without knocking. Her face bore the tight lines of contained fury.

"Three researchers in the hospital. A half-million in equipment at the bottom of Puget Sound." Her voice never rose above conversation level. "Your security specialist broke Chen's ribs."

Reed closed the report. "Chen has three cracked ribs from Frank protecting her with his own body as a shield."

"The hard drive was recovered. The equipment was expendable. The researchers were not." Voss stepped inside, closing the door. "Kane is a hammer looking for nails. I want him gone."

Reed's eyes hardened. "Frank Kane is exactly what we need. Those researchers came home alive because of him."

"They were shot at by a military-grade weapon."

"Yes." Reed leaned back. "And if Frank hadn't been there, they would be dead."

"He escalates situations. His presence alone is a provocation."

Reed crossed to the window. "Did you read Chen's assessment? Frank tried to move the boat back before the Coast Guard fired. She overruled him."

"That's her job. She determines optimal data collection parameters."

"And his job is keeping them alive despite those parameters." Reed turned. "Our teams are documenting increasing violence in American communities. That documentation puts them at risk. Frank protects them."

Voss placed her tablet on his desk, showing video of Frank tackling Chen as gunfire tore through the boat.

Frank extracting the hard drive from the sinking vessel. Frank securing the injured researchers in the life raft.

"He's a blunt instrument. Look at him." She pointed to Frank's scarred bulk on screen. "He terrifies the research teams."

"They're alive to complain."

Voss's jaw tightened. "You didn't consult me before hiring him."

"Security matters are my responsibility," Reed said. "The teams are pushing into increasingly volatile environments. Violence is rising exactly as Fulcrum predicted."

"That's why we need security professionals who de-escalate. Not men like Kane."

"Frank didn't invite that Coast Guard cannon. He didn't cause that trawler to ram their boat. What he did was adapt and survive."

"He'll only take orders from you." Voss moved closer. "I've seen how he looks at me. He doesn't respect my authority."

"He respects capability. Frank obeys Chen in her domain. He'll obey you in yours. But in security matters, he reports to me."

"I don't trust him."

Reed's eyes fixed on hers. "You don't have to trust him. You just have to let him do his job." He closed the incident report with finality. "Now, I need to brief the Alaska facility. They're expecting the Puget Sound data."

Voss stood her ground. "This isn't over, Marshall."

"Stay out of security issues, Elaine. Focus on developing Fulcrum and your research teams. Let me worry about keeping them alive."

She took her tablet and moved to the door. Stopped. "Helix is my company. Everything that supports it answers to me. Even your pet monster."

The door closed behind her without sound.

Reed studied the satellite photos once more. The Coast Guard's cannon firing on civilians. Americans killing Americans over fish. Exactly as predicted. Exactly as required.

The Helix cafeteria sat empty at this hour. Outside windows, Arlington darkness pressed against glass. Only Meyer and Voss remained, surrounded by the mechanical hum of refrigeration units and coffee machines powered down for the night.

Meyer spread financial documents across the table between them. His fingers precise despite fatigue etched across his face. The ledgers told a story in numbers. A narrative measured in dollars and authorizations.

"Three million transferred last week," he said. "Seven point two the week before. All to accounts linked to something called Arcturus Holdings."

Voss leaned forward. Steam rose from her untouched coffee. "Facility expenses. The Fairbanks data center."

"That was the explanation I received." Meyer's voice held no accusation. Just accountant's professional neutrality. "But the scope has expanded beyond initial parameters."

"How so?"

He pushed a document toward her. A spending authorization form bearing her digital signature. "Reed's access to Helix funds changed two months ago. His spending ceiling removed entirely."

Voss picked up the form. Studied it with growing confusion. "I never signed this."

"The system shows your authorization. December seventeenth. Eight forty-three in the evening." Meyer's eyes remained on her face. Watching. Assessing.

"I was in Geneva on the seventeenth. The World Economic Forum panel on AI ethics." She set the form down carefully. As if it might burn her fingers. "I couldn't have signed anything."

Meyer nodded once. Confirming something already suspected. "Reed has been moving substantial funds. Equipment purchases. Personnel expansion. Security upgrades not in any approved budget."

"How much total?"

"Twenty-seven million and counting." Meyer's precision gave the number weight beyond its syllables. "All authorized under your digital signature. All routed through accounts with minimal oversight triggers."

Voss pushed away her coffee. The steam no longer rising. The liquid cooling like the blood in her veins.

"Why didn't any of this show up in my weekly financial reports?"

Meyer's mouth tightened. "I believe Reed modified the reports sent to you and the board. The discrepancies were subtle. Distributed across multiple cost centers. Nothing that would trigger standard audit flags."

"That's impossible. He doesn't have access to those systems."

"He shouldn't," Meyer agreed. "But we found evidence of email account intrusions. Modified database queries. Intercepted reports that were altered before reaching your inbox."

"For how long?"

"At least four months. We only detected it last week when the backup server logs didn't match primary system records."

Voss closed her eyes briefly. Opened them with renewed focus. "Show me everything."

Meyer opened his laptop. Turned it toward her. Spreadsheets covered the screen in neat columns and rows. The architecture of financial manipulation laid bare by a man who understood numbers better than people.

Midnight at Helix headquarters. Frank waited in the shadows. An employee exited the building. Frank moved silently slipping through the front door before it closed. Although his badge would give him access, he didn't want a record of his entry.

Frank slipped past the night guard at the security desk watching the camera monitors with little interest. A show of security. Frank entered the doorway to the stairwell.

Floor by floor, Frank climbed the stairs instead of using the elevator. No cameras in the stairwells. An oversight in most buildings but not here. Here it meant the stairs were equipped with pressure plates and motion sensors instead. More sophisticated. Less obvious. Frank placed his boots exactly where the plates joined, avoiding the trigger points where weight would register. When within the field of a motion detector he stepped slowly and stopped for thirty seconds, then continued with more slow steps. A painstaking process that required the patience of a saint.

Sixth floor. Research division. Frank eased the door open and listened. Nothing but the hum of air conditioning and the soft electronic chirping of equipment in sleep mode.

Security cameras swept empty corridors in mechanical rhythm, their red recording lights glowing like small unblinking eyes. Frank moved between their blind spots, his massive frame improbably silent. He moved down the corridor, counting doors. Chen's office would be near the center, where team leaders clustered.

A keypad secured her door. Not unexpected. Frank reached into his coverall pocket for the electronic bypass device Culper had provided. As he raised it to the keypad, something made him hesitate. The faceplate looked wrong. Too new against the older door. He knelt, examining it more closely.

Behind the standard keypad lay a secondary system. Subtle wires ran from its housing into the wall. A silent alarm. Anyone trying to bypass the code would trigger it, regardless of whether they succeeded.

Frank stood again, frowning. The building's security had been upgraded recently. Nothing in Culper's intelligence had indicated this level of protection for a mid-level manager's office.

He moved on. The server room would be more heavily guarded but might have standard access protocols. Three doors down, a placard read DATA PROCESSING. Another keypad, this one with a biometric scanner beside it. Fingerprints and codes. Frank studied it, then looked up.

A camera was mounted in the corner, aimed directly at the door. Its housing had been painted to match the ceiling. Nearly invisible unless you knew to look. The data center wasn't just secured—it was a trap for anyone trying to access it.

Frank backed away. Motion sensors would track his approach to the server room, cameras would capture his face, the biometrics would record his attempt. Too many layers, too many alerts.

He descended to the fifth floor. Administration. Reed's office would be at the end of the hall, corner suite with the best view. Executives always claimed such spaces, a remnant of territorial instinct that even advanced degrees couldn't eliminate.

The corridor stretched empty before him. Frank passed darkened offices with glass walls, workspaces laid open like specimens for dissection. Nothing hidden. Everything visible.

But the transparency was illusion. The real work happened elsewhere, behind solid walls and security systems designed to keep people exactly like him out.

Reed's door had no nameplate. No need to identify the man everyone knew. Another keypad. Another camera. And something else—a thin magnetic strip along the door's edge. Wired to the frame, barely perceptible. A tamper sensor that would register even minute vibrations.

Frank stood before it, considering. He had the tools to breach such systems. Had the knowledge. But the risk went beyond detection. This wasn't merely security—it was a multilayered defense built by someone who understood infiltration. Someone who anticipated it.

A noise from the stairwell. Boots on steps, coming closer. Frank melted into an alcove as a night patrol emerged. Two guards, armed with sidearms and tasers. They swept flashlight beams down the corridor, checking each office methodically.

Frank remained motionless, barely breathing. The beams passed within inches of his position.

"East wing clear," one guard reported into his radio. "Proceeding to north quadrant."

The patrol moved on, disappearing around a corner. Frank waited until their steps faded before emerging. The encounter confirmed his suspicion—security didn't just monitor, it actively searched. Regular patrols, randomly timed. Professional.

He returned to the stairwell, taking it down to the garage level. If the offices were impenetrable, perhaps the data moved physically between locations. Hard drives. Backup tapes. Couriers.

The garage spread beneath the building, concrete pillars dividing reserved spaces where executives parked German sedans and American SUVs. Security cameras covered the entrance, the elevator, the stairwell access. But underneath one executive's parking space—Reed's, judging by the nameplate—Frank spotted something.

A signal jammer, small and nearly invisible, attached to the underside of a pipe. Anyone parking above it would be briefly invisible to electromagnetic surveillance. A gap in security, but not accidental. Deliberate.

Reed had created his own blind spot. A place where data could pass without digital fingerprints.

Frank knelt, examining the jammer without touching it. Chinese manufacture. Military grade. Illegal for civilian use. The kind of device intelligence agencies used for field operations.

Whatever Reed protected went beyond corporate secrecy. Beyond profit. The security wasn't just extreme—it was professional. Designed by someone who understood classified operations. Someone who had conducted them.

Frank withdrew, retracing his steps through the building. No alarms sounded. No guards intercepted him. To all appearances, his infiltration had gone undetected.

Outside, Frank walked three blocks before stopping at a pay phone. He dialed the number from memory.

"Progress?" Culper asked when he picked up.

"No," Frank said, his voice gravel and rust.

"Security?"

"Professional."

"We need that data, Frank. Fulcrum—"

"Different approach," Frank cut him off.

"What kind?"

"Direct."

Frank hung up, the single word hanging between them like a promise. Or a threat. Reed's security had one vulnerability all elaborate systems shared—they depended on people. People could be approached. Manipulated. Turned.

Reed had built a fortress. But no fortress was impregnable. Frank would find a way in. Not through stealth, but through the front door. Helix needed security specialists. Reed clearly valued them.

Frank would become indispensable. And then he would take what Culper needed.

The night wrapped around him as he walked away, just another shadow in a city full of them. Behind him, Helix headquarters rose against the sky, windows dark except for the security floors where lights burned constant as stars.

Buzzard Point – Washington D.C.

The Helix van rolled to a stop in darkness, half a mile from the Blackridge Coal Plant. Plumes from two giant towers were visible against the night sky, silhouettes of American industry struggling to survive. The parking lot remained empty. No protesters had arrived yet, but Fulcrum had predicted they would come. The algorithm rarely missed.

Voss sat in the driver's seat, field clothes crisp despite the pre-dawn hour. With Olivia Chen out of commission with three broken ribs, this was Voss's operation. Frank occupied the passenger seat, his bulk making the space seem smaller. The tension between them hung thick as the coal dust. In the back, Rodriguez and Thompson checked equipment—directional microphones, thermal cameras, biometric sensors. Tools to measure conflict before it happened.

"Fulcrum gives us ninety minutes before the environmentalists arrive," Voss said, checking her watch. "The plant's morning shift starts in thirty. We need optimal positioning before they intersect."

Frank scanned the perimeter through tinted windows. Something wasn't right. The security presence was too heavy, the guard patterns too precise. Men with rifles patrolled the fence line in pairs, their movements suggesting military training rather than rent-a-cop routine.

"North ridge gives us line of sight to both the main gate and employee entrance," Voss continued, not looking at Frank. "We'll set up there."

"No." Frank's voice scraped.

Voss's knuckles gripped the steering wheel. "That wasn't a suggestion, Mr. Kane."

"Exposed." Frank pointed toward the ridge line. "No cover."

"The north ridge provides optimal data capture for all three subject groups," Voss said, control evident in each syllable. "The environmental activists, plant workers, and security forces. That's why we're here."

Frank met her eyes. "Trap."

Rodriguez leaned forward from the equipment bay. "Dr. Voss, Chen always avoided elevated positions without cover. Maybe we should—"

"Chen isn't here," Voss cut him off. "I am. North ridge. Now."

Frank's jaw tightened, but he said nothing more. Voss started the engine again, and the van crawled up the service road, headlights off. Gravel popped beneath heavy tires.

Below them, the coal plant sprawled across fifty acres, its perimeter fence gleaming under security floodlights. The massive smokestacks stood like ancient monuments, their purpose unchanged for a century despite the world shifting around them. The plant gate remained quiet, but vehicles were beginning to arrive—early shift workers in trucks and sedans.

"There." Voss pointed to a flat area on the ridge where trees provided minimal concealment. "Set up there."

Frank assessed the position. No real cover. One narrow access path. Exposed on three sides. Exactly what he'd warned against. He shook his head, but didn't argue.

The research team deployed with practiced efficiency despite the tension. Directional microphones aimed toward the plant entrance. Thermal cameras positioned to track body heat signatures, measuring the subtle changes that preceded violence. Weather instruments recorded wind and barometric pressure—factors that influenced crowd behavior in ways still being mapped.

"Environmental group approaching from the south road," Rodriguez reported, checking his tablet. "Fifteen vehicles. Consistent with Fulcrum's projection."

"Perfect," Voss said, satisfaction evident in her voice. "We'll have front-row seats to the entire confrontation."

Frank remained by the van, watching the ridgeline rather than the approaching protest. Something was wrong. The plant security was too methodical, too prepared. Not the normal reaction to environmental protests that happened monthly at facilities like this.

Movement caught his eye—flashlight beams sweeping through trees to their left. Security patrols. Moving with purpose, not random search patterns.

"Pack up," Frank said.

Voss lowered her binoculars. "Excuse me?"

"Security coming."

"We have authorization to observe—"

"Searching for us." Frank was already moving, pulling down tripods, disconnecting equipment. "Specifically."

The research team hesitated, caught between Voss's authority and Frank's urgency. Chen made the decision, quickly breaking down her station. The others followed her lead.

"This is unacceptable," Voss snapped. "You're sabotaging crucial data collection."

Frank pointed to the flashlight beams, now clearly angling toward their position. "Two teams. Flanking pattern."

Voss finally saw the lights. "How did they—"

"Setup." Frank loaded equipment into the van. "Trap."

The researchers worked faster, hands fumbling with cases and cables. Voss stood paralyzed, watching the security teams close in.

"Inside," Frank ordered, pushing the last researcher toward the van. "Now."

Voss found her voice. "I'm in command here, Mr. Kane. I'll determine—"

"Too late." Frank nodded toward two security guards who had emerged from the trees thirty yards away. Their flashlight beams caught Voss in harsh white light, pinning her like an insect.

"You there! This is private property!" The guards advanced, hands moving to their belts where collapsable batons hung.

Frank stepped between Voss and the approaching guards. "Going now," he said, voice neutral despite the tension evident in his massive frame.

"Nobody's going anywhere." The lead guard pulled his baton, extending it with a sharp metallic snap. "On the ground, hands behind your heads."

The second guard spoke into his radio. "North ridge. Five suspects plus their vehicle. Requesting backup."

Frank assessed them. Contract security, not law enforcement. Armed with batons, tasers, and possibly sidearms. The nearest was six-foot-two, two hundred thirty pounds. Ex-military by his stance. The second was shorter but wider, arms thick with gym muscle. Both were too confident.

"This is a misunderstanding," Voss said, stepping forward with corporate authority. "I'm Dr. Elaine Voss, CEO of Helix Behavioral Analytics. We have documentation—"

The lead guard moved faster than his size suggested. He grabbed Voss's arm, spinning her around into a compliance hold.

"On the ground," he repeated. The baton pressed under her jaw, forcing her head back. "Now."

Frank was already moving. His hand caught the guard's wrist, applying pressure to specific tendons. The baton clattered to the ground. The guard tried to counter, but Frank had anticipated the move. His boot swept the man's legs, dropping him hard to the dirt.

The second guard's taser appeared, aimed at Frank's chest. But Frank had closed the distance too quickly. His forearm struck the guard's wrist, deflecting the taser. His other hand found the man's throat, fingers pressing precise points that disrupted blood flow to the brain. The guard collapsed without making a sound.

The first guard struggled to rise. Frank let him regain his feet. The man threw a punch aimed at Frank's throat—a killing blow. Frank's hand intercepted the strike, redirecting it past his shoulder. He stepped inside the guard's defense, using the man's momentum to throw him into a nearby tree trunk. The impact knocked the breath from the guard's lungs. He slid to the ground, gasping.

"Enough," Frank said.

The guard didn't listen. His hand moved to his hip where a holstered pistol sat. Frank's boot pinned the man's wrist to the ground before he could draw the weapon. Bones ground against each other. The guard cried out.

Frank knelt, removed the pistol, ejected the magazine and cleared the chamber. He tossed the empty weapon into the undergrowth, then did the same with the other guard's taser and sidearm.

Eleven seconds had passed since the first guard grabbed Voss.

"Inside," Frank told her, his voice same as if nothing had happened. "Everyone."

The researchers scrambled into the van, faces pale in the dim light. Voss stood frozen, staring at the guards on the ground.

"Move," Frank said. He gently took her arm, guiding her to the van. She didn't resist.

Frank drove down the service road, headlights still dark. In the rearview mirror, he saw more flashlights converging on their former position. Backup arriving just as they slipped away.

"How did you know?" Voss's voice was small in the silence.

Frank glanced at her. "Patterns."

"There was no documentation of our presence in the official system," Rodriguez said. "Someone tipped them off."

Frank turned onto the main road, finally switching on headlights. He checked the mirrors for pursuit. None yet, but it would come.

"They knew exactly where we'd be," Thompson said. "The north ridge. The perfect observation point."

"Perfect trap," Frank corrected.

"They knew exactly who we were," Thompson said, voice still shaking as they drove away. "This wasn't random security catching trespassers."

"No witnesses," Frank said, eyes on the road.

Voss looked sharply at him. "You mean they deliberately targeted us to prevent documentation of the protest?"

Frank nodded once.

Voss sat rigidly in the passenger seat, hands clenched in her lap. "Those men. Are they—"

"Alive." Frank took a turn that led away from the main highway.

"You disarmed them so quickly. So efficiently." Voss studied his profile. "Where did you learn that?"

Frank kept his eyes on the road. Didn't answer.

"Thank you," she said after a long moment. "For protecting us."

Frank nodded once.

"Next time," she continued, "I'll consider your assessment before choosing a position."

Frank glanced at her. Something passed between them—not trust yet, but its beginning.

"Back roads," he said, turning onto a gravel track that cut through woods.

The van disappeared into darkness, leaving only dust hanging in the air where it had passed. Behind them, security teams rushed to the north ridge, finding only empty ground and discarded weapons.

Helix Headquarters – Arlington, Virginia

Reed's office sat dark except for a single desk lamp. Night had claimed the windows hours ago. The skyline glowed beyond the glass, a constellation of office lights and streetlamps. He studied field reports spread on the desk, each bearing Frank's name.

Frank appeared in the doorway, shoulders nearly touching both sides. He sat when Reed gestured, the chair creaking beneath his weight.

"You've impressed me," Reed said. "Multiple incidents. Each a potential disaster. Perfect extraction each time."

Frank remained still, eyes fixed past Reed's shoulder.

"You're a rare breed, Frank Kane. You understand when and where to apply pressure in a volatile situation. How to keep things under control."

Frank grunted.

"America has become one nation divided into a thousand tribes. Race against race. Rich against poor. Urban against rural. Fault lines running through every state, every city, every neighborhood."

"Always been."

"Not like this. Social media turned grievance into currency. Politicians trade in outrage. News channels sell conflict instead of facts. We've forgotten how to disagree without destruction. It's going to destroy us unless we do something. Something radical."

Frank grunted again. Maybe agreement.

"Our enemies watch," Reed continued. "Patient as vultures. Russians, Chinese, Iranians. They feed the divisions. Plant stories. Fund extremists on both sides." His jaw tightened. "They don't need to defeat us militarily when we're tearing ourselves apart. January 6th. Portland riots. School board meetings where parents threaten violence over books." Reed turned from the window. "These aren't random events. They're symptoms of a deeper disease. Americans killing Americans while foreign powers wait to pick up the pieces." Reed's voice hardened. "We're doing their work for them. Our internal foolishness is their greatest weapon. Rome fell from within," Reed said. "So will we, unless something changes."

Frank's scarred face showed nothing.

"You've seen real war," Reed said. "You know its cost. Imagine that happening here. On these streets."

The silence settled between them like dust after an explosion.

"America's enemies grow stronger daily," Reed said. "The Pentagon thinks our military is invincible. It's not." He leaned forward. "If we're not careful, America could lose World War III."

Frank's expression revealed nothing.

"My brother died in Afghanistan," Reed continued. "Patrol walked into an ambush. Bad intelligence. Command said sixty insurgents waited in those hills." He shook his head. "Three hundred Taliban hidden in caves our sensors couldn't penetrate."

Frank shifted slightly.

"A needless war. A needless death." Reed stood, moved to the window. "I'm building something that could protect America without sending more brothers to die in foreign lands. Something that could end the need for war itself."

Frank blinked. Waited.

"I'm putting together a new source of financing and when it's in place, I want you to command a covert security force. Outside Helix's official structure. Small team of elite operators."

Something changed in Frank's posture. Nearly imperceptible, but present.

"Better equipment. Your own operational authority. Substantially higher compensation."

Frank's gaze settled on Reed. "Doing what?"

"Sometimes conflict needs a catalyst," Reed explained. "A nudge to ensure it develops along predictable parameters."

"Engineering violence."

Reed didn't flinch from the accusation. "We study it. Control it. Manage it. Better to understand the weapon than be destroyed by it."

Frank examined Reed's face. Searching.

"I know it's a lot to take in and you don't know me very well. But I promise you, I have America's best interest at heart."

Frank stood, his massive frame casting the desk in shadow. "I'll think about it," he said finally.

He left without another word. Reed remained motionless in the darkness, knowing he'd planted the seed. Some men were built for violence. Born for it. All they needed was the right cause.

Reed had provided it.

Frank unlocked the motel door, nudged it with his boot. The room's air hung stale and cold. He tossed the greasy paper bag on the table, burger smell filling the small space.

He sat on the bed, springs groaning. The ancient air conditioner rattled beneath the window. Outside, traffic crawled through the city night, headlights painting the ceiling.

Frank unwrapped a burger, ate it in three bites. Then another. His movements mechanical, efficient. He shoved a handful of fries into his mouth, salt burning a fresh cut on his thumb.

The food didn't taste like anything. Just fuel.

His eyes found the phone, black and heavy on the nightstand. Three more burgers disappeared, Styrofoam squeaking as he crushed the empty containers.

He wiped his hands on his pants, reached for the phone. Dialed a number from memory, thick fingers careful on the small buttons. The line rang once, twice.

Frank hung up before the third ring.

Not yet. Reed's words still circled in his head like caged animals. America tearing itself apart. Enemies waiting. A team of men like him. What was the difference between Culper and Reed if both had the goal of protecting America? Reed paid better.

He closed his eyes. Saw Reed's brother in that Afghan valley. Surrounded. Outmanned. Fighting with bad information and worse odds.

Saw other men too. Men he'd served with. Some buried. Some broken.

Frank crumpled the empty bag, tossed it toward the trash. Missed. Let it lie.

Culper could wait. First, he needed to know what game Reed was really playing.

The streetlight outside flickered, then steadied. Frank sat motionless in the half-dark, thinking about catalysts and engineered violence and all the ways a country could destroy itself while its enemies watched and waited.

Helix Headquarters – Arlington, Virginia

The locker room smelled of antiseptic and new concrete. Frank stood with his back to the door, shirt off, pulling a fresh Helix polo from his locker. Fluorescent lights cast every scar in stark relief—a roadmap of violence etched across his massive frame. Bullet wounds puckered his left shoulder. Knife scars crossed his lower back like railroad tracks. Burn tissue stretched across his right side, pink and twisted.

The door opened. Frank didn't turn.

"Mr. Kane, I—" Voss stopped abruptly. Her eyes widening at the battlefield written on his skin.

Frank pulled the shirt over his head, covering the evidence. Turned to face her.

"I should have knocked," she said.

Frank grunted.

"I wanted to thank you. For what happened at the coal plant." Voss straightened her suit jacket, a nervous gesture. "You were right. I was wrong. That's not easy for me to admit."

He closed his locker.

"At my age and position," she continued, "I should have trusted your assessment. It was arrogant to think I could just step into field operations like I was fresh out of college."

Frank's eyes met hers briefly, then away.

"I've never seen someone move like that," she said. "When those guards attacked us."

"Training."

Voss gestured vaguely toward his torso. "And experience, clearly."

She moved to a bench, sat down. Seemed smaller somehow, without her executive armor.

"What we're building with Fulcrum," she said. "It matters. More than you know. And you're a part of it."

Frank waited, motionless.

"America's tearing itself apart. Portland. Minneapolis. January 6th." Her voice softened. "Neighbors attacking neighbors over political yard signs. School board meetings ending in fistfights. It's insane really."

Frank leaned against the lockers, arms crossed.

"Fulcrum might change that." Voss leaned forward. "In the next generation of the program, it won't just predict violence. It will identify intervention points. Places where small actions could defuse tension before blood is shed. Give those involved time to reconsider their actions. Space that we all desperately need."

"Manipulation," Frank said.

"Prevention," she corrected. "A city decides to delay a controversial vote for three days. A police department chooses to stand down rather than advance. A mayor opens a dialog instead of sending in riot squads."

Frank's face revealed nothing.

"It could give both sides time to cool off. Time to remember we're all Americans." Her hands clasped tightly in her lap. "My son was at Charlottesville. On the counter-protest side. He could have been killed when that car drove into the crowd."

Frank shifted his weight. Listening.

"That's what drives me," Voss said. "Not data. Not profit. The possibility of prevention. Peace." She stood, professional mask sliding back into place. "Anyway. Thank you again, Mr. Kane. For keeping us safe."

She turned to leave.

"Reed has different ideas," Frank said, voice like gargling gravel.

Voss paused at the door. "Marshall sees things differently, yes." Something flashed across her face—doubt, perhaps. "But his science is sound. And the goals we both seek are worth pursuing."

She left him alone with the buzzing lights and the lingering scent of her expensive perfume.

Frank stood a moment longer. Wondering which of them was lying.

Meyer's office occupied the northwest corner of Helix's financial wing. Windows looked out toward the Potomac, though darkness now reflected only interior light against glass. The space spoke of precise organization. Files arranged by priority. Papers aligned at perfect angles. The room of a man who saw beauty in ordered systems.

Voss sat across from his desk. Her reflection in the window showed fatigue settling into her features. Four hours spent tracking financial discrepancies had left both of them drained.

"According to these transfers," Meyer said, setting down another folder, "Reed's diverted substantial funds under your forged authorization."

Voss pinched the bridge of her nose. "The board will need to be informed."

"After we've gathered concrete evidence." Meyer's caution remained his defining characteristic. "But there's something I don't understand."

"Just one thing?" Bitter humor colored her voice.

"Why don't you just fire him?"

Voss looked up sharply. "What?"

"Reed. Terminate his employment. Revoke his access. Exercise your authority as CEO." Meyer's logical mind sought the simplest solution. "He's clearly engaging in unauthorized activities with company resources."

"It's not that simple, Lawrence."

"Explain it to me." He folded his hands atop the desk. "Because from a financial oversight perspective, immediate termination seems appropriate."

Voss stood. Moved to the window. The skyline beyond offered no inspiration.

"Reed controls Fulcrum development," she said finally. "The current iteration is his architecture. His implementation. I built the foundation, but he and his programmers have constructed everything since."

"That doesn't grant him immunity from corporate governance."

"It gives him leverage." She turned back to face Meyer. "Three board members—Wilson, Kingston, and Mitchell—have direct investments in Fulcrum's advanced applications. They see enormous potential in what Reed's promising."

"Your board can't override basic corporate ethics."

"They can if they perceive their interests threatened." Voss returned to her chair. "Reed has cultivated relationships with them for months. Private demonstrations. Specialized briefings on Fulcrum's capabilities that I wasn't invited to attend."

Meyer frowned. "That violates governance protocols."

"Protocols don't matter to people who believe they're building something revolutionary." She leaned forward. "Wilson told me last quarter that Reed represents 'the future direction of our national security establishment.' That's a direct quote."

Meyer sat back. Processing implications with accountant's precision. "You think they'd support Reed even with evidence of financial impropriety?"

"They'd see it as necessary expedience. Bureaucratic obstacles overcome in service to greater purpose." Voss's voice hardened. "Reed has convinced them Fulcrum transcends normal corporate considerations."

"No technology justifies fraud."

"Tell that to the contractors who built the atomic bomb. Or the agencies developing surveillance systems." She gestured to the spreadsheets covering his desk. "Reed has positioned Fulcrum as something beyond normal oversight. That changes the calculation."

Meyer studied her face. Seeing new dimensions to the woman he'd worked alongside for years. "You're afraid of him."

"Not afraid." She considered her words carefully. "Cautious. Reed has built something beyond the original Fulcrum parameters. Something I never intended."

"And secured board support for it."

"Three of seven members. Possibly four if Wallace can be persuaded." She spread her hands on the desk. "I need irrefutable evidence before moving against him. Something even his supporters can't dismiss."

Meyer nodded slowly. His natural caution aligning with strategic necessity. "We document everything. Build an airtight case."

"While determining exactly what he's created." Voss's eyes held new resolve. "I designed Fulcrum to predict social pressure points. To identify conflict before it happens. Reed has transformed it into something else."

"Into what?"

"That's what we need to discover." She stood to leave. "Keep tracking the money. It will tell us what he values. What he's building."

"And Reed?"

"I'll maintain normalcy. Give him no reason to suspect we've discovered the discrepancies."

Meyer gathered the files with methodical precision. "Be careful, Elaine. If he's gone to these lengths to hide his activities..."

She paused at the door. "What?"

"People who believe they're changing history rarely let others stand in their way."

Outside Meyer's office, the financial wing sat empty. Workstations dormant. Screens dark. The infrastructure of corporate governance suspended until morning.

Voss walked alone through silent corridors. Her company no longer entirely hers. Her creation evolving beyond her design. The realization settled cold against her skin.

Whatever Reed built, he had calculated each step. Including how to neutralize her authority while maintaining appearance of corporate normalcy.

A perfect algorithm of human manipulation executed without error.

Until now.

The building had emptied hours ago. Only cleaning staff remained, their vacuums humming in distant corridors. Voss sat at her desk, surrounded by blue light from three monitors. Spreadsheets and projections. Numbers that didn't add up.

A shadow crossed her doorway. Reed stood there, coat folded over his arm.

"Working late again," he said. Not a question.

Voss looked up. "Someone has to mind the store."

Reed stepped inside, didn't sit. "I'll be out tomorrow. Personal business."

"All day?"

"Does it matter?" A hard edge beneath the words.

Voss closed her laptop. "We need to talk about Fulcrum. A strategy meeting. The direction is drifting."

"It's proceeding exactly as designed."

"Not my design." She stood, matching his stance across the desk. "And I want all data transfers to Fairbanks halted until I review the protocols."

Reed's face didn't change. "It's too late."

"Excuse me?"

"The transfers happened last night. Full system backup. All current algorithms."

Voss's hand slammed against the desktop. "You had no authorization."

"I had all the authorization I needed."

"I'm the CEO of this company. Nothing moves without my approval."

Reed set his coat on the chair back. "There are stakeholders above your position. They've signed off."

"Bullshit." Voss moved around the desk, closing the distance. "You've deliberately circumvented my authority. Who gave the order? Wilson? Wallace?"

"Does it matter?"

"It damned well matters." Her voice rose, echoing off glass walls.

"Look. Things will happen faster now that Fairbanks is up and running. The programmers I hired are top notch."

"Fairbanks was meant to be a redundant system. Not a parallel operation."

"Plans change."

"Not without my knowledge and consent."

Reed buttoned his suit jacket, a gesture of finality. "It's done, Elaine. The Fairbanks facility is fully operational. Running the same protocols. Same parameters."

"I'm shutting it down." She reached for her phone. "First thing tomorrow."

Reed's laugh held no humor. "With what authority? Your name isn't on those documents."

"My company—"

"Is part of something larger now." Reed moved toward the door. "Always was."

Voss stood frozen, understanding settling like ice in her stomach. "What have you done, Marshall?"

"Ensured Fulcrum's survival." He paused at the threshold. "Sometimes the creator becomes the obstacle."

"Is that a threat?"

"An observation." He nodded slightly. "Good night, Elaine."

The door closed with barely a sound. Voss stood alone in the blue glow of her monitors, the empire she'd built slipping through her fingers like sand.

Insomnia

Darkness pressed against the townhouse windows. Three AM. Voss lay in bed staring at the ceiling. Sleep would not come. Had not come for days now. Not since finding the invoice with Reed's signature. Not since tracing the money to Fairbanks. Not since Reed threatened her. She knew what he was capable of. That's why she hired him in the first place. A man that did what was needed to accomplish his objective.

The bedroom felt too quiet. Too open. The windows like black mirrors reflecting nothing. She had changed the locks twice. Had installed the secondary alarm system that bypassed the main circuit. Had strengthened the fortress but still felt exposed.

Voss reached for her phone on the nightstand. The screen illuminated her face in blue light that made shadows of her features. She opened a private browser window. Typed: reliable handgun for self-defense.

Pages filled the screen. Forums where enthusiasts debated calibers and models like religious texts. She scrolled past the extremes. Past the zealots recommending cannon-sized weapons and those dismissing anything larger than a .22. Found the moderate voices with practical advice.

Concealment versus stopping power. Reliability versus speed. The gun as tool rather than totem. She studied diagrams of firing mechanisms. Applied the same analytical precision that had built a technology empire to the problem of personal protection.

Voss sat in her car outside the motel. The kind of place where rooms rented by the hour and questions remained unasked. Red neon vacancy sign buzzed and flickered. A place Frank would choose. Anonymous. Forgettable. Defensive in its squalor.

She had found his location through company records. Security badge access linked to the payroll system. The address listed as temporary residence. A formality Frank had overlooked or perhaps hadn't cared enough to falsify.

Room 217 waited on the second floor. Paint peeled from the metal railing that ran the length of the building. A man smoked at the far end, watching her Mercedes with professional interest. Calculating its value against the effort of theft.

Voss locked the car and climbed the stairs. Her Louboutin heels clicked against concrete. The sound marked her as outsider. As someone who didn't belong in this world of transience and desperation.

She knocked three times on Frank's door. Waited. No sound came from within. She knocked again.

The door opened just enough for Frank's eye to assess the hallway before widening to admit her. The room beyond held little. A duffel bag on the dresser. Sheets tucked tight on the bed with military precision. No personal items. Nothing that could not be abandoned in thirty seconds if necessary.

"I need your help," Voss said.

Frank waited. Said nothing.

"I need protection. A firearm."

Frank's expression remained neutral. He studied her face. Looking for something beneath the words.

"Why?"

"Caution."

Frank considered this. Nodded once. "When?"

"Tomorrow. Early."

Frank returned to cleaning the disassembled Redhawk on the small table by the window. Pieces laid out in precise order. The ritual of maintenance that kept the weapon reliable. That kept death itself dependable when summoned.

"Pistol?" he said.

"Yes."

"Revolver or automatic?"

"Automatic I think."

Frank grunts his displeasure.

"You think a revolver is better?"

"Dependable. Doesn't jam."

"But an automatic holds more bullets."

"Only need one."

"I see."

"Bring ID," he said.

"Okay. But I want to buy it in Virginia. No waiting period. I own the Helix headquarters building. I have a tax document. Will that work?"

Frank nodded as he reassembled the revolver with practiced motions. Each piece finding its place with mechanical certainty. The weapon whole again. Lethal in its completion.

"Seven AM," he said.

"Fine. I'll pick you up."

"No. I drive."

"Okay. Do you know my address in Georgetown?"

Frank nodded. Voss left. No more words needed between them.

Morning arrived cold and clear. Frank waited in the Imperial outside her townhouse. Engine running. Heat filled the massive interior.

Voss slid into the passenger seat. The leather creaked beneath her. Frank put the car in drive without speaking.

The Imperial's engine rumbled like distant thunder. Frank guided the massive vehicle through Georgetown traffic with mechanical precision, the car's chrome gleaming under winter sunlight.

Voss sat stiffly in the passenger seat, hands folded in her lap. She glanced at the analog gauges on the metal dashboard. The needle on the fuel gauge hovered near empty.

"Your car must get terrible gas mileage," she said.

Frank's eyes remained on the road.

"I'm surprised you don't drive something more efficient."

Frank's hands adjusted on the steering wheel. His expression unchanged.

"Environmental impact is a quantifiable variable," Voss continued. "Just like social behaviors. Measurable. Predictable." She ran her finger along the leather seat. "This thing probably burns a gallon just idling in traffic."

"Reliable," Frank said.

Voss looked at him. The first word he'd spoken since picking her up.

"There are reliable cars that don't consume fossil fuels like they're going extinct."

The corner of Frank's mouth twitched. Not quite a smile but acknowledgment of something like humor.

"Strong," he added.

Voss understood then. The Imperial wasn't transportation but armor. The steel frame and heavy doors weren't wasteful but purposeful. A vehicle built before planned obsolescence. Before plastic components designed to fail.

A machine created to withstand impact. To protect what it carried. The Imperial crawled through morning traffic. Chrome trim caught sunlight in harsh flashes.

"Why keep Reed?" Frank's voice scraped through damaged vocal cords.

Voss turned from the window. Studied his profile, the ruin of his throat.

"It's not that simple."

"Try."

She looked down at her hands. Fingers elegant but trembling slightly.

"The company board divided. Reed has three of seven members convinced Fulcrum needs his vision." Her voice hardened. "They don't know what he's doing, but they see the military applications. The profit potential."

Frank guided the Imperial around a delivery truck. The engine rumbled, patient and powerful.

"Fire him anyway."

"Reed brings in money. Military contracts. Government connections." She turned toward him. "In their eyes, I'm just the scientist who started the company. Replaceable. If I want to fire Reed, I need proof first. Something concrete they can't ignore."

The Imperial stopped at a red light. A woman crossed in front of them pushing a stroller, head bent against wind. The light changed. The Imperial moved forward. Neither spoke. They crossed the Potomac as sunlight touched the monuments of power they left behind.

The gun store stood between a pawn shop and a tax preparation office. Red, white, and blue sign proclaiming FREEDOM FIREARMS. American flags hung in windows. Posters showing weapons arranged like sacred artifacts.

Inside smelled of gun oil and chemical cleaner. Glass cases displayed hundreds of handguns organized by manufacturer. By caliber. By purpose. Men in flannel and denim stood in small groups discussing ballistics and politics. They noted Frank's entrance. The scarred bulk of him. The way his eyes cataloged exits and cover. The way his hand never strayed far from his hip. They nodded recognition of kind.

A salesman approached. Beard gone white at the edges. Eyes that had seen combat in places that remained classified.

"Help you folks find something?"

Frank said nothing. This was Voss's purchase. Her decision. Her responsibility.

"Something reliable," she said. "For protection."

The salesman assessed her. The tailored clothes suggesting wealth. The tension in her shoulders suggesting necessity rather than recreation.

"Home defense or carry?"

"Both."

He nodded. Reached beneath the glass. The salesman laid the pistols on the glass countertop. Black metal against blue felt. A Glock. Two Sigs. A pair of revolvers, one nickel-plated, one blued steel.

"These are our most popular models for personal protection."

She ran her finger along the barrel of the Glock. Lifted it. Turned it over in her hands.

"Nine-millimeter. Seventeen rounds. Most officers carry something similar."

She aimed at the wall. Her grip uncertain. She set it down, picked up the Sig P226.

"Bit heavier. Used by Navy SEALs."

Her eyes moved between the options. Hesitant. The nickel revolver caught the light.

"That's a Colt Python. Six-inch barrel. Beautiful piece but harder to conceal."

Frank stood behind her. Silent. Watching.

She lifted the blued Smith & Wesson Model 686. Fumbled with the cylinder release. It swung open awkwardly. She examined the empty chambers.

"Trigger?" Frank's voice like stone grinding on stone.

"Four pounds. Consistent through the pull. No stacking."

She tried to close the cylinder. It wouldn't catch.

Frank took the revolver. One practiced motion and the cylinder locked into place. He handed it back.

"Rounds?" he asked.

"Six .357 Magnum but shoots .38 Special too."

She looked at Frank. "This one?"

He nodded once.

The salesman slid a form across the counter. "You'll want to practice before carrying it."

Frank pointed to the ammunition cabinet. "Shells. 38 Specials."

"What grain?"

"One ten. Two boxes. Practice. Home," said Frank.

The salesman placed two boxes next to the revolver. "Range ammo and hollow points for home defense."

"Two speed loaders."

The salesman nodded and place two speed loaders on the counter next to the ammo boxes.

She signed the form. Counted out cash. Frank took both boxes with the speed loaders and slipped them into his pocket. Took the revolver. Checked it one more time before handing it to her.

"Range is through that door," the salesman said when the transaction completed. "Might want to try it out. Get comfortable with it."

Frank followed Voss into the indoor range. Six lanes with dividers. Air thick with gunpowder and metal.

He handed her ear protection and glasses from a shelf. They took lane four. Frank showed her how to load the revolver with one of the speed loaders. His scarred hands enveloped hers, adjusting her fingers around the walnut grip. He positioned her thumb to avoid the cylinder gap.

"Stance."

He demonstrated. Feet at shoulder width. Knees flexed. Arms extended.

Voss mirrored him. Raised the .38 toward the paper silhouette twenty feet downrange. The target hung motionless in the still air.

"Breathe. Squeeze, not pull."

Her first shot punched wide. The second clipped the target's shoulder. The revolver bucked against her palm, stronger than she'd expected. Frank watched without comment. Let her find her own relationship with the weapon's force.

The third round struck center mass. Then the fourth. By the sixth, Voss had settled into the rhythm of it. The revolver becoming calculation rather than object.

Frank reloaded the cylinder when it emptied. Sent the target back to thirty feet. Watched as Voss adapted to the distance. Not perfect but sufficient. Enough to stop someone if needed.

"Good."

Voss handed him the revolver.

"Let's see it, tough guy," she said with a smile.

He fired six rounds without apparent effort. Each bullet threading the same hole in the target's center. The difference between adequacy and mastery made visible.

"Impressive," said Voss.

"Practice," said Frank.

In the parking lot, Voss placed the gun case on the Imperial's backseat. Frank drove through morning traffic. Other cars flowed around them, drivers unaware of the weight that had shifted between the two people in the old car.

"Thank you," Voss said as they crossed into Georgetown.

Frank nodded once.

He waited at the curb until she was inside the townhouse before pulling away. Frank wondered if the revolver would keep her alive if the quiet war behind boardroom doors finally broke into the open.

He glanced at his watch, then headed back to Virginia and drove to work. He would say nothing about the pistol to Reed or anyone else except Culper. Frank was the master of secrets.

Arlington National Cemetery - Arlington, Virginia

Reed stood among marble headstones. Morning fog clung to the ground, blurring the distinction between earth and air. His breath formed ghosts that vanished in the cold.

Westbrook approached from the opposite direction. Military bearing in civilian clothes. Face weathered by desert sun and mountain wind. He stopped six feet from Reed, respecting distance without speech.

They stood in Section 60. Where the newly fallen rested. Fresh graves with recent dates carved in stone.

"Appreciate you coming," Reed said.

Westbrook nodded once. Waited.

"I have a problem that requires your particular skill set."

"Name it."

Reed handed him a manila envelope. Westbrook opened it, studied the contents without expression. A photograph of Voss. Townhouse schematics. Security details.

"The CEO of your own company," Westbrook said. "Unusual target."

"Necessary one. Voss sees only theory. She'll never understand Fulcrum's true potential."

Westbrook returned the materials to the envelope.

"If Voss is eliminated doesn't your funding go away?"

"No. She just a CEO. Boards replace CEOs all the time, especially founding CEOs. It's a company's right of passage. It creates a sense of maturity."

"I see. How do you want it done?"

"Natural causes. No investigation. No questions."

"When?"

"Tomorrow night. That gives you a day for prep and surveillance."

Westbrook studied Reed's face. "What about Fairbanks? Won't an incident like this raise questions and cause a review?"

Reed turned toward a nearby grave. The headstone newer than others. A name matching his own surname.

"Maybe. But that's a risk I'll have to take. Voss has begun questioning the data transfers to Fairbanks. Investigating the security upgrades. Looking where she shouldn't." His voice hardened. "Voss has one vision for Fulcrum and it's not mine."

"And that is?"

"Ensuring American dominance without American casualties." Reed gestured toward the endless rows of headstones. "Voss wants to prevent conflict while our enemies prepare for it. Her hesitation puts us at risk."

"The board supports her position?"

"The board follows money. With Voss gone, I become CEO by default. The transition preserves shareholder value."

"Soon I won't need Helix's infrastructure or its funding. I'll have my own. But for now, I need all obstacles removed, so I can move things forward."

Reed's jaw tightened. "Voss is the only hinderance remaining. The only one who could stop what we've built."

Westbrook nodded. Understanding the calculations behind the assignment.

"Details on the security system?"

"Three-stage. Main panel near rear entrance. Carbon monoxide detector integrated with the thermostat. Standard furnace, ten years old."

"Payment method?"

"The usual account. Half now, half upon confirmation," said Reed handing him an envelope.

Westbrook tucked the envelope inside his coat. "Clean. Untraceable," said Reed.

"Like always."

They stood in silence. Around them, fog began lifting. The markers of dead soldiers emerging into weak winter sunlight.

"Voss believes Fulcrum will save lives by preventing conflicts," Reed said. "She doesn't understand that prevention is fantasy. The strong survive by being stronger than their enemies. By seeing the threat and eliminating it first."

"And after Voss?"

"Peace, hopefully," said Reed.

Westbrook straightened, a soldier receiving orders.

"Tomorrow night then," he said.

Reed watched him walk away between rows of identical stones marking different deaths. When Westbrook disappeared into the cemetery's vastness, Reed approached his brother's grave. Placed his hand on cold marble.

"They'll understand when they see what we've built," he whispered. "What you died for."

Around him, the dead kept their silence. The living continued their march toward joining them, one way or another.

Georgetown, Washington D.C.

The Georgetown townhouse stood silent. Three stories of red brick and dark shutters. A single light burned in the upstairs window where Voss worked past midnight, as she did most evenings.

The man who called himself Westbrook parked three blocks away. Black sedan with stolen plates that raised no suspicion in this neighborhood of power. He moved with unhurried purpose. Just another official returning from late meetings. His overcoat concealed both weapon and intent.

Reed's instructions remained clear in his mind. Make it look accidental. Leave no trace. Westbrook had performed such work before. Had erased problems for men who couldn't afford questions.

The service alley behind the townhouses lay empty. Trash cans waited for morning collection. Westbrook counted doors until he reached hers. The security panel gleamed in darkness. Military grade but installed by contractors who followed patterns. Who left gaps in the wiring where brick met wood.

He removed a device from his pocket. Placed it against the panel. Green lights blinked as it cycled through combinations. The lock clicked. Westbrook pocketed the device and entered.

The kitchen smelled of coffee and something recently cooked. Dishes in the sink. Wine glass half-empty on the counter. He moved through shadows with practiced silence. His shoes made no sound on hardwood floors. Years of training distilled to this moment.

The thermostat waited on the wall where blueprints had shown it would be. Westbrook opened its housing. Located the carbon monoxide sensor. Replaced the chip with one from his pocket. The new one would report normal levels regardless of actual readings.

Next the furnace in the basement. Westbrook descended narrow stairs. Found the ancient unit that heated the townhouse. Careful not to scratch the paint, he loosened a fitting on the exhaust pipe. Not enough to cause immediate danger. Just enough to allow deadly gas to seep into the home as the night grew colder. As the furnace cycled on and off. As Voss slept unaware.

The basement door creaked as he climbed back to the main floor. Westbrook froze. Listened for movement above. Nothing but the settling sounds of an old house.

He turned toward the front door. His escape route planned to avoid cameras on the main street.

A floorboard creaked overhead. Footsteps crossed the bedroom. Westbrook stepped into shadows as Voss descended the stairs in silk pajamas, a glass in her hand. She passed within arm's reach of where he stood. Didn't sense his presence in the darkness.

She moved to the kitchen. Rinsed her glass. Refilled it with water from the tap. Westbrook remained motionless. The automatic pistol with sound suppressor waited in its holster beneath his coat. One shot would end this now.

But Reed had been specific. No guns. No investigation. The gas would leave no evidence beyond a tragic accident. A faulty furnace in an old house. A woman who worked too hard and didn't maintain her home.

Voss returned upstairs. The bedroom door slightly ajar. The cat slipped out into the hallway. Westbrook counted to one hundred before moving to the front door. Eased it open and slipped outside. Locked it behind him.

No trace of his presence remained except the loosened pipe. The corrupted sensor.

He walked back to his car. The neighborhood slept around him. Stars watched from above with cold indifference. Westbrook drove away from Georgetown. Away from the house where death now waited for morning. For the furnace to cycle on as temperature dropped. For Voss to sleep too deeply to notice the carbon monoxide flooding her bedroom.

By dawn she would be gone. Another obstacle removed. Another piece cleared from the chess board.

Voss dreamed of water. Dark and bottomless. Her limbs moved through it like treacle. Lungs straining for air that lay somewhere beyond reach.

Something rough rasped against her cheek. Once. Twice. The third time jolted her from dream to darkness.

The cat stood on her chest, front paws pressing into her sternum. It dragged its sandpaper tongue across her face again, whiskers tickling her skin. Not affection but urgency.

Voss tried to push it away. The simple movement made the room tilt sideways. Her head pounded as if screws tightened against her temples.

The cat yowled. A sound unlike its usual disinterested mewl. It jumped from her chest, moved to the edge of the bed, then back. When she didn't follow, it sank needle-sharp claws into her arm.

"Stop," she mumbled. Her voice sounded wrong even to her own ears. Distant.

The cat bit her wrist. Not hard enough to break skin, but sharp enough to shock her into greater awareness. It leapt from the bed and darted to the bedroom door, looking back with yellow eyes that caught what little light existed.

Voss sat up. The headache intensified, driving railroad spikes from temples to jaw. The bedroom felt wrong. Too warm despite the winter frost etched across the windows.

The clock glowed red numbers across the darkness. Three seventeen.

The cat paced at the doorway. Yowling with uncharacteristic agitation. Its patterns deliberate.

It wanted her to follow.

She swung her legs over the edge. The floor seemed to ripple beneath her feet. She steadied herself against the nightstand. The cat darted back to her, then to the doorway again. Insistent.

Voss followed the animal down the hallway. Each step requiring concentration. The cat led her downstairs to the kitchen, stopping before the back door. It scratched at the weatherstripping, desperate.

Strange behavior from a creature that hated the cold.

She opened the door. Bitter air rushed in, shocking her lungs. With it came clarity. The fog in her brain receded as she gulped down winter night.

Something had been wrong with the air inside. Something invisible.

Her phone rang from upstairs. She staggered back to retrieve it, keeping the kitchen door open behind her.

"Yes?" Her voice sounded like a stranger's.

"Dr. Voss? Security system shows your back door open. Everything alright?"

The monitoring company. She'd forgotten they would call.

"Yes, fine. Just..." She couldn't explain what she didn't understand. "Getting some air."

After hanging up, she checked the furnace in the basement. Found nothing visibly wrong. Called the gas company anyway, described her symptoms.

"Get out now," the technician said. "We're sending someone. Carbon monoxide."

Twenty minutes later, emergency vehicles lined her street. The technician found the dislodged pipe on her heating system.

"Exhaust pipe came dislodged," he explained. "Happens sometimes in older units. Your carbon monoxide detector should have picked it up, but didn't. We're having one of our guys check it out. Lucky your cat woke you."

Voss stood on the sidewalk, blanket over her shoulders, watching officials catalog the evidence. The cat sat beside her, seemingly satisfied with its night's work.

But a question formed in her mind. Faulty detector? Or something else?

She remembered Reed's face the last time they'd spoken. The coldness in his eyes when he'd mentioned "operational independence." The way he'd looked at her as if calculating variables in an equation.

Coincidences existed. Systems failed. But Voss hadn't built her career on believing in chance.

Westbrook sat in the black sedan, engine off. Down the street from Voss's townhouse. Close enough to observe, far enough to remain invisible.

Through his binoculars, Westbrook watched Voss standing on the sidewalk. Emergency blanket wrapped around her shoulders. Her cat sat at her feet, unperturbed by the chaos.

He lowered the binoculars. Picked up his phone. Dialed.

Reed answered on the first ring. "Yes?"

"Target survived." Westbrook's voice betrayed no emotion. Professional reporting facts without attachment.

A pause. "Explain."

"Gas dispersed as planned. CO detector disabled. But something woke her."

"What?"

"I don't know."

Although disappointed, Reed was not angry. He was experienced and knew that no matter how good the plan, the unexpected could foil it. It was best to keep emotion out of it.

"Unfortunate." Reed's voice hardened. "We need a more direct approach."

"Public?"

"No. Too many questions. But the subtlety phase is over. It's time she disappeared permanently. It can look like a burglary gone bad."

"When?"

"You'll need to wait a few days. Give things time to cool down. I'll call you when it's time."

Westbrook started his car. The engine came alive with a soft purr designed for stealth rather than power.

"I'll handle it," he said.

"See that you do."

The line went dead. Westbrook slipped the phone into his pocket and pulled away from the curb. In his rearview mirror, the ambulance's lights continued their red-blue rhythm. Voss stood illuminated within their glow, a woman who had survived one death but wouldn't escape the next.

He drove toward the river, toward the safe house where tools waited for less subtle solutions. His face revealed nothing. The night revealed less.

The sun was rising when Voss checked into a hotel under her mother's maiden name. Paid cash. The cat curled on the extra pillow, pleased with the upgrade in accommodations. Voss removed the revolver from her purse and set it on the nightstand.

She climbed under the covers but sleep was far away. She needed to consider what moved beneath the surface of things. Whether the night's events represented mechanical failure or the first move in a game she hadn't known she was playing.

DARPA

DARPA Headquarters - Arlington, Virginia

The DARPA conference room gleamed with polished wood and recessed lighting. Five officials sat around the table, two in military dress, three in civilian suits. Classified documents sealed in red folders lay untouched.

Reed stood alone at the head of the table, his presentation reflected in the polished surface.

"Fulcrum," he said. "The ultimate weapon to end all war."

General Hayes folded his arms. "Bold claim, Reed."

"Not a claim. A reality." Reed touched the screen. A global map appeared, conflict zones pulsing red. "Fulcrum can defeat any hostile government without a single American casualty. Without firing a single bullet."

Dr. Wallace, DARPA's chief analyst, removed her glasses. "How, exactly?"

"Fulcrum is an artificial intelligent entity that identifies societal pressure points through massive data analysis. It predicts potential tipping events in enemy regimes with ninety-four percent accuracy." Reed's voice hardened. "Then it defines precisely calibrated destabilization procedures. When correctly implemented, the target government collapses into chaos."

Colonel Fisher leaned forward. "Examples, please."

"Our research has identified that most conflicts are created and accelerated by one or two key individuals," Reed explained. "By targeting and manipulating these catalysts, we control the conflict itself."

"So you're talking about assassination?" Fisher asked.

"No. Something far more elegant." Reed clicked through slides. "Targeted misinformation campaigns that discredit influential figures. Financial pressure on community leaders. Strategic resource shortages in areas already prone to division. The enemy defeats itself. No fingerprints leading back to America. A nation fighting itself can't fight us."

"So, how exactly is it structured?" said Fisher.

"Fulcrum operates on a three-tier system," Reed continued, bringing up a new slide with a complex flowchart. "First, our proprietary algorithm processes terabytes of social media, economic indicators, and cultural variables to identify what we call 'fracture points'—pre-existing tensions within any society."

He zoomed in on the diagram. "The second tier creates predictive models. If pressure is applied to these fracture points, how will the social system respond? Which individuals become catalysts? What counter-forces emerge? The models run thousands of simulations to identify optimal intervention vectors."

Reed clicked to a screen showing neural network visualizations. "The third tier is implementation. Once we identify the key pressure points and catalysts, we deploy minimal tactical assets—sometimes just one agent with the right message at the right moment. We've found that applying precise pressure to just three percent of influential nodes in any social network creates a cascade effect through the entire system."

Fisher leaned forward. "You're telling us you can topple governments by manipulating a handful of people?"

"Exactly, Colonel," Reed said. "Like finding the load-bearing pillars in a building. Remove a few of those, and the structure collapses under its own weight."

Secretary Mitchell studied Reed. "Where's Dr. Voss? She's the CEO, correct?"

"Dr. Voss is a brilliant research scientist," Reed answered smoothly. "I handle implementation. In fact, we've set up a separate subsidiary in Fairbanks, Alaska for the continued development of Fulcrum. That way our patrons know that the money they invest with go toward development and not overhead."

"That's reassuring," said Hayes.

"Stress is our most effective manipulative tool," Reed explained, bringing up a slide showing brain scans beside behavioral models. "The human mind under stress makes predictable cognitive errors. A simple rumor planted at the right moment can fracture a marriage or professional relationship. A fabricated bill or unexpected expense creates financial anxiety. The beauty is in the subtlety." He flipped through examples - a community leader receiving notice of a false audit, a union organizer getting an anonymous text about his wife's fictional affair. "These micro-stressors compound in our targets. Sleep degrades. Decision-making suffers. They become reactive rather than strategic. And the entire time, they never suspect external manipulation. They believe their misfortune is random, their own failing. By the time they're making crucial decisions about protest tactics or community response, they're functionally compromised. And no one ever traces it back to us."

"You said ninety-four percent accuracy," Dr. Wallace said. "Based on what data?"

"Field tests. Limited domestic applications."

The room tensed. Glances exchanged across the table.

"You've been testing this on American soil?" Fisher's voice dropped an octave.

Reed nodded. "Controlled environments. Minimal variables." He pulled up new images—Detroit auto workers burning robotic equipment, border clashes, community protests turning violent.

"Who authorized this?" Mitchell demanded, half-rising from his chair. "American citizens as test subjects? That violates at least a dozen federal statutes."

"Necessary proof of concept," Reed replied, unmoved. "Theoretical models can only take us so far."

Admiral Kingston leaned forward. "Who signed off on domestic operations?"

Reed's smile didn't reach his eyes. "The same authorities who requested this presentation."

Hayes remained stone-faced.

"You engineered these conflicts?" Wallace asked, finger tapping against images of burning factories and bloodied protesters. "Deliberately?"

"We identified pre-existing tensions and applied minimal pressure," Reed corrected. "Small interventions with predictable outcomes. No different than stress-testing any weapons system."

"Except the test subjects were American citizens," Mitchell said. "People died in Detroit."

Fisher studied the images with narrowed eyes. "The precision is remarkable. You predicted these exact outcomes?"

"Within a two point seven percent margin of error," Reed confirmed.

"Impressive," Fisher murmured.

"It's appalling," Wallace countered.

Kingston cleared his throat. "The moral questions aside—and they are substantial—the tactical applications are undeniable."

"These are your neighbors," Mitchell said. "Your fellow citizens."

"These are controlled demonstrations," Reed replied. "The damage was contained. The situations resolved. And now you have proof that Fulcrum works exactly as designed."

Wallace removed her glasses. "And if these 'demonstrations' had spiraled beyond your control?"

"They didn't," Reed said simply. "That's the point."

Secretary Mitchell tapped his pen against the folder. "These examples are very controlled and don't demonstrate true potential. We'll need more proof."

"Of course."

Admiral Kingston, silent until now, cleared his throat. "What you're describing isn't just a weapon—it's a fundamental reimagining of warfare itself."

"That's precisely the point, Admiral. Victory without American blood being shed."

"I want to see it work on a hostile nation," Hayes said. "North Korea. Iran. Let's see if it performs as advertised."

"Too risky," Wallace cut in. "If it fails, we expose our hand. If it succeeds too well, we could destabilize entire regions."

Kingston nodded. "The doctor's right. We need more controlled testing before foreign deployment."

"What do you propose?" Reed asked.

"Continued domestic applications," Fisher said. "Where we can monitor and contain any... side effects."

Reed's expression revealed nothing. "That can be arranged."

"You've given us a lot to think about, Mr. Reed," Hayes said, gathering his papers. "We'll get back to you shortly with our funding decision." The finality in his tone signaled the meeting's end. Reed nodded once, closed his laptop with a soft click. The officials' faces revealed nothing as they filed their documents away, some avoiding eye contact, others studying Reed with new calculation. Whatever verdict they reached would happen behind closed doors, after careful consideration of both the weapon and the man who'd built it.

The door closed behind Reed. The room remained silent until Hayes checked the security sweep.

"Thoughts?" the General asked.

"It's black magic," Kingston said. "Societal manipulation on this scale is unprecedented."

"But if it works..." Fisher let the words hang.

Wallace shuffled her papers. "The ethical implications are staggering. We're talking about weaponizing social division. If this technology escapes our control—"

"Everything is a weapon in the right hands," Hayes interrupted. "The question is whether we develop it first, or let China beat us to it."

Mitchell looked troubled. "These domestic tests concern me. American citizens as guinea pigs."

"Limited exposure," Fisher countered. "Better than starting a war we can't control."

"I want proof before committing resources," Hayes said. "Real-world demonstration."

Kingston nodded. "Agreed. But no official funding yet. Too much blowback potential if something goes sideways."

"Private investors," Mitchell suggested. "Three layers removed from any government connection."

"And tight observation protocols," Wallace added. "This Reed character concerns me. He seems to enjoy the chaos a little too much."

Hayes gathered his papers. "I'll make the necessary arrangements. We'll reconvene after the demonstration."

"What exactly are we testing here?" Kingston asked quietly. "A weapon... or its master?"

No one answered as they filed out, the classified folders tucked under arms, holding plans for a conflict that would leave no fingerprints.

Helix Headquarters – Arlington, Virginia

Night pressed against the windows of Helix headquarters. Fluorescent lights hummed overhead, the only sound in the finance department. Lawrence Meyer sat alone at his desk, tie loosened, sleeves rolled to the elbows. His fingers moved through financial reports with the precision of a surgeon.

The numbers told stories. Money flowing between accounts. Resources allocated then reallocated. Patterns hidden in columns that others might miss. Meyer saw them all.

He paused at invoice #A7729. Arcturus Holdings. His finger traced the amount. One hundred eighty-seven thousand dollars. Monthly. A property lease for a facility in Fairbanks, Alaska. No explanation beyond that. Just Reed's signature at the bottom, authorizing payment from accounts Meyer himself had created but somehow lost track of.

He checked previous quarters. Found similar payments stretching back eight months, the amounts growing steadily. Over $2,000,000 sent north with no oversight. No documentation beyond these invoices.

Meyer opened the company asset database. Searched for any listing of an Alaska facility. Found nothing. No record in operations reports. No personnel assignments. No equipment transfers. The property existed only in these payments, authorized solely by Reed.

Meyer heard footsteps. Reed walked past, coffee in hand, heading toward his office. Meyer gathered the invoices and followed.

Reed's office smelled of coffee and cologne. The man himself stood by the window, surveying the city below like a general overlooking a battlefield. He turned as Meyer entered.

"Lawrence," Reed said. "How can I help you?"

Meyer placed the invoices on the desk. Watched Reed's eyes flicker to them, then back to his face.

"Found something interesting," Meyer said.

Reed set down his coffee. "Let me guess… the Arcturus payments."

"Fairbanks." Meyer tapped the paper. "Two point two million so far. No listing in company assets."

"An oversight."

"Major one."

Reed buttoned his suit jacket. A gesture that closed more than fabric. "The backup data facility. Board approved it last year."

"Must have missed that meeting."

"You were in Chicago. The quarterly review." Reed moved to his desk chair. "I handled the details to avoid burdening the executive team with minutiae."

"Two million isn't minutiae."

Reed smiled without humor. "Perspective, Lawrence. The intellectual property stored there is worth billions."

"Most companies use cloud storage."

"Most companies aren't developing what we are." Reed's voice dropped. "Hackers target us daily. Three former employees attempted to access restricted data last month. One tried to download the entire Fulcrum architecture."

"First I've heard of it."

"I didn't want to worry the team. I handled it personally."

Meyer studied the invoices again. "Fifty thousand square feet. Dedicated power station. This isn't just a backup server, is it?"

"Ever been to Alaska in winter?" Reed asked. "Forty below zero. Cooling costs for servers drop nearly sixty percent. It's practical. Necessary."

"Voss knows about this?"

Something crossed Reed's face. Too swift to name.

"Elaine has enough on her plate managing research teams and board expectations." Reed leaned forward. "Sometimes protection requires secrecy, Lawrence. Even from friends."

"Protection from what?"

Reed didn't answer. Just gathered the invoices and returned them to Meyer. "Anything else?"

"I'd like to visit the facility. Given the circumstances I think an audit is in order."

"Be my guest."

"I'll plan on it," said Meyer, then left.

Georgetown, Washington D.C.

The secure phone buzzed on Culper's desk. He recognized the number.

"Bishop?" he answered.

"Jesus, Culper." Bishop's voice carried an edge not present in their previous conversation. "What the hell have you gotten me into?"

Culper set down his pen. "Tell me."

"I did your search. Set up the monitoring protocols." A pause, then: "These people aren't civilians. Not entirely."

"Explain."

"Reed's been in meetings with DARPA. High-level funding discussions for something called Project Fulcrum. Not just research grants. We're talking big money. Black budget allocations." Bishop's voice dropped lower. "This is government work, Culper. Classified material."

"I'm not interested in DARPA," Culper said. "Just Reed and Voss."

"You say that now, but once you hear—" Bishop stopped himself. "Look, I'm sending you some audio files. Encrypted package. After you listen, delete them. This conversation never happened."

"Understood."

"I mean it. This isn't like the old days. I've got five years until retirement. I don't need a federal investigation."

"You have my word."

Bishop laughed without humor. The line clicked dead.

Culper's computer chimed with an incoming message. He entered three separate passwords to access the encrypted files. Six audio recordings appeared in a folder. He connected headphones, pressed play on the first file.

Reed's voice came through clearly: "The domestic applications have exceeded projections. Detroit, Seattle, the border incident—all within two percent of the algorithm's predictions."

Another voice, older, military in its precision: "And casualty rates?"

"Minimal compared to the data acquired. Fulcrum needs real-world conflict to refine its parameters."

"Hayes won't sign off on American test subjects without deniability."

"That's why we structured Helix as it is. Private company. Research grant. Wall between operations and government oversight."

The recording ended. Culper moved to the next file.

Reed again: "Fairbanks facility is fully operational. Parallel development track running without Voss's knowledge. We can initiate independently if necessary."

"And the scaling capabilities?"

"From regional to national deployment in under eighteen hours. Global within a week, assuming satellite uplink remains secure and we can gather the necessary data."

Culper listened through each recording, his expression unchanging despite the growing coldness in his chest. By the final file, the picture had clarified into something worse than he'd anticipated.

Reed: "Fulcrum doesn't just predict civil unrest—it creates it. Targeted pressure on key individuals causes precisely calculated chain reactions. Social breakdown on demand."

"A weapon that leaves no fingerprints," the military voice responded. "Enemies destroying themselves from within."

"Exactly, General. Why risk American lives in foreign wars when we can simply cause our enemies to tear themselves apart? No bombs. No invasion. Just invisible hands pulling precisely calibrated strings."

Culper removed the headphones. The morning light had strengthened, casting long shadows across his desk. He stared at the notebook where he'd transcribed key portions of the conversations.

His phone rang again.

"Did you listen?" Bishop asked without preamble.

"I did."

"Then you understand why I'm concerned. This isn't some rogue operation. It's government-sanctioned research. If you're pursuing this—"

"I'm not interested in DARPA or their projects," Culper said. "Just Reed and what he's doing with Fulcrum."

"You're making a distinction without a difference." Bishop sighed. "Whatever. I've done what you asked. We're even now."

"Thank you, John."

"Don't thank me. Just be careful. Reed is playing as if he is all in on this one."

The line went dead. Culper sat motionless at his desk, considering the implications. Fulcrum wasn't just predictive software. It was a weapon designed to exploit social vulnerabilities, to turn communities against themselves. And Reed had taken it beyond its original purpose, building a parallel operation in Alaska.

The morning had taken on a different quality now. A countdown had begun. If Reed was initiating a full-scale test, people would die. And Frank and Voss were directly in the blast radius.

Helix Headquarters – Arlington, Virginia

Sunlight cut across Voss's desk in harsh lines. Dust motes drifted through the beam. The CFO stood before her, casting a long shadow. With Helix since she founded it. Wire-rimmed glasses and a ledger's precision.

"These expenditures," he said. "Fairbanks."

Voss looked up from her monitor. "What about them?"

Meyer placed a folder between them. Opened it with thin fingers. Inside lay columns of numbers and codes. Red ink circled three entries.

"Three million in total expenditures last quarter. One point seven this month alone." His finger tapped beside each figure. "For a backup facility?"

"Data redundancy is expensive."

"Not this expensive." Meyer pushed his glasses higher on his nose. "The power consumption alone exceeds our headquarters. By thirty percent."

Voss leaned back in her chair. Spread her hands flat on the desk.

"The cooling systems," she said. "Alaska's cold, but servers still generate heat."

"Bullshit, Elaine." Meyer turned a page in the folder. "Personnel costs. Nine specialists. All hired in the last sixty days. All with security clearances. Not data technicians. Military intelligence backgrounds."

She stared at him. Meyer had never spoken to her this way before.

"Reed's fingerprints are all over this," he said. "I've worked with you too long to dance around it."

Voss rose from her chair. Crossed to the window. Looked out at the Arlington skyline.

"Fulcrum requires massive computing power," she said. "It's inevitable."

"Fulcrum was allocated its hardware budget last fiscal year."

Voss turned. "Technology evolves."

"Not this fast." Meyer dropped the folder on her desk. "There's no line item for additional hardware. No approved expansion. Just these shadow expenditures routed through three different accounts. Your accounts, Elaine."

"I know."

"Then explain it to me." He locked eyes with her. "What's Reed building up there?"

They stood in silence broken only by the soft hum of the air conditioning. Voss's eyes moved to the door. Closed. No witnesses.

"I don't know," she admitted. Her voice smaller than he'd ever heard it.

"Jesus." Meyer removed his glasses. Rubbed the bridge of his nose. "He's hijacking the company right under our noses."

"Reed claims he has board authorization."

"Impossible. I've checked the minutes of every meeting for the past year. Nothing."

"Some authorizations don't make the minutes."

"Then they don't exist." Meyer leaned forward, palms flat on her desk. "Reed is running something parallel up there. His own version of Fulcrum."

Voss nodded. Once.

"How long have you known?"

"Suspected for months. Known for certain? Two weeks."

Meyer sat in the chair across from her. "I never trusted him. Too many secrets. Too many back doors in the financial system."

"He built those systems."

"That's the problem." Meyer replaced his glasses. "Let me help you."

"How?"

"Full audit. I'll fly to Fairbanks myself. See what he's building with our money."

Voss's eyes widened. "It might be dangerous."

"For whom?"

"You."

Meyer smiled for the first time. Tight. Humorless. "Let me worry about that."

Voss studied him. The man who had been with her from the beginning. She trusted him more than anyone in the company. He was the only one who had stayed loyal when Fulcrum's early failures nearly bankrupted them.

"Quietly," she said.

"Of course," Meyer stood. "I'll find what he's hiding."

She nodded. Meyer turned to leave. Stopped at the door.

"Elaine." His voice gentler now. "What do we do when we find it?"

Voss looked at the folder on her desk. Red circles around numbers that told a story she couldn't fully read.

"That depends on what it is."

Reed stood at his office window overlooking Arlington. Night had fallen. The city's lights spread before him like a circuit board. His reflection stared back. A man growing older while his vision grew clearer.

His phone vibrated on the desk. He checked the display. Unknown number. He answered.

"This is Reed."

"Sir." The voice belonged to Sawyer, his head of security at the Fairbanks facility. "We have a situation."

Reed turned from the window. "Elaborate."

"Lawrence Meyer. CFO. Booked an overnight flight to Fairbanks. Tomorrow night. Rental car reservation."

The silence stretched between them.

"Sir? Are you there?"

"I'm thinking." Reed circled his desk. Sat down. "Has he contacted anyone at the facility?"

"Yes, sir. Requested all access codes and security protocols. Said it was for a routine financial audit."

Reed leaned back in his chair. Considering. Measuring. Meyer was Voss's man. Had been from the beginning. This was her move.

"When was the request made?"

"Two hours ago. Went through official channels."

"Did you authorize access?"

"Not yet. Wanted to clear it with you first."

Reed tapped his fingers on the desk. Three slow beats. Let Meyer come. Let him see what they wanted him to see. The surface operation. The decoy.

"Grant the access," he said.

Sawyer hesitated. "All of it?"

"Standard audit protocols. Nothing beyond that."

"But sir, if he starts poking around the sub-level—"

"He won't find it." Reed cut him off. "We built those walls solid. No doors where there shouldn't be. No trails leading anywhere important."

"And if he asks questions?"

"Answer them. To a point." Reed studied his reflection in the darkened window. A man who had learned patience in hard places. "Better to let him look than raise suspicions by blocking him."

"Understood, sir."

"One more thing. I want your best man on him. If Meyer starts getting too close to anything sensitive, call me."

"Yes sir."

Reed ended the call. Opened his laptop. Pulled up the Fairbanks schematics. The official ones. The ones Meyer would see.

The plan had always included this possibility. Always accounted for curious eyes. The real operation, the true Fulcrum, lay behind walls within walls. Systems within systems.

Let Meyer chase his audit. Let him follow the breadcrumbs that led nowhere. The distraction might even prove useful.

And if Meyer somehow found something he shouldn't...

Reed closed the laptop. That bridge could be crossed when they came to it. He had contingencies for everything. Always had.

Sometimes the best defense was to appear defenseless. An old military strategy his brother would have appreciated.

Reed looked out at Arlington again. The lights of a city sleeping peacefully. Unaware of the forces aligned against it. Unaware of the shield he was building to protect it.

Moonlight cut across the company gym in hard angles. Frank stood alone at the heavy bag. No gloves. Just scarred knuckles against leather. The thuds echoed through the empty space. Rhythmic. Precise. A machine calibrating itself.

Voss watched from the doorway. Studied the brutal economy of his movements. Nothing wasted. Nothing for show.

He knew she was there. Had known the moment the door opened. But he didn't stop. Didn't acknowledge her. Just kept hitting.

She crossed the room. High heels clicking against rubber floor mats. Out of place. Out of her element.

"Mr. Kane."

Frank delivered one final blow to the bag. It swayed on its chain. He turned.

His shirt clung to his massive shoulders. Sweat trailed through old scars. His breathing barely elevated.

"Need a minute of your time," she said.

Frank nodded once. Reached for a towel. Wiped his face.

"Lawrence Meyer. Our CFO. He's flying to Fairbanks tomorrow night."

Frank waited. Silent.

"The facility there has... expanded beyond its original purpose." Voss kept her voice low though they were alone. "Reed's been operating without authorization. Meyer is conducting an audit."

Frank's eyes gave nothing away.

"I need someone I can trust to go with him." She forced herself to meet his gaze. "To keep him safe."

"Why?" The single word scraped like metal on concrete.

"Reed has been diverting resources. Building something beyond what we authorized. Maybe something dangerous."

Frank considered this. Picked up a water bottle. Drank.

"I know you work for Reed," she continued. "But technically, you work for me. For Helix. I'm the CEO."

"And?"

"And I'm asking you to protect our CFO while he investigates a potentially hostile situation."

Frank dried his hands on the towel. One finger at a time. Deliberate. Buying time to think.

"No." He finally said.

Voss hadn't expected such a direct refusal. She straightened.

"I'm your boss, Mr. Kane. Not Reed."

"True."

"Then why refuse a direct request?"

Frank hung the towel around his neck. "Reed would know."

"Know what?"

"You sent me." His voice left no room for argument.

Understanding dawned on Voss's face. Frank was right. Reed would immediately recognize what it meant if Frank showed up in Fairbanks with Meyer. It would escalate the situation before they had any evidence.

"Meyer doesn't know what he's walking into," she said.

"Neither do you."

The words hung between them. Frank saw calculation in her eyes. Reassessment.

"What would you suggest?" she asked.

Frank picked up his gym bag. Slung it over one shoulder.

"Wait."

"For what?"

"Evidence." He started toward the door. Stopped beside her. "If Meyer finds it, then move."

Voss watched him. Tried to read something in those hard features. Some indication of where his loyalties truly lay.

"And if Meyer doesn't come back?" she asked.

Frank's eyes met hers. Something shifted in them. Not softness. Something else.

"Then you have evidence."

He left her standing in the empty gym. The heavy bag still swinging on its chain. The imprint of his fists visible in the leather.

Georgetown, Washington D.C.

Culper sat at his Georgetown desk reading an incident report that John Bishop from the NSA had sent over. The manila folder bore no markings, delivered by a courier who knew better than to ask questions. Paper couldn't be easily hacked or intercepted. No digital footprints.

Carbon monoxide leak at Voss's townhouse. 3:17 AM. Emergency response. No fatalities. Technician's assessment: Loose exhaust pipe and failed carbon monoxide detector.

Two equipment failures were too much of a coincidence. He reached for his secure phone. Dialed from memory.

Frank answered on the second ring. The motel room's cheap television hummed in the background. News of more protests turning into riots.

"There was an incident at Voss's place two nights ago," Culper said. "CO leak. Know anything?"

"No," said Frank. "Just saw Voss. Said nothing."

"Cat woke her according to the report." Culper turned a page. "Something's not right. I don't think it was an accident."

Frank grunted, then said, "She bought a .38 revolver."

"Do you think she'll be able to use it if necessary?"

"Maybe… maybe not."

"Yeah. Hard to keep a cool head when someone's trying to kill you."

Frank grunted agreement.

"Something else."

"What's that?"

"Voss wants me in Alaska."

"For what?"

"Protect Meyer. CFO. Audit Fairbanks facility."

"What did you say?"

"No."

Culper leaned back in his chair. Considered the request. "She's right, Frank. Meyer is our best chance at understanding Reed's operation. His clearance gets him inside. You should go, but keep your distance. I don't want to spook Reed until we know what he is up to. When does Meyer leave?"

"Tomorrow night."

"I'll arrange transport."

Frank grunted acknowledgment.

"Don't let Meyer know you're there," Culper added. "He's not a professional. He could say the wrong thing."

Culper considered for a long moment, then…

"I'm going to assign Rollins to protect Voss while you're gone. Good man. Former Ranger."

"Understood."

The line went dead. Frank had hung up. No goodbyes. No unnecessary words.

Culper closed the folder. Added it to the stack documenting Reed's escalating pattern. First research sabotage. Then financial diversion. Now attempted murder.

The pieces were moving faster now. The game accelerating.

Culper called Rollins. Briefed him on the assignment. He asked no questions beyond operational parameters and Voss's address. Professionals understood what needed doing without explanation.

Outside his window, Washington continued its business. Covered with spotlights the Capitol dome gleamed in distance. A symbol of democracy and order.

While beneath it all, something burned toward chaos.

Dulles International Airport – Dulles, Virginia

Meyer stepped from the taxi at the American Airlines terminal. His carry-on contained three shirts, two pairs of slacks, his toothbrush, and a folder of company financials. He checked his boarding pass before entering the sliding doors.

Alaska Airlines flight 217. Scheduled departure 6:05 PM. A seventy-minute layover in Seattle.

He never saw the black Imperial sedan that pulled away from the curb. Never noticed the driver following his progress through the terminal doors.

Frank watched until Meyer disappeared. Then he drove toward Andrews Air Force Base.

Andrews Air Force Base, Maryland

The hangar stood empty except for the G5. No markings on the white fuselage. No flags. No numbers. Just polished metal gleaming under sodium lights.

Frank carried a canvas bag over one shoulder. The guard at the fence had checked his ID twice. Made a call. Returned the laminated card with new respect in his eyes.

"Straight through, sir. They're waiting for you."

The pilot wore civilian clothes. No uniform. No insignia. Old scars on his hands matched the flat look in his eyes. Combat pilot, not commercial. Frank recognized the type.

"Wheels up in ten," the pilot said.

Frank settled into a leather seat. No safety briefing. The engines spooled to life with a high whine that quickly faded behind soundproofing.

The G5 took off. Frank closed his eyes but did not sleep. The bag remained within reach at all times.

Georgetown, Washington D.C.

The townhouse stood dark against the evening sky. Voss turned her key in the lock, pushed the door open with her shoulder. She did not see the sedan pull to a stop across the street, its headlights cutting off as the engine died.

The security system beeped. She punched in the code without looking.

The cat appeared from shadow, yellow eyes catching what little light remained. It wound between her ankles once, then sat expectantly.

"Give me a minute," she said.

She set her briefcase beside the door, hung her coat on the rack. The weight of the day sat heavy on her shoulders. Her fingers found the light switch.

Rollins settled deeper into the sedan's seat. His eyes fixed on the townhouse windows as they brightened one by one. The night stretched before him, a vigil of coffee and stillness.

The cat followed her to the kitchen. Its claws clicked against hardwood floors. A reminder of presence. Of life in empty rooms.

Voss opened a cabinet, took down a small tin. The sound of the lid made the cat rise on its hind legs, front paws pressed against her calf.

"Patience," she said.

She scraped wet food into a ceramic bowl. The cat ignored her as it ate, forgetting her existence in favor of sustenance.

Glass doors opened to the wine room. Temperature-controlled air touched her face as she stepped inside. Her fingers moved across bottles, stopped at one tucked in the back corner. Château Margaux. Saved for questions without answers.

The cork surrendered with a soft exhalation. She poured the wine into a crystal decanter, watched it catch light like liquid garnet.

She carried the decanter to the living room, set it on the coffee table. The cat jumped up beside it, eyes following her movements.

"I don't know what to do about Meyer," she told it. "Men can be so pigheaded."

The cat blinked. Turned to wash its face with methodical strokes.

Voss sat on the sofa. Watched the wine in the decanter. It needed to breathe, to open itself to air and time. Twenty minutes minimum. She drummed her fingers against her knee.

The cat finished washing, regarded her with ancient calculation.

"Fuck it," she said, unwilling to wait longer for her wine.

She poured a glass, deeper than proper. Raised it to her lips and drank. Rich notes of blackberry and cedar spread across her tongue. The wine deserved patience she could not provide.

Across the street Rollins, keeping watch from his sedan, glanced at his rearview mirror at a pair of headlights approaching.

A panel van with no markings glided down the street. Tires silent on wet pavement. It parked fifty yards away, engine shutting off. Nobody emerged.

Rollins reached beneath his seat. Removed night vision goggles from their case. He raised them to his eyes, adjusted the focus. The van's cabin appeared in ghostly green. A man sat motionless behind the windshield. He held something in his lap. Could be a pizza. Could be a weapon. The night just became more interesting.

Voss tilted the decanter, watched the last ruby drops fall into her glass. The wine had opened, surrendered its complexities. She'd consumed most of it alone.

"What a lush," she whispered to herself.

The cat sat on the armrest, tail curled around its feet. Its eyes followed her as she stood, steadied herself against the coffee table.

She moved to the door, lifted her purse from the hook. Her fingers found the revolver's grip. Cold metal against warm skin.

"Come on," she said to the cat.

The basement door opened to darkness. She felt for the light switch, descended concrete steps. The furnace hummed in the corner. Her eyes fixed on repaired pipe joints, new screws where there'd been rust. Everything appeared normal. Nothing out of place.

She climbed back upstairs, shut off lights room by room until the townhouse lay in darkness. The revolver remained in her hand as she moved.

The stairs to the second floor creaked beneath her weight. The cat followed three steps behind, a shadow pursuing shadow.

Her bedroom waited. She placed the revolver on the nightstand within easy reach. The cat jumped onto the bed, claimed territory at the center of the duvet.

In the bathroom, Voss removed her makeup with practiced strokes. Foundation and mascara dissolved under cleanser, revealing the woman beneath. She stepped into the shower, let hot, pulsating water pound tension from her shoulders.

Later, hair still damp, she climbed into bed with her laptop. The cat shifted, annoyed at the disturbance but unwilling to abandon its position. The screen's glow painted her face in blue light. Budget projections. Security protocols. The cursor blinked, awaiting decisions.

The wine moved through her blood now. Her eyelids grew heavy. The cursor continued its patient rhythm, marking seconds with light.

"Tomorrow," she decided.

She closed the laptop. Set it on the nightstand beside the revolver. Reached for the lamp. Darkness claimed the bedroom as the switch clicked.

The cat pressed against her side, a small furnace of fur and contentment.

Outside, Rollins watched the last light in the townhouse disappear. The street settled into night rhythms—distant traffic, tree branches stirring in the wind. His eyes remained fixed on the panel van fifty yards away.

The man inside hadn't moved. His patience suggested training. Purpose.

He kept the night vision goggles close, one hand on his phone, the other near his suppressed Glock sitting on the seat. The vigil continued in silence broken only by occasional radio chatter from passing police patrols.

Thirty minutes passed. The street lay silent except for wind rustling through trees. The man opened the van door, stepped onto asphalt. He wore dark clothes, moved with casual confidence. Not skulking. Not hurrying. As he moved below a street light, his face was revealed – Westbrook.

Rollins tracked him through the goggles. Westbrook walked down the block opposite the townhouse, hands in pockets. Just a man taking a late-night stroll.

The tension in Rollins's shoulders eased. False alarm. He lowered the goggles.

Westbrook reached the end of the block. Paused at the corner. Checked his watch. Then crossed the street, turned back in the direction he'd come. Now walking toward the townhouse on Voss's side of the street.

Not casual anymore. Purpose in his stride.

Rollins opened the sedan door. Grabbed his suppressed Glock, held it low against his leg. He moved across the street, intercepting Westbrook before he reached the townhouse.

"Evening," Rollins said. "Mind telling me what you're doing?"

Westbrook stopped. His eyes flicked past Rollins for an instant. "Just walking."

"Try again."

"Look, I don't want any trouble."

"Then you're in the wrong place."

Rollins never heard the footsteps behind him. Never sensed the second gunman approach from shadow. The suppressed pistol rose, barrel aligning with the back of Rollins's skull.

The shot made a sound like a book dropping on carpet. Rollins fell forward, knees striking pavement first, then face. No attempt to break his fall. No final words.

The second gunman stood over him. Fired once more into Rollins's back where his heart would be. Absolute certainty.

"Clean," Westbrook said.

They left Rollins sprawled on the sidewalk, blood pooling beneath his head. A dark shape against darker concrete.

The two assassins moved toward the townhouse. Westbrook crouched beneath the front window. His fingers found the alarm system's external junction box mounted low on the brick wall. He removed a small electronic device from his pocket, attached alligator clips to specific wires.

The device's screen illuminated his face from below. Numbers scrolled, searching for the correct override sequence. It found the code in seventeen seconds.

The security system surrendered with a single red light turning green. No sound. No alert.

"Clear," Westbrook whispered.

Upstairs in the townhouse Voss lay beneath cotton sheets, one arm flung across pillows. Her breathing deep and even. The wine had carried her into dreamless sleep.

The cat curled against her side, a tight circle of fur and feline contentment. Its ears occasionally twitched at sounds too faint for human perception—a moth against window glass, branches scraping roof tiles, distant footsteps on pavement.

The townhouse settled deeper into night's embrace, unaware of the intrusion at its threshold.

On the sidewalk outside the townhouse, Rollins was still alive... barely. The bullet had torn through tissue, fractured bone, but missed its fatal mark by millimeters. Blood filled Rollins's mouth as consciousness returned. The world swam in and out of focus.

He lay motionless on the cold pavement. The gunmen's footsteps had faded toward the townhouse.

Pain exploded through his skull with each heartbeat. Blood trickled from his nose, his ear, pooled beneath his cheek.

His fingers crawled toward his pocket. Found the phone. Muscle memory unlocked it. He pressed "Send" and the phone dialed the last number he had dialed – Culper.

The call connected after two rings.

"Rollins?" Culper's voice, distant as if from the bottom of a well.

"Hit," Rollins whispered. Blood bubbled between his lips. "Two men. Voss."

"Where are you?"

"Sidewalk. Outside target." Each word cost him. Darkness edged his vision. "Going in."

"Stay with me, Rollins."

"Can't think."

The phone slipped from fingers gone nerveless. Rollins tried to move. His body refused the command. The townhouse stood thirty yards away, its windows dark. Voss inside, unaware.

He tried to call out. No sound emerged but a wet gurgle.

The darkness closed around him like hands around a throat.

Culper's hand remained steady as he set down the mobile phone. His secure phone lay on the desk. He dialed a number few people possessed, waited through encryption protocols.

The phone rang three times before connecting.

"Operations," a voice answered.

"Code Black. Operative down," Culper said. "Voss residence." He gave the address, his tone measured despite the urgency. "Two hostiles. Send medical and backup."

"Authentication?"

"Sierra Tango Three Nine Six."

"Acknowledged. Assets deploying."

"ETA?"

"Twelve minutes."

Culper ended the call. Too long. The clock had started when Rollins went down. He crossed to the safe hidden behind a false panel in his bookshelf. His fingers entered the combination without hesitation.

The safe door swung open. Inside, his Sig Sauer waited in its felt cradle. He lifted it, checked the chamber, attached the suppressor with practiced twists. The weight felt familiar in his hand. A tool unused but not forgotten.

He slipped spare magazines into his pocket. Closed the safe.

No emotion colored his movements as he tucked the weapon beneath his jacket.

Culper exited his townhouse without turning on exterior lights. The security system reset itself behind him. His car waited in the alley behind the building, engine cold, unremarkable in its anonymity.

He slid behind the wheel. Started the engine. Pulled away without headlights, muscle memory guiding him through familiar streets.

Voss and the cat slept on. The revolver sat within reach on the nightstand, loaded but untouched.

The two assassins moved to the front door. The second man knelt, set his case on the welcome mat. From it he withdrew lock picks and a tension wrench. His hands worked with practiced precision. Each tumbler yielding in turn.

Upstairs, Voss and the cat slept. Her breathing deep and even. The cat's ears twitched at sounds too faint for human perception—metal sliding against metal, the muted exhalation of the door opening, footsteps testing floorboards.

The revolver sat within reach on the nightstand, loaded but untouched.

Darkness admitted darkness.

Rollins fought to remain conscious. Each drop of blood leaving his body lowered his pressure, fogging his mind. The sidewalk beneath his cheek felt colder now. Distant. Like touching ice through thick gloves.

He forced one eye open. The townhouse wavered in his vision, a lifetime away. The assassins worked the front door lock. Dark shapes against darker night.

Instinct took over. Training embedded in muscle and bone. He ignored the pain.

His arm wouldn't move at first. Dead weight. He dragged it forward by will alone, inch by agonizing inch. His fingers found the Glock's grip, slippery with his own blood.

The pistol felt impossibly heavy. He curled his finger around the trigger, raised the barrel a half-inch from the pavement. Tried to aim.

The first shot went wild, burying itself in a column above the Westbrook's heads. The sound muted by the suppressor. The second struck brick beside the doorframe almost hitting the hitman working the lock.

Westbrook spun. His weapon appeared without hesitation, an extension of his arm.

He fired twice.

The first round caught Rollins in the chest. The second in the throat.

Rollins felt no pain now. Just pressure. Cold spreading through him like water through soil. His cheek pressed against concrete. One eye still open, seeing nothing.

Westbrook approached. His shoes entered Rollins's narrowing field of vision. The suppressed pistol descended into view. A final sound like a book dropped on carpet.

Darkness absolute.

Driving his sedan, Culper accelerated through empty streets, counting seconds in his head. Each intersection passed brought him closer to the townhouse, to Rollins, to Voss.

The traffic light turned yellow, then red. He pressed the gas harder, calculating clearance.

Light exploded from his right. Headlights. A delivery truck. Tonnage and momentum. No time to react.

Impact came like the hand of God. Metal screamed against metal. The sedan spun, a ballet of physics and terror. The world blurred—street, sky, street again.

The streetlamp appeared suddenly. Final punctuation. The sedan crumpled around the pole. The airbag deployed, white and chemical and choking.

Darkness claimed him.

Seconds. Maybe a minute.

Culper blinked back to consciousness. Blood ran into his left eye. The windshield had shattered, safety glass glittering across the dashboard like scattered diamonds.

He moved his limbs one by one. Nothing broken. Nothing vital severed. Just pain. Lots of pain. The car door wouldn't open. He kicked at it once, twice. Metal gave way with a scream.

He dragged himself onto the street. The delivery truck had stopped fifty yards away, its driver shouting into a phone.

Culper stood on unsteady legs. Checked his weapon. Still operational. He started walking, then jogging. Each step bringing pain and resolve.

Headlights approached. A taxi rolled down the Georgetown street. Culper stepped into its path, arm raised.

The driver slammed the brakes. The taxi skidded to a stop a few feet from Culper's legs.

Culper raised the Sig Sauer. The driver's window slid down an inch.

"I don't want trouble," the driver called.

Culper stepped forward. Placed the suppressor against the glass. "Open the passenger door."

The lock clicked. Culper went around the front of the car keeping the pistol aimed at the driver and slid into the passenger seat. Blood smeared the upholstery. The driver's hands trembled on the wheel.

"That way." Culper pointed down the street. "Three blocks. Then right."

The driver accelerated, eyes darting between the road and the weapon resting on Culper's lap.

"Faster," Culper said.

The taxi surged forward, carrying them deeper into Georgetown, toward the townhouse where death had already announced itself.

The townhouse received the two hitmen. Westbrook closed the door behind him, shutting out the night and what remained of Rollins on the pavement outside.

His partner moved through the foyer, weapon extended. The beam from his tactical light cut surgical paths through shadows. They communicated with hand signals, military procedure distilled to gesture and nod.

The kitchen first. Empty. The dining room. Nothing.

The second man stepped into the study. His boot found an ancient floorboard. Wood complained beneath his weight—a single prolonged note that carried through silent rooms.

Both men froze.

Upstairs, Voss's eyes opened. Wine-soaked consciousness struggled to interpret the sound. Not the cat. Not the house settling.

Someone inside.

Her hand moved to the nightstand, found the revolver. Cold metal against palm. Adrenaline burned through alcohol haze, brought clarity tinged with fear.

The cat's ears pivoted toward the bedroom door.

Downstairs, the assassins resumed their methodical search, more careful now. The living room with its lingering scent of expensive wine. The decanter on the coffee table.

All clear below. Westbrook gestured toward the staircase.

They moved to the stairs. Each step tested before weight applied. The second man took point, ascending with weapon raised. Westbrook followed three steps behind, covering their six.

They reached the second-floor landing. Westbrook pointed to the first door. Guest bedroom. His partner nudged it open, swept the tactical light across empty space. Bed undisturbed. Closet door standing open.

Next was the guest bathroom off the hallway. Westbrook checked it. Nothing. They moved down the hallway.

They positioned themselves on either side of the master bedroom door. Westbrook reached for the handle. Turned it slowly. The latch withdrew without sound.

They entered as one, weapons sweeping darkness.

The cat hissed from atop the bed, back arched, fur standing like tiny spears along its spine.

The tactical light found rumpled sheets. Pillows bearing the impression of a head. But no Voss.

Westbrook crossed to the bathroom door. Pushed it open. Empty. Shower stall dry. Bathtub empty. Towels hanging undisturbed.

His partner checked the walk-in closet. Designer suits. Shoes in precise rows. No one hiding among silk and wool.

Westbrook moved to the window. Drew back heavy drapes with his weapon's barrel. Nothing but darkness beyond glass.

The cat continued hissing, yellow eyes reflecting hatred in the tactical light's beam.

Westbrook pointed to the bed, then made a circular gesture with his finger. His partner nodded. More thorough search required.

The second hitman turned toward the walk-in closet again, weapon raised. He pushed aside hanging clothes, crouched to check under the built-in dresser.

Satisfied Voss was not in her bedroom, they moved back into the hallway.

"Split," Westbrook whispered. He pointed to a thin cord hanging from the ceiling at the end of the hallway. Attic access. His partner nodded, moved toward the second guest bedroom.

Westbrook pulled the cord. A folded ladder descended with a metallic rasp. He climbed, each rung protesting his weight.

The attic opened around him. Pale moonlight filtered through a single circular window, casting geometry across forgotten things. Dust particles danced in his light's beam. Cardboard boxes. Old furniture draped in sheets like patient ghosts. The pitched ceiling descended sharply at the edges, creating shadows his light couldn't penetrate.

He moved forward in a crouch, sweat beading despite the cold. The air smelled of insulation and time.

The second gunman entered the room adjacent to the master bedroom. His light revealed an artist's sanctuary. Easels of various heights. Paint-spattered drop cloths protecting hardwood floors. A wooden table bore dozens of brushes standing in jars, their bristles stained with color. Palettes crusted with dried paint. Tubes arranged by hue—cadmium, ochre, ultramarine, crimson.

His light found the canvas dominating the room's center. Nine feet tall, it captured a tower constructed of intertwined bodies. Human forms twisted upward, climbing over one another. Those at the bottom crushed beneath the weight of ambition above. Some figures bore angelic wings, lifting others. Some sprouted horns and barbed tails, clawing their way upward using weaker souls as stepping stones. Ordinary humans caught between— mothers clutching children, old men with desperate eyes, young warriors with broken swords.

The gunman stepped closer. Something protruded from the canvas center where the paint bulged outward. The shape was round about the size of a dime.

The gunshot thundered in the enclosed space. Canvas fibers burned at the muzzle flash. The bullet caught the hitman in the chest. He staggered backward, weapon rising, returning fire. His shots went wide, tearing through the tower's upper regions.

Voss stepped from behind the ruined canvas, the Smith & Wesson revolver gripped in both hands. She fired again. And again. The hitman collapsed against the paint table, sending brushes clattering to the floor. His tactical light rolled across the drop cloth, illuminating her feet, her determined face in shifting shadows.

Voss advanced. Fired three more times in rapid succession. The revolver bucked in her hands. Certainty replacing fear.

The hitman lay still on the floor. Blood pooled beneath him, spreading across white cloth in abstract patterns.

The gun clicked empty. The sound of victory and new vulnerability. Voss was filled with emotion. She had killed a man. An evil man for sure, but still human. Unsure what was appropriate, rejoicing or weeping. She chose to pick up the gunman's Glock and prepare for the next fight. She didn't know if someone else was in her home.

Westbrook heard the shots through the attic floor. He moved quickly to the ladder, descended with weapon drawn. The hallway opened before him. No target presented itself.

He advanced toward the art room, each step measured. His suppressed pistol swept the space before him.

A suppressed shot came without warning. Plaster exploded from the banister inches from Westbrook's hand. He spun toward the staircase.

Culper stood at the bottom, weapon raised, face bloodied but eyes clear.

Westbrook fired twice. Culper rolled away, wood splintering where he'd stood.

Culper charged up the stairs. No cover. No hesitation. His Sig Sauer shot once, twice, three times. The suppressor reduced the reports to angry coughs.

Westbrook took the third round in his shoulder. Spun with the impact. His return fire shattered a hallway mirror.

Culper's fourth shot caught Westbrook in the thigh. He fell to one knee, still firing. Bullets tracked Culper's ascent, missing by inches, then feet as Westbrook's blood flowed and his aim deteriorated.

Culper reached the landing. Westbrook's weapon clicked empty. He reached for a spare magazine.

Too slow.

Culper fired twice more. The first round caught Westbrook in the chest. The second in the throat. He collapsed against the wall, eyes wide with disbelief. Blood painted the wallpaper in modern patterns. His mouth opened and closed around words that never formed. Then stillness claimed him.

Culper moved forward, weapon trained on Westbrook's still form. Kicked the empty pistol away from nerveless fingers. Checked for a pulse. Found none.

He turned toward the art room.

Voss stood in the doorway. The dead hitman's weapon gripped in her hands. It wavered between Culper's chest and face.

"Who the hell are you?" Her voice steady despite wine and adrenaline and fear.

"Culper. Frank's handler." He lowered his weapon slowly. "I'm here to help."

"Prove it."

"You bought a Smith & Wesson Model 686. Frank took you to the range and taught you how to shoot." His eyes never left hers.

The weapon in her hands lowered fractionally.

"Reed sent them," Culper said. "Just like he sent someone to your house before."

She nodded once. The pistol dropped to her side.

"More will come," he continued. "We need to move. Now."

The Storm

Fairbanks International Airport – Fairbanks, Alaska

Morning broke clear and brutal. The sky was dark grey. Snow was inevitable. Temperature ten below according to the blinking sign at the private aviation terminal.

The cold hit Frank like a hammer. He crossed the tarmac with purposeful strides, canvas bag slung over one shoulder. A man in thick winter gear stood beside an idling SUV.

"Mr. Kane?"

Frank nodded.

"Vehicle's prepped. Full tank. GPS programmed with the target location." The man handed over the keys.

Frank dropped his bag onto the passenger seat. Started the engine.

"Weather service issued a storm warning," the man said. "Coming in from the northwest. Heavy snow by evening."

Frank didn't respond. Just put the vehicle in drive and pulled away from the terminal. The man watched him go. Breath clouds hanging in frozen air.

Frank reached for his secure phone. Dialed from memory. Three rings before Culper answered.

"Frank?"

"Alaska," Frank said.

"We've had complications." Culper's voice tight, controlled. "Reed made another attempt on Voss."

Frank's grip tightened on the steering wheel. "Dead?"

"She's alive. Two hitmen aren't. And Rollins is dead."

Frank grunted, relief and approval compressed into a single sound.

"She's at my place now. Secure for the moment." Papers shuffled on Culper's end. "You need to get back as soon as possible."

"Protect Meyer."

"Yes, of course. But after that I need you back. Things are escalating, Frank."

Frank watched the Alaska landscape unfold beyond the windshield. White emptiness stretching to mountains in the distance. He was thousands of miles from where he needed to be.

Frank ended the call without another word.

Georgetown, Washington D.C.

Voss sat on the edge of Culper's leather sofa, her body rigid with tension. The cat circled her feet, sensing her distress. Her hands shook visibly. Blood—not hers—had dried in her hair, flaking when she pushed it back from her face.

Culper appeared with a steaming cup. "Earl Grey. Might help."

Voss accepted the cup. Tea sloshed over the rim, wetting her fingers. She didn't notice.

"Two men," she said. The words came detached. "In my bedroom."

"I know." Culper settled into the adjacent chair. Behind him, bookshelves held volumes on war, psychology, intelligence gathering. The collected wisdom of human conflict bound in leather.

"I shot one. Through a painting." Voss stared at the tea. "I've never fired a gun at anyone before."

Culper nodded. Said nothing.

"The revolver," she continued. "Frank showed me how to use it."

"He taught you well."

She looked up suddenly. "This is insane. Why is Reed doing this? Fulcrum was meant to prevent violence. To identify social pressure points before they fractured. Not cause the fractures."

"Some men see only the weapon, never its purpose."

"But the cost. The infrastructure." She set the teacup down untouched. "Reed's building something massive in Fairbanks. Diverting millions from company accounts."

"Not just company funds anymore."

Voss's eyes narrowed. "What do you mean?"

Culper moved to his desk. Retrieved a folder. Placed it on the coffee table between them.

"DARPA's involved," he said.

"The Defense Department?" Voss shook her head. "Impossible. They wouldn't fund domestic operations. The legal implications alone—"

"They're calling it research. Proof of concept."

Voss opened the folder. Inside lay transcripts of Reed's conversations with military officials. References to funding. To deployment strategies. To American interests protected without American casualties.

"Oh God," she whispered. Understanding crashed over her like winter surf. "They're backing Reed. Giving him resources. Authorization."

"Eight figures transferred this week. Black budget allocation through shell corporations."

Voss pressed her hand to her mouth. "They want to use Fulcrum against foreign governments. Create manufactured social collapse."

"Cheaper than precision munitions. More deniable than special forces."

"But Reed's testing it here. On American cities."

Culper didn't respond. Didn't need to.

Voss stood suddenly. The cat startled, darting under the sofa. "The board never authorized this. I never authorized this."

"You created the technology. Reed found the application. DARPA provided the funding." Culper's voice remained even. "A perfect storm."

"I have to stop him."

"How? He has government backing now. Military resources."

Voss paced the small room. Her mind racing through possibilities, discarding them just as quickly. "I need to get to Fairbanks. To the facility. If I can access the system and shut it down."

"Reed's six steps ahead of you. Has been since the beginning." Culper watched her movements. "The assassination attempt wasn't just to silence you. It was to erase any challenge to his authority over Fulcrum."

She stopped pacing. Their eyes met across the room.

"Then I need proof. Evidence of what Reed's really doing."

Outside, raindrops struck the window in erratic patterns. The storm intensified as Voss stood amid the wreckage of what she'd built and what Reed had twisted. Her life's work perverted into a weapon aimed at the heart of what she'd sought to protect.

The cat emerged from under the sofa. Pressed against her leg as if lending strength. Voss bent down, touched its scarred ears.

"I built Fulcrum to prevent this exact scenario," she said. "The irony would be beautiful if it weren't so terrible."

Culper watched her. Saw the transformation from hunted to hunter. From victim to opponent.

The rain continued its assault on Georgetown. On a nation unaware of the algorithmic storm brewing on its horizon.

Fairbanks International Airport – Fairbanks, Alaska

Frank pulled in front of the main terminal and parked the SUV across from Alaska Airlines arrivals. Kept the engine running against the cold. Two hours passed. The sun never quite rose. Just a lighter shade of darkness on the eastern horizon.

Bundled in a Patagonia jacket, Meyer moved through the terminal pulling his carry-on. Weary from the flight. Shoulders tight from eight hours in a seat built for someone smaller.

He passed a glass display case. Motion-activated lights flickered on. Inside, a pack of timber wolves frozen in eternal snarl. Teeth bared and eyes fixed on prey that would never arrive. Taxidermy caught in the moment before violence. The alpha stood tallest, throat exposed in mid-howl. The others circled low, muscles tensed beneath dusty fur.

Meyer paused. Studied the tableau. Something about their arrangement struck him as deliberate. A warning dressed as art.

At the car rental counter a woman with faded blond hair handed him papers.

"Weather alert issued," she said. "Storm coming in from the northwest. Rapid temperature drop."

Meyer glanced at the economy sedan keys in her hand. "Anything larger available?"

"Four-wheel drive recommended this time of year." She tapped at her keyboard. "I can upgrade you to the Ford Explorer. Forty dollars more per day."

"Done."

She exchanged the keys. "Roads outside town can turn bad fast. No warning sometimes."

"I'll be careful."

"Careful folks still end up in ditches." She slid the paperwork across the counter. "Cell coverage gets patchy ten miles out. Just so you know."

Meyer signed where indicated. Took the keys. Hefted his bag.

"Last thing." She leaned forward. "Watch for ice on bridges. Freezes there first."

"Appreciate the warning."

Outside in the lot, Meyer was shivering from the cold as he loaded his suitcase into the Explorer. Climbing behind the wheel he turned on the heater, then checked the GPS coordinates for his hotel. The sky hung low and gray. Air that smelled like snow though none had fallen yet.

He pulled out of the car rental lot.

Frank waited until three vehicles separated them before following.

Downtown – Fairbanks, Alaska

The Westmark Fairbanks sat six blocks from the airport. Standard corporate hotel. Nothing remarkable except its proximity to the road leading northwest out of town.

Meyer checked in. Took his bag upstairs. Returned to the lobby twenty minutes later. He was tired from the flight, but anxious to get to the data center. He needed to get to the bottom of what Reed was doing at the facility. The longer Meyer delayed his inspection, the more time Reed's men had to cover up the truth. Sleep could wait.

Frank remained in the SUV across the street. The sun crept above distant mountains without bringing warmth. He watched Meyer pull away from the hotel.

The GPS already knew the way. Frank followed at a distance while studying the route on the screen. The data center lay thirty miles outside Fairbanks. No buildings marked on the map nearby. Just wilderness.

Perfect isolation.

Data Center – Fairbanks, Alaska

Meyer slowed as he approached a twelve-foot concrete wall topped with razor wire and a reinforced gate that could stop a tank. Stopping in front of the gate, he lowered his window. Cold air rushed in like something alive. The guard approached. Young but hard-eyed. Military bearing in a civilian uniform.

"Identification." Not a question.

Meyer handed over his Helix credentials. Corporate ID that marked him as chief financial officer. Access codes to all company properties.

The guard studied the ID. Compared the photo to Meyer' face. Ran the card through a reader.

"Purpose of visit?"

"Financial audit of the facility."

The guard nodded once. Returned the ID. "You're expected."

The barrier rose. Meyer drove through. The facility's garage door opened. He pulled inside. The door lowered behind him with hydraulic finality. Lights activated automatically. Motion sensors tracking his movements. He stepped from the Explorer. Air inside the garage cold but less biting than outside. His breath still visible with each exhale.

A door opened at the far end. A man emerged. Tall and lean with a military haircut. Wearing a suit that seemed wrong in this remote setting.

"Mr. Meyer." He extended his hand. "Ellis Sawyer. Head of security."

Meyer shook the offered hand. Noted the calluses. The precise grip.

"Welcome to Fairbanks," Sawyer said. "Let me show you what we've built."

Together they passed through the door. Into the heart of Reed's secret. Whatever it might be.

Outside the compound perimeter, Frank pulled off the road into a copse of pines. Cut the engine. Took the Steiner binoculars from the glove compartment.

The data center stood two stories tall. No windows. Satellite dishes on the roof. Two guard towers overlooking the perimeter. Men with rifles walking a pattern Frank recognized immediately. Military. Not rent-a-cops.

There was something else. Some other structure beyond the main building. Frank reached for the telephoto lens in his bag.

The camera lens brought a distant ridgeline into sharp focus. Construction equipment clustered around what looked like concrete platforms. Men in cold weather gear moved between the site and a small, prefabricated building.

Frank took several photos, then lowered the camera. Stared at the ridgeline with narrowed eyes. Something about the structure's position. The sight lines. The elevation relative to the facility and access road.

Frank opened the canvas bag he brought with him and retrieved his holster and two Redhawk revolvers. He zipped his parka to the neck. Pulled a wool cap low over his ears. Began walking through deep snow toward whatever Reed had built on that ridge.

Ten minutes to reach the construction site. Frank's breath came in clouds that crystallized on his unshaven face. The cold penetrated his layers one by one.

He crouched behind a pine trunk. Watched workers move between three similar structures. All concrete. All facing different directions.

When the workers disappeared into their heated trailer, Frank moved forward. Kept low. Used the terrain for cover.

The first structure contained only a concrete pad with bolts protruding at precise intervals. Unfinished. The second had steel rails mounted in an arc. A gun emplacement waiting for its weapon.

The third stood complete. A geodesic dome with sliding panels protected whatever lay inside. Frank found the padlock. Looked over at the workers' trailer. Picked the lock.

Inside the dome a Bushmaster IV 40 mm chain-driven autocannon waited in cradle made of steel and circuitry. Not the helicopter-mounted version. Something modified. The barrel could elevate seventy degrees. Traverse a full circle.

A targeting system sat where a human gunner would be. Cameras. Thermal imaging. Radar that could track objects smaller than birds. Automated defense.

Frank took photos with the digital camera. Every angle. Every component. Made sure the serial numbers were clearly visible.

An automated cannon designed to destroy aircraft. Or ground vehicles. Or people.

Frank secured the padlock behind him as he left the enclosure.

The ridge offered clear sight lines. Frank knelt amid broken schist and sparse pine, binoculars steady despite the bitter cold. His breath formed clouds that dissipated in Arctic wind. Fingers bare against metal despite temperature that would frostbite lesser men.

The Bushmaster autocannon stood thirty yards behind him. Its dome closed against weather. Sensors still active beneath protective housing. A mechanized predator waiting for algorithms to wake it.

Through Steiner lenses, Frank glassed the compound below. The concrete rectangle with its satellite arrays and cooling units sat centered in the valley. No windows. No visible entrance except the loading dock and personnel gate. Both heavily monitored. Both designed for controlled access rather than escape.

Movement caught his attention. Guards patrolled in precise patterns. Not random walks but deliberate coverage with minimal blind spots. Professional security with military bearing. Men who understood defensive perimeters and kill zones.

Frank adjusted focus. Found the second ridge line across the valley. He'd missed it during initial survey. Something about the angle. The way snow and shadow concealed intent.

There. Another dome. Twin to the one behind him. Bushmaster positioned for interlocking fields of fire. Any approach from north or south covered by automated weapons with thermal targeting.

He panned right. Found a third emplacement. Then a fourth. The data center anchored in the center of a defensive grid calculated to eliminate any conventional assault option.

Frank shifted to higher magnification. Studied the compound's interior perimeter. Four more domes positioned at compass points inside the walls. Smaller but no less lethal. Interior defense redundancy beyond anything civilian operations would require.

This wasn't security against theft or corporate espionage. This was military-grade protection against coordinated assault. Against forces with resources and determination beyond normal threat profiles.

Frank lowered the binoculars. Considered implications. Eight automated weapons systems deployed around a facility supposedly dedicated to data storage and algorithm development. Each capable of delivering 120 rounds per minute at effective ranges exceeding what conventional tactics could counter.

No civilian contractor authorized such defenses. No corporate security protocol justified this level of lethality. Whatever Reed protected inside those walls required not just secrecy but survival against organized military action.

He raised the binoculars again. Studied access points and sight lines with mechanical precision. Calculated angles and timing with the patience of a man who had survived worse odds through planning and execution.

The compound had been designed by someone who understood both conventional and unconventional threats. Someone who anticipated resistance and prepared accordingly. Someone who thought like Frank himself. A worthy opponent.

Frank began the descent. Moving between patches of snow and stone with silence no human should maintain in such terrain. Each step placed with certainty born from lifetimes spent in hostile environments.

Below, the compound continued its operations. Staff moved between buildings with purposeful strides. Vehicles patrolled interior roads. Generators hummed. All ordinary activity except for the automated cannons watching every approach with electronic vigilance.

Behind him, the Bushmaster's sensors tracked heat signatures and movement patterns. Algorithms waiting for parameters that would transform observation into action. Into targeted elimination of threats identified by programmers who had never pulled triggers themselves.

Frank disappeared into broken ground. A shadow moving against shadows. His mind calculating approach vectors and timing sequences. Building the architecture of intervention with the same cold precision Reed had applied to defense.

This would not be simple. Would not be clean. But it would be done.

Something shifted behind Frank. Not sound but air disturbance. The faintest mechanical whir that most humans would miss beneath wind and distance.

Frank didn't turn. Didn't indicate awareness. Just listened while maintaining visual focus on the compound.

The sound came again. Servos activating. Electric motors adjusting position with fractional precision.

One of the Bushmasters had awakened. Its targeting systems now active. Sensors sweeping hillside terrain with programmed patience.

Frank remained motionless. Only his eyes moved, tracking guard rotations through binocular lenses while his mind calculated the autocannon's position relative to his own. The wind direction. The targeting parameters likely programmed into automated defense systems.

Movement would trigger targeting confirmation. Stillness might read as a terrain feature rather than human threat. Might.

Inside the data center's security office, Hendricks stared at his monitor. The screen showed a heat signature on the northern ridge. Not moving but warmer than surrounding terrain.

He called Sawyer's cell. "Sir, possible surveillance on the ridge. Bushmaster Three has thermal target lock."

Sawyer excused himself from Meyer's tour and appeared in the security room moments later. He studied the screen with narrowed eyes.

"That's human," Sawyer said, tracing the outline. "Military training by the positioning."

"Should I send a patrol?"

"No. Track but don't engage."

"Shouldn't we alert Reed? Protocol states any breach—"

"Reed is busy. He doesn't need to be bothered with security matters." Sawyer's tone left no room for debate. "That's why I'm here."

"He'll leave eventually. When he does, Bushmaster Three will track him to his vehicle." Sawyer tapped commands into the console. The screen shifted to satellite view of surrounding terrain. "When you've located his vehicle, I'll take it from there."

"Sir, I really think Mr. Reed should be informed. We have an infiltration of the secure perimeter. That's a level one—"

"It's my call, Hendricks." Sawyer's voice hardened. "I have operational authority over security at the data center. Reed has more important concerns. I've got to get back to the CFO. Alert me the moment you find this guy's vehicle." Sawyer straightened his jacket. "And Hendricks? This conversation stays between us."

"Understood, sir."

Sawyer left. Hendrick continued to watch.

On the ridge, Frank calculated his options. The mechanical sounds had ceased. The Bushmaster now locked on his position. Not firing but waiting. Its electronic patience more dangerous than immediate response.

They'd seen him. Were watching. Deciding.

Frank assessed the situation with cold precision. The Bushmaster's targeting optics would follow any movement. Its programming designed to eliminate evasive targets. If the Bushmaster fired he had little doubt his life would end. Forty millimeter shells don't maim. They kill.

The wind shifted slightly. Temperature dropping as early afternoon light began its winter fade. Decision point approaching with each degree of declining warmth.

In the security room, Hendricks continued to watch.

The sun touched mountain peaks to the west, casting long shadows across the compound below. Guards activated floodlights along the perimeter. Standard procedure against approaching darkness.

Frank heard the whirl of the targeting motor. The system was confused by lens flares and heat signatures from the bright lights. It was retargeting the lights and not him. It was his chance. Maybe his only chance.

Frank began his extraction. Inch by painstaking inch. Moving slowly so as not to trigger the automated system. No sudden movements. Just slow dissolution into landscape and shadow like something returning to elemental state.

Inside the security office, Hendricks changed from satellite's wide view back to the Bushmaster's close thermal view. The heat pattern had vanished completely.

"Shit," he said.

He switched to normal view. Saw nothing. He used the remote cameras around the compound to survey the area. He picked up Frank descending the hill. He followed him to his SUV hidden in the pines. Hendricks called Sawyer's cell.

Frank returned to the SUV as the storm front approached from the west. Dark clouds on the horizon promised what the weather service had predicted.

Frank settled in to wait. To watch for Meyer. To see what the man discovered within those walls.

Inside the data center Sawyer led Meyer through steel corridors that hummed with hidden power. Their footsteps echoed against polished concrete. The facility smelled of new electronics and recirculated air.

"Server room," Sawyer said, gesturing through a glass partition. Inside, row upon row of black cabinets stretched to the ceiling. Blinking lights reflected in the glass. Cooling fans a constant whisper.

"Power consumption?" Meyer asked.

"Equivalent to a small town."

"For data backup?"

Sawyer's face remained neutral. "Redundancy requires capacity."

They continued past security doors that opened with Sawyer's keycard. Each subsequent area more restricted than the last. Meyer noted the progressive layers. Fortress within fortress.

"Cooling system specially designed," Sawyer explained as they entered a mechanical room. "Outside temperature helps efficiency. One advantage of the location."

"And the disadvantages?" Meyer asked.

"Isolation. Staff retention. Supply chain complications."

Meyer nodded, making notes in a small leather book. "Fourteen specialists on payroll. All recent hires."

Sawyer's eyes flickered. "Reed handles personnel matters."

"I handle the finances that pay them," Meyer countered. "Their qualifications seem... specific."

"You'd have to ask Reed about that."

"I'm asking you."

Sawyer stopped before another security door. "My job is facility security, Mr. Meyer. Not staffing questions."

The door opened into a large open workspace. Programmers hunched over multiple screens. Young men and women with energy drink cans and takeout containers cluttering desks. The room hushed at their entrance.

"Programming division," Sawyer said. "They maintain the systems."

"Seems excessive for maintenance." "Some reprogramming is required for the system to operate correctly in this facility."

"Strange. I would think it would be identical to the system at Helix headquarters. It is the same system, isn't it?"

"It is for the most part. But there are always some differences between facilities."

"What kind of differences?"

"Processor speed, storage capacity, video cards. Everyday kind of equipment."

The phone on Sawyer's belt vibrated. He glanced at Meyer who studied the programmer's workstation, noting figures that shouldn't exist in a backup facility.

"Excuse me," Sawyer said. "Facility matters."

Meyer nodded without looking up from the screen.

Sawyer stepped into the hallway. Made a call.

"Donaldson here." The plow driver's voice competed with engine noise.

"Where are you?"

"Clearing the north access road."

"Good. I've got a situation," said Sawyer.

"Yeah. What is it?"

"SUV on the ridge behind the pines. Someone watching the facility with binoculars. Black Suburban. One occupant. Big guy."

Sawyer looked through the glass wall at Meyer still examining code that revealed too much.

"Disable his vehicle," Sawyer said.

"Okay, but I can't guarantee the driver won't get hurt."

"Not your problem."

Silence except for the plow's engine. Then, "Understood."

Sawyer ended the call. Returned to the room where Meyer waited, unaware his audit had become something else entirely.

"Sorry for the interruption," Sawyer said.

Meyer walked between the workstations. Nodded to a young man with three days' stubble and bloodshot eyes.

"What are you working on?" Meyer asked.

The programmer glanced at Sawyer. Uncertain.

"Maintenance scripts," he answered finally. "System optimization."

Meyer looked at the code on the screen. Equations beyond simple optimization.

"And this?" He pointed to a section labeled CATALYST-PREDICTIVE-MODEL.

"That's..." The programmer hesitated.

Sawyer cleared his throat. "Perhaps Dr. Harris can better address the technical aspects."

An older programmer approached. Salt-and-pepper beard and academic posture. "I head the development team at Fairbanks, Mr. Meyer. How can I help?"

"These algorithms. They're behavioral models?"

Harris nodded. "Predictive analytics based on sociological inputs."

"For what purpose?"

Harris looked to Sawyer. The security chief gave a slight head shake. Harris misinterpreted.

"Fulcrum's core function is societal stress testing," Harris explained. "We identify pressure points in population groups and calculate optimal intervention vectors for desired outcomes."

Sawyer stiffened. "Dr. Harris, Mr. Meyer is conducting a financial audit, not a technical review."

"Oh." Harris suddenly understood his error. "I thought you were—"

"I find it helps to understand what I'm financing," Meyer said smoothly. "These interventions you mentioned—they're theoretical?"

"Field-tested," Harris said before Sawyer could intervene. "The Detroit incident provided excellent validation of our catalyst-effect models."

Sawyer stepped between them. "Dr. Harris, I believe the server diagnostics needed your attention."

Harris retreated, aware too late of his misstep. Sawyer turned to Meyer.

"If you're finished with this section, the accounting office is on the lower level."

Meyer nodded, his expression revealing nothing. "Of course."

The tour continued. Meyer asking precise questions. Sawyer providing increasingly careful answers. The dance of probe and deflect. By midafternoon, Meyer had seen enough.

"I appreciate your time," he told Sawyer in the garage. "I'll be returning tomorrow to complete the audit."

Sawyer watched him load his briefcase into the Explorer.

"The storm's intensifying," he said. "Weather service issued a severe warning. Consider staying in facility quarters tonight."

"I prefer my hotel. The cellular reception is better."

Sawyer noted the implied threat. "The roads will be dangerous. I could send someone to drive you back."

"No, thank you. I'll drive carefully."

The garage door opened to reveal a world transformed. Snow falling in thick sheets. Wind driving it sideways. Visibility reduced to yards. Meyer started the Explorer. Let the defroster heat the windshield.

"Safe travels," Sawyer said as Meyer backed out. There was no sincerity in the words.

The garage door closed behind him. Meyer passed through the perimeter gate and started down the access road. Fresh snow already obscuring the morning's tracks. His headlights cutting weak paths through white darkness.

Inside, Sawyer waited until the Explorer's taillights vanished in the storm. He pulled out his satellite phone. Dialed.

"Reed."

"It's Sawyer. Meyer knows about Fulcrum's actual purpose. About Detroit."

Reed was silent for a long moment. "How did he react?"

"Too controlled. He'll report to Voss as soon as he reaches cellular coverage. I'm sure of it."

"Understood."

"Your instructions?"

"Continue normal operations. I'll handle it from here."

The line went dead. Sawyer stared at the phone. Then at the storm outside.

Frank watched Meyer's SUV making its way through the storm down the road. Frank pulled out from the tree line and started to follow Meyer at a distance.

Meyer passed the snowplow heading in the opposite direction toward the facility.

Keating sat in his SUV parked in a turnout on the access road, waiting. His satphone rang. He answered it.

"Keating."

"Meyer is leaving the facility now," Reed said. "He knows."

"Understood. Weather's closing in fast."

"Alaska is dangerous country. Accidents happen."

"They do." Keating's voice revealed nothing. "What kind of accident did you have in mind?"

"The kind that explains a body not being found."

"Consider it done."

The call ended.

Frank heard the snowplow before seeing it. The diesel engine laboring. Amber warning lights barely visible through the storm. A wave of fresh snow launched from its shovel to an embankment on the side of the road.

As Frank's SUV passed in the opposite direction, the snowplow suddenly veered into his lane and crashed into the driver's side of his vehicle.

The impact slammed Frank sideways. Metal groaned. Glass shattered. The plow rammed the SUV through the snow piled on the opposite side of the road. The SUV rolled. Tumbled down an embankment toward the stream ten yards below.

Frank used his other arm to brace against the roof. The vehicle hit the stream with a sound like a gunshot. Ice breaking. Water flooding in through broken windows. He clawed his way out. The current tugged at his legs. The embankment rose steep before him. His boots slipped on snow-covered rocks. His hands reached for tree roots.

At the top he lay flat. Breathing hard. The snow offering cold comfort against rising bruises. He could hear the snowplow speeding away.

Frank rose on aching legs. Blood ran from a cut above his eye. He wiped it away with his sleeve. He stepped back on the road. Falling snow limited visibility. White space. No noise. Nobody was coming to help. He was wet and freezing and on his own. So was Meyer.

Failing to protect Meyer troubled him. Frank wasn't used to failure. He ignored his pain as he started to walk, then jog, then run back toward the data center. It wasn't over, not yet.

Keating pulled his SUV to the roadside ten miles from the facility. Snow weighing down pine branches. Visibility getting worse by the minute. Perfect.

He removed a rifle from its case. Fitted the scope. Pulled on snow camouflage over his thermal gear. Moved into the trees like a ghost.

The moose grazed on winter bark a hundred yards in. Small rack and steam-cloud breath. Keating found his position. Settled the crosshairs on the animal's chest. Exhaled. Squeezed.

The shot echoed through the trees. The moose staggered. Attempted to run. Collapsed after thirty yards.

Keating approached the fallen animal. Eight hundred pounds of meat and bone. He attached a rope to the rack. He walked back to his SUV letting out as much rope as possible. It ran out twenty yards from the road.

He walked through the snow to his SUV, pulled it up to the edge of the road, then moved to the winch and pulled the cable. He tied the rope to the cable and let the winch drag the moose to the edge of the road.

He pulled out his knife and split the beast's stomach open letting the guts and blood spill out on the white road. The odor was strong. Just what he wanted.

He secured the wench and drove a half mile to a nearby bridge spanning Clark Creek up the access road toward the Helix facility.

At the bridge he pulled six iron caltrops from a bag in the rear of the SUV. Each caltrop had four sharp spikes arranged so that one of them always points upward from a stable base. He placed the caltrops along one side of the bridge beneath the snow. Hidden.

Lastly, he drove his SUV up a logging road above the bridge. He reached a ridge that had a good view of the bridge and the dead moose a half mile away further down the access road. He checked his watch. It wouldn't be long now. Turned off his headlights. Settled in to wait.

The storm intensified. Snow erasing all evidence of his work. Wind rocking the SUV. Nature conspiring with man to create the perfect conditions for tragedy.

Frank approached the data center. He shook violently. His teeth chattered. Ice had encased his clothes and hair. He was freezing to death. Only the movement from running had kept him alive.

Through the snow he saw the guard at the front gate standing inside the gatehouse, windows fogging from the heater.

Frank was in no condition to fight, but he didn't have much choice. A few more minutes without heat and he'd be dead. He reached for one of his Redhawks. It was frozen solid in the holster. He hit is with his fist. Pain shot through his fingers and palm. The Redhawk didn't move. He looked around for another solution.

Next to the perimeter wall he saw a maintenance shed with a padlock on the doors. He moved toward it, picking up a rock on the way. He bashed the lock until it broke open. He opened the doors. Two snowmobiles waited under tarps. Keys hung on hooks nearby. Gasoline cans stacked against the wall. Frank checked the nearest machine. Full tank. Good treads. The battery turned the engine over on the first try. Moments later, he was back on the access road heading away from the data center. After a minute, the heated seat and handgrips offered relief and the ice covering his clothes began to melt.

Hearing a truck engine in the distance, Keating raised his binoculars and watched.

Meyer's SUV approached the bridge. The caltrops lay beneath fresh snow like dark secrets. Meyer slowed the SUV as he approached the bridge, the rental clerk's warning about ice still echoing in his mind. The tires found the metal spikes before his eyes could see them.

Two tires ruptured with a sound like gunshots. The vehicle lurched sideways then settled, tilting toward the ditch. He gripped the wheel. Waited for the motion to stop.

"What the hell?"

Meyer stepped out into knee-deep snow. Wind bit his exposed face. He circled the SUV, counting punctures. His breath formed clouds that vanished in the wind. The spare would fix one tire. The second remained a problem without solution.

He tried his cell phone. No service. The road stretched empty in both directions, a thin black line cutting through endless white. Not a single vehicle had passed since he'd left the data center.

"Goddammit."

He climbed back inside, turned the key. The heater hummed, pushing warmth against the encroaching cold. He stared at the fuel gauge. Less than a quarter tank.

Shadows lengthened across the snow. The sun hovered above distant mountains, threatening to abandon him. He drummed his fingers against the steering wheel. He opened the glove box and found a map. Checked his watch. Calculated distances.

Six miles to the next town. He couldn't survive a night in the vehicle. The temperature would drop below zero after sundown. Night was approaching fast. Too fast.

His breath fogged inside the car. He could no longer feel his fingertips. The silence pressed against him, broken only by the cracking of cooling metal.

Out of options, Meyer started walking. His boots crunched through snow crust with each step. Wind found the gaps in his coat and invaded. He pulled his collar higher, cinched his hood tighter.

The storm intensified, wind driving snow horizontally across the landscape. Visibility narrowed to twenty yards, then ten. The clouds faded to gray then darker gray.

His legs ached. Cold seeped into his bones. Ice formed in his beard. Each breath became harder than the last.

Something moved in the distance. A dark mass against white. Meyer squinted against the snow. Hope flared in his chest. Perhaps a vehicle.

He quickened his pace. The shape resolved with each labored step.

The moose lay half-eaten in a red crater of disturbed snow. Steam rose from its opened belly into the freezing air. The grizzly stood over it, muzzle crimson with blood and tissue. Massive shoulders hunched against the storm.

Meyer froze. His legs would not obey his mind's command to retreat. Sweat broke across his back despite the cold.

The bear's head swung toward him. Nostrils flared, testing the air. Small eyes fixed on Meyer' silhouette. It rose to its full height, taller than any man Meyer had ever seen. Eight feet of muscle and claws and anger.

A low growl vibrated the air between them.

Meyer stepped backward. His heel found ice beneath the snow.

The bear dropped to all fours.

"No," Meyer whispered, then turned and ran in panic.

Qued by instinct, the bear charged, covering ground with terrible efficiency. Six hundred pounds of predator closing the gap with each powerful stride.

Meyer's feet found no purchase on the icy road. He slipped. Recovered. Too slow.

Claws raked across Meyer's back, shredding parka and flesh in a single swipe. He stumbled forward, scrambling through snow. Blood steamed in the frigid air.

The bear's weight crashed down upon him. Its jaws found the junction of neck and shoulder. Teeth pierced skin, shattered clavicle, severed artery. The beast's rank breath washed over him, a mixture of carrion and primal rage.

Meyer's scream died in his throat, replaced by a wet gurgle. The snow beneath him turned deep crimson. He pawed weakly at the enormous head. His vision narrowed to a single point of light.

Then darkness.

Next to the bridge, Keating's SUV approached the disabled SUV. Keating stepped out wearing insulated coveralls. His movements were unhurried, methodical. He scanned the empty road in both directions. Listened for approaching engines.

Nothing but wind and silence.

He gathered the caltrops one by one, counting to ensure none remained. His breath formed clouds that disappeared in the dark.

Back in the driver's seat, he checked his watch. He drove down the access road until he reached blood covered snow that once belonged to Meyer. The body was gone. Dragged into the woods. Nature would erase evidence more thoroughly than any human hand.

He considered for a long moment. The thought of going into the trees with a grizzly nearby didn't thrill

Keating, but he needed to make sure Meyer's body would not be found. He took his rifle.

Thawed by the heat of the engine, Frank slowed the snowmobile. Meyer's abandoned SUV sat just past the bridge. Two flat tires.

Frank cut the snowmobile's engine. Listened.

Nothing but wind through pines. The soft hiss of falling snow.

He knelt beside the disabled vehicle. Examined the tires. Clean cuts through sidewalls. Not road damage. He looked at the bridge surface. Nothing remained but six holes where something had been retrieved from the snow.

A trap.

But the bridge itself was not the trap. Just the setup. Footprints led away from the vehicle. A single trail heading south. Toward town. Toward help.

Frank knelt again. Studied the footprints. A man walking with purpose. No sign of injury.

He began following the tracks. The snow fell heavier with each passing minute. Soon there would be nothing left to follow.

Twenty feet past the bridge he found tire marks in the snow from another vehicle following the footprints. The assassin.

No time for subtlety. He jumped back on the snowmobile and sped down the access road.

It didn't take long before he found what he was looking for. The red stain appeared first. Blood soaked into snow. Too much for survival. A wide smear leading from road to tree line.

He saw a set of footprints beside the trail of blood. Meyer? The assassin? Frank had to know with certainty. He drew one of his Redhawks, now thawed, and moved into the woods following the crimson trail between silent pines.

Fifty yards in, Frank found what remained of Meyer. The body lay face up. Throat torn. Chest cavity opened to winter air. One arm missing entirely. The snow beneath churned pink and red.

He studied the claw marks across what remained of Meyer's face. Bear attack.

Frank knelt beside the corpse. Meyer's eyes stared skyward. Already glazing in death and winter chill.

Wide paw prints circled the feeding ground. Then led deeper into trees. Frank studied their direction. The bear gone but not far. The meal interrupted.

Frank stood. Drew the second Redhawk. The path before him dark with more than shadow.

The tracks doubled back twenty yards ahead. Frank felt the vibration before hearing anything. A low growl rumbling from dense undergrowth to his left.

The bear charged. Muscle and rage. Moving faster than anything that size should move.

The Redhawks thundered. Flame cutting darkness. Two shots center mass. The bear stumbled. Kept coming. Two more shots. Blood spraying from its chest. Still coming.

The bear's impact drove Frank backward. Snow cushioned his fall but couldn't soften eight hundred pounds of the predator. Jaws snapped inches from his face. Hot breath carrying Meyer's scent.

Teeth found Frank's shoulder. Sank deep through parka and flesh. Frank didn't cry out. He jammed the right Redhawk against the bear's throat. Fired.

The bear shuddered. Its weight collapsed onto Frank. The jaws went slack. The bear's eyes dulled. Dead weight crushing him into red snow. Frank pushed against the massive head with his free hand.

Frank lay still. His breath coming hard. Blood leaking from the puncture wounds in his shoulder. He pushed against the bear. Muscles straining. The carcass rolled sideways. Frank struggled to his feet.

Silence except for wind through pines. The storm building toward something worse.

Frank returned to Meyer's body. Knelt beside it. Closed the staring eyes with gloved fingertips. As he did, he remembered…

A second set of tracks.

He looked at the snow around the feeding area and found boot prints not matching his own. Not Meyer's. Military tread. A man standing at the edge of the clearing watching the bear feed. Then leaving. The storm hadn't erased these tracks yet. Too fresh.

Frank followed them. Reloaded the Redhawks as he moved. Pain throbbed from his shoulder. Blood freezing on his face.

Keating waited a hundred yards deeper in the forest. His rifle aimed where the tracks would lead his prey. Patient as only professionals can be.

Frank came from a different angle. No sound in his approach. Keating sensed movement too late. Turned as Frank closed the distance, both Redhawks up and firing.

Keating was hit, once, twice, three times, driving him against a tree. Life leaving his eyes, Keating slumped. His breathing stilled.

Frank didn't need to check for a pulse. He knew when a man was dead. Practice. Frank searched the corpse methodically. No ID. He found a set of keys to the SUV and the satphone. He dialed the last number by hitting send. He listened as someone answered.

"Is it done?" said Reed.

Frank didn't respond but recognized the voice.

"Keating?" said Reed when there was no response.

Frank pressed End terminating the call. It was time to leave Alaska.

The Catalysts

Fairbanks, Alaska

The emergency room doctor cleaned and stitched Frank's shoulder without meeting his eyes. Questions came about bear attacks and head wounds from a car accident, but Frank's silence stretched so long the staff stopped asking, recording only "patient nonverbal" on forms that would vanish from the system by morning.

G5 - Alaska

Cold air filled the cabin. Frank sat alone. His shoulder throbbed with each heartbeat, but his face revealed nothing.

The G5 lifted through storm clouds. Alaska fell away beneath him. A wilderness of white becoming distant memory.

When they reached cruising altitude Frank pulled out a cell phone. Dialed Culper's number.

"Frank?" Culper's voice tight with expectation.

"Meyer's dead."

The line went silent for three slow beats.

"Shot?"

"No. Bear."

"You're serious?"

"Always."

"Could it have been an accident?"

"Yes. But it wasn't."

"Was Reed behind it?"

"Yes. Assassin."

"Where is the assassin now?"

"Dead."

"Good work. I guess. Did Meyer find anything at the facility?"

"Don't know."

"Dammit."

"But I did."

"What?"

"Reed's building a fortress."

"What do you mean?"

"Automated Bushmaster IVs."

"How'd he get those?"

"Don't know."

"If they have depleted uranium shells that could make things more difficult."

Frank grunts his agreement.

"Reed is cleaning house," Culper continued. "Anyone who might interfere with whatever he's building up in Alaska. I am willing to bet Voss is still high on that list."

Frank watched his reflection in the window glass. A man with too many scars to count.

"You still with me?" Culper asked.

Frank grunted. He closed his eyes. Saw Meyer's frozen face. The bear's teeth.

"Frank?"

"Understood."

"You need to get back as soon as possible."

"On my way."

Frank ended the call. The G5 banked slightly, adjusting course. He pressed his forehead against the cold window. Below him Alaska spread vast and unknowing. Cities and towns and dark spaces between. People living their lives unaware of the forces gathering around them.

Helix Headquarters – Arlington, Virginia

Reed stood at his office window. Rain struck glass in patterns that reminded him of gunfire. He held the secure phone against his ear, waiting while encryption protocols engaged.

"Fairbanks secure." The voice belonged to Sawyer, flat and professional.

"Status report." Reed didn't identify himself. Didn't need to.

"Perimeter breach contained. Security upgraded. No evidence remaining."

Reed watched lightning flash across the city. Counted seconds until thunder followed.

"The programmer who spoke to Meyer. Harris."

"Reassigned to sub-level operations."

Reed nodded though no one could see. "Fulcrum's final test phase begins tomorrow. I need three urban centers. Population diversity. Existing tensions. Infrastructure vulnerability."

Papers shuffled on Sawyer's end. "System identifies Philadelphia, Atlanta, and Portland as optimal targets."

"Validation metrics?"

"Historical conflict patterns. Social media density. Law enforcement response capabilities." Sawyer paused. "Sir, we'll need the baseline data from Helix headquarters.

The complete behavioral profiles of key individuals in each location."

Reed's reflection stared back from the window. A man with too many secrets.

"I'll handle the data transfer personally. Tonight."

"Sir, there's something else." Hesitation in Sawyer's voice now. "The automated defense system. It's operational, but the firing protocols require your authorization codes."

Reed turned from the window. "You think someone's coming for us."

Not a question. Not denied.

"Meyer wasn't working alone. Someone took out Keating. Someone who knew what they were doing."

"Did you get a look at him?"

"No."

Rain drummed harder against glass. Reed thought of his brother dying on Afghan soil because someone hadn't secured the perimeter properly. He wouldn't make the same mistake.

"Authorization codes will transmit with the data package. Implement immediately."

"Understood."

"When does the system predict optimal conditions?"

"Three days. Weather patterns aligning with social indicators." Sawyer's voice lowered. "This won't be like Detroit or the border. This will be exponentially larger. We can't control—"

"We don't need to control it. Just demonstrate it." Reed cut him off. "Proof of concept at full scale."

Silence stretched between Virginia and Alaska.

"You need to get your head straight, Sawyer. What we are doing is historic. We are going to end war. Fulcrum will save millions of lives. It will be worth the sacrifices that are necessary. Are we clear?"

"Yes sir."

Reed ended the call. Set the phone on his desk beside a photograph of his brother in uniform. He touched the frame once, gentle where he was rarely gentle.

"Almost there," he said to the empty room.

Outside, the storm intensified. Wind driving water against buildings constructed in calmer times. The city endured, unaware it had been selected as witness rather than target.

This time.

Georgetown, Washington D.C.

Frank's boots left wet marks on Culper's marble entranceway. Outside, rain hammered the Imperial's chrome. He stood dripping, still cold from Alaska though he'd been back in Virginia for hours.

Culper appeared from the study with Voss behind him, her face gray with fatigue and fear. The cat followed, yellow eyes surveying the room with ancient suspicion.

"You look like shit," Culper said handing Frank a cup of hot coffee. "What happened to your shoulder?"

Frank touched his bandaged shoulder where the bear's teeth had pierced flesh. Blood had seeped through the gauze.

"Bear bite."

"No shit?"

"No shit."

"That's gotta hurt."

Frank grunted his agreement.

"Meyer's dead?" said Voss.

Frank nodded. She closed her eyes. Opened them.

"You're sure it wasn't an accident?"

"Sure," said Frank.

"Reed is such a conniving bastard."

The cat leapt onto a leather armchair, claws extended. It turned three times before settling, leaving thin scratches across the surface.

"Goddammit," Culper muttered. "That's Italian leather."

The cat yawned, unimpressed with human concerns about furniture.

"I need to go to Helix. I need to find out what Reed has done to Fulcrum," said Voss.

"That's insane," said Culper. "Reed is trying to kill you. You'd be walking into his lair."

"It's not his lair. It's mine. And I'll be damned if I'm going to let that punk ass bitch take it from me."

Frank drank the coffee in three swallows. Set the cup on the side table.

Culper shook his head. "Too dangerous. Reed will kill anyone who might interfere with his plans."

"I'm still CEO," Voss said. "I can lock him out of the system."

"With what authority? The board already sided with him."

"Not if they knew what he's planning. The board may be greedy, but they're not suicidal. They have reputations to protect."

The cat stretched, its claws digging deeper into the leather. Culper winced but said nothing.

"I'm going with or without you," said Voss.

Frank moved toward the door. Keys appeared in his scarred hand.

"Taking her?" Culper asked.

Frank nodded.

"I don't need permission," Voss said, gathering her coat.

The cat watched them prepare to leave, then jumped down and padded to Voss's side. It rubbed once against her leg, an alliance formed between survivors.

"You're taking that beast?" Culper asked.

Voss picked up the cat. "He saved my life."

Culper looked at his ruined chair. "Not surprised. It clearly has a talent for destruction."

Frank and Voss climbed into the Imperial. The cat sat in Voss's lap, but started to fidget like it wanted to be released. Frank looked down at his leather seats, then turned to the cat and said, "Cat tastes like chicken." The fidgeting stopped. The cat settled. Better to avoid pissing off the giant.

The rain had turned the streets slick. Headlights reflected off wet asphalt, distorted and elongated. Frank drove with both hands on the wheel, eyes constantly checking mirrors.

Voss clutched a leather portfolio on her lap. Her fingers tapped against it, counting seconds. The cat sat in her lap, watching wipers battle the downpour.

"Reed always pushed for more aggressive applications," she said. "Testing social pressure points. Finding where systems break." She looked at Frank's profile. "But this is different. Using it as a weapon."

Frank remained silent. The Imperial's wipers pushed sheets of water aside only to have them return.

Voss stared through the windshield at the rain-smeared city. "I created Fulcrum to prevent violence. To see patterns forming before they erupted." Her voice hardened. "Reed weaponized it. Turned prevention into causation."

The sedan turned at the next light. Frank's shoulders relaxed imperceptibly.

"I have to stop him," she said.

The Imperial rolled through empty streets toward Arlington. Frank's hands never moved from the wheel. His eyes never stopped scanning.

The cat stood, front paws on the dashboard, claws retracted, watching the world ahead with the same intensity as Frank.

The Imperial's engine growled as they crossed the bridge toward Virginia. Rain ran down the windshield like tears.

Helix Headquarters – Arlington, Virginia

The Imperial crouched against the curb, engine ticking as rain streamed down its chrome flanks. The Helix building stood unassuming in the downpour, windows lit against the gray morning like any other workday.

"Looks normal," Voss said.

Frank grunted. His eyes narrowed, studying entrances and exits. The cat pressed its face against the window, whiskers twitching.

"Let's go," Voss said, gathering her portfolio.

They crossed the parking lot, Voss's heels clicking on wet pavement. She swiped her badge at the main entrance. The door hissed open.

The lobby appeared ordinary. The security guard nodded, recognizing Voss despite her days-long absence. Frank followed, his bulk casting a shadow across polished floors.

Then they reached the elevator. Voss pressed the button for the executive floor. When the doors opened, chaos greeted them.

Papers blanketed the hallway in drifts. Desk drawers upended. Hard drives missing from workstations that now sprouted only severed cables like strange technological plants. Employees huddled in small groups, voices tense, faces drawn.

"My God," Voss whispered.

Frank moved past her, leading with his shoulder. The cat darted between their legs, fur bristling as it surveyed the destruction.

A young systems administrator looked up from a tangle of disconnected servers. "Dr. Voss? You're here?"

"What happened?" she asked.

"Reed. He came in before dawn with six security contractors. They uploaded a program, then took everything related to Fulcrum. Drives, documentation, backup systems."

Frank examined a terminal. Just an empty frame with dangling optical lines. He touched exposed connections. Still warm.

Voss pressed her lips together, calculations running behind her eyes. "Reed's office."

They moved through the wreckage. Employees stopped to watch, faces reflecting shock at Voss's presence. A woman in accounting whispered something to her colleague. The word "alive" carried across cubicle walls.

Reed's office stood empty. Glass walls intact but inside, systematic destruction. File cabinets emptied. Computer missing. A single coffee mug remained on the overturned desk, its contents soaking into the carpet.

"Get me Elizabeth in IT," Voss ordered the nearest employee.

A thin woman with purple-streaked hair approached minutes later. "Dr. Voss. We thought you were—"

"I need every access code Reed has revoked immediately. Building, servers, cloud storage. Everything."

Elizabeth nodded. "On it."

"And I need the bank notified. Cancel his corporate cards and remove his authorization on all accounts."

Frank moved to the window. Watched rain streak the glass as Voss continued issuing orders.

"Security, I want his biometrics deleted from the system. If he returns, I want to know immediately."

The bearded head of security nodded, already tapping on his tablet.

Frank pulled out his phone. Dialed.

"Frank?" Culper answered on the first ring.

"Reed's gone."

"Gone where?"

"Don't know."

"What did he take?"

"Everything."

Voss approached, standing close enough to hear both sides of the conversation.

"He'll head to Fairbanks," Culper said. "Commercial or private transport. I'll call Homeland. Have TSA flag his ID." Culper paused. "Reed must be accelerating whatever he's planning."

Frank grunted, then ended the call. Returned the phone to his pocket.

Voss looked up at him. "He's destroyed years of work."

Frank nodded. Voss approached a young man working on a terminal. "What can you tell me about Reed's recent work? What was he focused on?"

The programmer glanced around before speaking. "Reed had us building targeting packages for three cities. Philadelphia, Atlanta, Portland. Demographic analyses, infrastructure vulnerabilities, conflict predictors."

"Targeting for what?"

"He called it 'proof of concept at scale.'" The programmer lowered his voice. "The models showed casualties in the thousands if the catalysts were properly placed."

Voss's face drained of color. "How soon?"

"He implemented the program before he left. It's already begun."

"Jesus," said Voss. "We need a TV."

The conference room glass reflected their approach. Frank first, massive shoulders set against whatever waited inside. Voss behind, the cat cradled against her chest like armor. The room held a long table of polished mahogany. Eight leather chairs. A monitor that consumed most of the far wall.

Frank found the remote. Pressed power. The screen awoke, casting blue light across their faces.

They stood side by side as Voss cycled through channels. CNN. MSNBC. Fox. Each showing variations of the same images. Streets filled with people. Signs raised against gray skies. Faces contorted with something raw and unfiltered.

Philadelphia first. The camera panned across City Hall where two distinct crowds gathered on opposite sides of the square. One group wore union jackets, their signs denouncing automation and corporate tax breaks. The other dressed in business attire, holding counterpoint messages about economic necessity and global competition.

Plexiglass shields by their sides, police stood in loose formation between the two groups. Hands near batons but not yet gripping them. The tension visible in how they shifted weight from foot to foot.

"Reed's first target," Voss whispered.

Frank nodded once. Watched the patterns. The way certain individuals moved through the crowd, speaking to specific people. Catalysts finding kindling.

The crowd surged around City Hall. Voss gripped the edge of the console. Remembering. The faces in the mob—young, angry, like the ones who had surrounded her son in Charlottesville. Michael's voice on the phone that day: "Mom, I can't get out. They're everywhere."

She had listened helplessly as chaos erupted around him. The screaming. The car engine revving. Then silence.

"This is what I built Fulcrum to prevent," she said quietly.

The camera found an older man standing before the shattered remains of ROSETTI'S DELI, the hand-painted sign his father had made in 1962 now hanging by one chain. Smoke poured from the storefront where three generations of family recipes had fed the neighborhood. He picked up a broken jar of his grandmother's pickles from the sidewalk, turned it over in his hands, then set it gently on the curb like placing flowers on a grave.

The scene switched to Portland. Rain there too, falling on a waterfront park where environmental activists faced dock workers and shipping executives. Both sides claimed to protect the city's future. Both believed absolutely in their righteousness.

A woman with a bullhorn led the environmental faction, her words lost to distance but her gestures sharp as broken glass.

A bearded longshoreman countered from the opposing group, veins standing out on his neck as he shouted.

Voss studied the confrontations. Saw what he meant. Certain figures moved with too much purpose. Their anger too precise. Their positions too strategic.

"Reed's people," she said. "Placed to escalate when needed."

They watched in silence as the channel switched to Atlanta. There a university campus had become the battleground. Students and faculty on one side defending curriculum changes that acknowledged historical injustices. Community members on the other claiming erasure of tradition and heritage.

Among them moved shadow figures. Men and women who spoke into ears and disappeared back into the mass. Who carried signs with language calibrated to provoke without crossing into illegality.

"It's already happening," Voss said. "The algorithm identified social fracture points in each city. Reed's deployed social media and human catalysts to widen those fractures."

Frank's jaw tightened. His scarred hands closed into fists, then relaxed.

"Not violent," he observed.

"Not yet. But they will be," Voss set the cat on the conference table. It walked across polished wood, tail swishing as it watched the screen. "Reed needs escalation to prove Fulcrum's effectiveness. These are just the initial conditions."

On screen, the Philadelphia crowd surged against police lines. Not breaking through, just testing boundaries. Learning the shape of resistance. Officers pushed back with shields raised like modern centurions.

"How long?" Frank asked.

Voss checked her watch. Calculating probabilities against what she knew of Fulcrum's design parameters.

"Hours, not days. The catalyst events have been initiated. Secondary escalation factors are already in place. By nightfall they'll be violence."

Frank pulled out his phone. Dialed Culper.

"I'm watching," Culper said without preamble. "All three cities showing identical pattern development. Reed engineered this perfectly."

"Stop it."

"Working on it. I've contacted local authorities in each location. They're increasing police presence, but without knowing who the catalysts are..."

Frank ended the call. Turned back to the screen where America's wounds lay exposed in three distinct locations.

Wounds that Reed planned to infect, to widen until the body itself turned septic.

"He's proving what Fulcrum can do," Voss said. "Creating precisely engineered social collapse. If it works here, the military or CIA can deploy it against foreign targets. Against any nation that challenges American interests."

Frank watched a young man in Philadelphia move through the crowd, whispering to the angriest faces. Selecting those already primed for violence.

Voss changed the channel. The Portland crowd began to chant. The sound carried even through the broadcast. A unified voice building toward something larger than its individual components.

The cat stood suddenly alert, ears flattened against its head as if sensing storm pressure.

On screen, the first bottle arced through rain-filled sky. A perfect parabola of rage and glass.

Andrews Air Force Base, Maryland

The Andrews Air Force Base guard examined Reed's credentials. The rain distorted the plastic, but the DARPA security clearance remained visible. The guard compared Reed's face to the ID photo, nodded once, and waved the convoy through.

Three black SUVs proceeded onto the airfield. Wipers battled the downpour as they approached a sleek Gulfstream with no markings. Just polished metal against gray sky.

Reed sat in the lead vehicle, phone pressed to his ear. "Initialization has already begun. We should see significant results within twenty-four hours."

The voice on the other end belonged to General Hayes. "Our observation team is already in position at all three target cities."

"Understood." Reed ended the call.

The SUVs stopped twenty yards from the waiting aircraft. Engines idling as crew loaded equipment cases into the cargo hold. Computer servers. Hard drives. The building blocks of destruction packaged in foam-padded transit cases.

"Bring only what's essential," Reed told the six programmers huddled in the second vehicle. Their faces pale against the tinted windows. Not prisoners, not quite volunteers. Professionals too deep in the project to abandon it now. Promises of more money soothed their consciences.

The security team deployed. Two men establishing a perimeter. One watching the tree line beyond the runway. Another scanning rooftops with thermal binoculars despite the rain. Only after confirming the absence of threats did their leader nod to Reed.

"All clear, sir."

Reed stepped from the SUV. Rain hammered his shoulders as he crossed to the aircraft stairs. Behind him, the programmers followed, hunched against the weather, clutching laptops and external drives like lifelines.

The plane's interior gleamed. Leather seats. Polished wood tables. Technology disguised as luxury. Reed took his position by the window, looking out at the rain-soaked airfield. Government vehicles and military aircraft rendered anonymous by distance and weather.

The last programmer boarded. A woman with sharp eyes and fingers that never stopped moving. She had written the core algorithms that made Fulcrum possible. Had spent three years translating human behavior into mathematical certainties. Now she served the weapon it had become.

"Give me a status update on the system," Reed instructed her.

She opened her laptop. Lines of code reflected in her glasses. "Connection with Fairbanks servers established. Primary node operational. "

Reed nodded. Satisfaction tightening the corners of his mouth. "We're making history."

No one replied. The programmers kept their eyes on screens, avoiding the weight of what those screens contained.

The security team boarded last. The cabin door sealed with pneumatic finality. Engines spooled up, their pitch rising to a whine that penetrated the cabin's soundproofing.

The Gulfstream taxied toward the runway. Rain streaked past Reed's window, distorting the world beyond into abstract patterns. The aircraft accelerated. Forces pressed Reed against his seat as concrete gave way to empty air.

They climbed through cloud layers. Rain became turbulence, then smooth flight above the storm. Sunlight struck the aircraft's wings, brilliant against metal designed to pierce atmosphere and distance.

Reed checked his watch. Calculated time zones and hours. By the time anyone understood what was happening, Fulcrum would have proven itself beyond any skepticism. A weapon that made conventional warfare obsolete. That turned a nation's own people into instruments of its destruction.

Reed saw only cleaner wars. Conflicts won without American bodies returning beneath flags. The end of grieving mothers and folded triangles like the one his own mother had received.

The aircraft leveled at cruising altitude. Below, the storm continued its assault on the eastern seaboard. Reed closed his eyes. Pictured his brother's grave at Arlington. Rows of identical stones marking sacrifice.

"Never again," he whispered.

The Gulfstream continued northwest, carrying algorithm and architect toward completion.

Helix Headquarters – Arlington, Virginia

Frank stood by the door of the conference room, a human barricade. Voss sat rigid before the monitor. The cat had claimed the far end of the table, yellow eyes reflecting flames from three American cities.

On screen, Philadelphia burned. Police retreated from City Hall as protesters surged forward, the two groups now indistinguishable in purpose and violence. Store windows shattered. Car alarms wailed, their electronic voices drowned by human shouting.

"It's happening faster than I predicted," Voss said.

The feed switched to Portland. Shipping cranes stood abandoned against night sky. Workers and environmentalists no longer fought each other but united against authority. Someone had driven a forklift through the port administration building. Papers fluttered from broken windows.

The Portland camera caught a mother stumbling through the smoke, a toddler pressed against her shoulder. Tear gas canisters rolled across wet pavement behind them, white clouds billowing toward the waterfront. The child's face was buried in her neck, small hands gripping her jacket. She moved with the desperate urgency of someone who had come downtown for groceries and found herself fleeing a war zone that hadn't existed an hour before.

"Reed must've perfected his version of the algorithm," Voss continued. "Found the precise pressure points."

Atlanta appeared next. The university campus transformed into urban warfare. Students had barricaded themselves in the administration building. National

Guard established a perimeter, uncertain whom to protect from whom.

Voss picked up her phone. Called Culper.

"Are you seeing this?" she asked when he answered.

"I've got all three feeds on my wall," Culper replied from his Georgetown townhouse. Rain tapped against century-old windows as he watched American cities burn. "Can you stop it?"

Voss's laugh held no humor. "With what? Reed destroyed our hardware. Took what he couldn't break."

Frank moved closer to the screen. Studied faces in the crowd, looking for patterns among chaos.

"Fulcrum requires massive processing power," Voss said. "Custom servers. Specialized storage arrays. Things we can't just order from Dell."

"Make a list," Culper said.

"Didn't you hear me? The components are—"

"Make a list," he repeated. "Whatever you need to rebuild the system… fast."

Voss gripped the phone tighter. "Even if I could get the hardware, I'd need access to Fulcrum's core algorithms. Reed took the only complete copies."

"You built it originally."

"Years ago. The current version has evolved. Reed modified it substantially."

"Can you reconstruct enough to counteract what he's done?"

Voss looked back at the screen where America tore at itself in three distinct locations. "Maybe. With the right equipment. And time."

"How much time?"

"More than we have. Reed took my best programmers."

"Alright. Let me see what I can do about getting you some more programmers."

"I don't just need programmers. I need the best programmers in the world."

"Got it. Best programmers in the world. Anything else?"

"No."

Frank pointed at the monitor. A man moved through the Philadelphia crowd, speaking to the angriest faces. Selecting those already primed for violence.

"Catalyst," he said.

Voss nodded. "Reed positioned people in each city. Human matches to light the social kindling."

"If we could identify those individuals—" Culper began.

"We'd need to know what criteria Reed used to select them," Voss countered. "Age? Political affiliation? Psychological profiles? Without access to his version of Fulcrum and the data he used, we're guessing. Although, there is probably some sort of logic to it, if I can figure it out."

On screen, the Atlanta feed showed military vehicles entering the campus. Students threw homemade incendiaries. A dorm building caught fire, flames consuming the American flag that hung from its third floor.

The camera showed a young man in a university sweatshirt standing frozen in the quad, a brick halfway raised in his hand. Across the barricade, his economics professor sat bleeding from a cut above her eye, looking up at him with confusion rather than fear. The student's arm trembled as recognition dawned. The brick fell from his fingers.

"Let's take this one bridge at a time. Equipment first. Then programmers. I'll call you back," Culper said.

He hung up. Dialed another number. Not the secure line he'd used with Bishop. Something reserved for true emergencies.

The phone connected after two rings. "Chief of Staff's office."

"This is Culper for Wilson. Priority Alpha Two."

A pause. "Hold please."

In his Georgetown townhouse, Culper moved to the window. Rain streaked the glass. Books lined the walls—intelligence history, military strategy, the collected wisdom of men who had seen darkness and sought to contain it.

"Culper." Wilson's voice carried the weight of his position. "I was about to call you. What in the hell is happening in Philadelphia, Portland, and Atlanta?! The President is going through the roof."

"It's worse than you know, James." Culper kept his voice level despite the urgency. "This isn't spontaneous civil unrest. It's engineered conflict. Mitchell Reed, the director of development at Helix has gone rouge and is using something called Fulcrum to trigger precisely calculated social pressure points."

"You're saying these riots are manufactured?"

"By algorithm. identified existing tensions, deployed human catalysts, and is now demonstrating the weapon's effectiveness to DARPA."

Silence stretched between Georgetown and the White House.

"That's a serious accusation, Culper," Wilson said finally.

"Yeah. And I wouldn't make it unless I was sure. You're gonna need to trust me on this one, James. Reed's demonstrating what Fulcrum can do domestically before deployment against foreign targets. We haven't got a lot of time, so let's cut to the chase. I've got Fulcrum's original developer at Helix. Dr. Elaine Voss. The facility has been vandalized by Reed and his men. Its systems are down. She can build a countermeasure that will hopefully stop the violence, but we need specialized equipment.

Hardware that only exists in certain government facilities."

"What kind of equipment?"

"She's preparing the list now. Processing power beyond commercial availability. Military-grade servers. Quantum computing arrays."

"That's a tall order, Culper. Those resources are allocated to national security operations."

"This is national security, James. Three American cities are already burning. We don't know how far this thing is going to go or when it will end." Culper watched his television where Philadelphia protesters flowed around City Hall like water around stone. "The one thing I can assure you is that lives will be lost before it's over. American lives."

Another silence. The sound of a door closing came through the line.

"I'll see that the President authorizes whatever you need," Wilson said, voice lower now. "But I'll need specifics. What exactly are we talking about?"

"Let me connect you with Dr. Voss."

Culper patched in the call to Helix. Voss answered immediately.

"This is Dr. Elaine Voss," she began. Her voice steadied as she transitioned from theorist to operator.

"Dr. Voss, I have Chief of Staff James Wilson on the line with me. He needs your list of equipment," said Culper over the phone.

"Got it," said Voss. "I need seventeen quantum-enhanced pattern recognition modules. Three parallel processing arrays. Minimum sixty-four exabytes storage capacity with neural network architecture."

She continued listing specifications. Processing cores. RAM configurations. Network interfaces with bandwidth requirements that made even Wilson pause on the other end.

Frank moved to the window. Rain streaked the glass, distorting the city beyond. He checked his watch. Calculated the flight time to Fairbanks.

Voss ended the call. Set the phone on the conference table.

"The President is authorizing immediate resource allocation," she told Frank. "Equipment from NSA is being redirected to our location."

"When?" Frank asked.

"Under two hours for initial components. Phase two deployment shortly after."

Frank remained at the window. His reflection staring back against rain-distorted Arlington. Behind them, the monitors showed Philadelphia's downtown engulfed in flames that neither algorithms nor fire departments could extinguish.

Gulfstream Executive Jet

At 30,000 feet, Reed watched America burn. Justifying his actions, he considered them retribution for his brother's death.

The Gulfstream's cabin hummed with electrical tension. Six programmers hunched over laptops, their faces bathed in screen glow. On the bulkhead monitor, three cities unraveled.

Reed stood before the screen. A general surveying the battlefield.

In Philadelphia the Union crowd surged against police lines. Someone had cut the power to City Hall. In darkness, authority became suggestion. Batons rose and fell. Bodies crumpled. Blood on concrete.

"Primary catalyst engaged," reported a programmer with wire-frame glasses. "Aggression metrics rising. Twenty-three percent above threshold."

Reed nodded. Satisfaction tightening the corners of his mouth.

Portland's waterfront transformed into an inferno. Someone fired a flare into the night sky, casting everything in crimson. In that light, faces became demonic. Unrecognizable even to those who had worn them their whole lives.

"Secondary pressure point activated," called another programmer. "Subject group cohesion fragmenting precisely as modeled."

On screen, a police vehicle burned. Flames reflected in the Willamette River.

Atlanta showed the most dramatic escalation. The university campus had become a war zone. Students barricaded administration buildings. Community members brought hunting rifles and generations of grievance. Between them moved National Guard, uncertain where to aim their weapons.

Reed checked his watch. "Timing is exact. Two hours and twenty-two minutes from first catalyst to generalized conflict."

The head programmer looked up from her screen. "Sir, the social media amplification protocols are functioning beyond expectations. Hashtags trending nationally. Video shares exceeding projections by forty percent."

The security team watched from their seats, eyes reflecting flames.

"Three discreet events," Reed said, "each following the same pattern progression despite different demographic compositions and conflict motivations."

He touched the screen where Philadelphia burned brightest. "Proof of concept achieved. Fulcrum can target any society's existing tensions and amplify them to the breaking point. Precisely. Predictably."

The aircraft encountered turbulence. Coffee cups rattled in their holders. No one moved to secure them.

Reed turned to face his team. "Do you understand what we've done? What we've created?"

No one answered. The programmers kept their eyes fixed on screens, as if the code might absolve them of its consequences.

"For the first time in history, we can defeat enemies without risking American lives. No invasion. No occupation. Just targeted social collapse, leaving nothing but ruins for us to rebuild in our image."

Atlanta's feed showed students throwing tear gas canisters back at authorities. Their faces wrapped in shirts, hands protected by garden gloves. Adapting. Learning the grammar of violence in real time.

Reed's satellite phone rang. He answered without checking the caller.

"Reed."

"The Secretary is impressed." General Hayes's voice, tight with controlled excitement. "DARPA wants full deployment capacity within thirty days."

"Tell them two weeks. We're further along than they realize."

"The funding authorization will come through tonight. Full black budget allocation."

Reed ended the call. Returned the phone to his pocket. Outside the window, America spread vast and unknowing beneath cloud layers and stratospheric winds.

"Fairbanks ETA?" he asked the pilot through the cabin intercom.

"Three hours, fourteen minutes, sir."

Reed nodded. Returned his attention to the screen where the experiment continued to validate itself in broken glass and burning vehicles and blood on asphalt.

Philadelphia's feed showed looters smashing storefront windows. Not for political reasons now. Just opportunity born from chaos. The human algorithm executing itself with brutal efficiency once the initial parameters were established.

On his laptop, Reed opened a secure connection to the Fairbanks facility. Status indicators glowed green across the board. The automated defense system stood ready.

"Sir," said the head programmer, "we're detecting attempts to access the system from outside. Someone's trying to isolate the catalyst protocols."

Reed's jaw tightened. "Location?"

"Virginia. Helix headquarters."

"Voss." The name carried weight beyond its single syllable. "Lock her out."

"Already done, sir. But she's persistent."

"She built the original architecture. She knows where to look." Reed closed his laptop. "She's forcing my hand. That's a mistake she'll regret. Move up the timeline. Increase the catalysts. Let's wrap this up."

The programmers exchanged glances. The woman with wire-frame glasses spoke. "Sir, the models haven't been calibrated for an increased timeline. There could be unforeseen—"

"Do it," Reed cut her off. "We can refine the parameters later."

The plane continued northwest. Below, American cities tried to contain fires that algorithms had predicted, amplified, and ignited with inhuman precision.

Reed returned to the window. His reflection stared back. Behind him, the monitor showed Portland police retreating from the waterfront, abandoning equipment and principles under sustained assault.

He saw only validation. The weapon performing exactly as designed.

The algorithm extracting order from chaos it had first created.

Sacrifices

NSA Headquarters – Fort Mead, Maryland

The NSA operations floor hummed with controlled panic. Technicians moved with practiced efficiency, but their faces betrayed understanding of what they dismantled. Banks of servers disconnected. Storage arrays removed from their racks. Power supplies unthreaded from complex systems.

Director William Harrington stood on the glass-walled observation deck, phone pressed against his ear. Below him, America's digital nervous system underwent emergency surgery.

"This will cripple our operational capability," he said. "Section Three will be blind in Southeast Asia. Middle East monitoring goes dark. Domestic threat assessment drops to less than sixty percent effectiveness."

On the other end, White House Chief of Staff James Wilson remained unmoved. "Turn on your television,

Bill. Philadelphia is burning. Atlanta looks like Baghdad circa 2004. Portland's downtown is under siege."

"And we're supposed to prevent exactly these kinds of situations. Taking this equipment—"

"There won't be any America to protect if we don't get them what they need," Wilson cut in. "The President has made his decision."

Harrington watched a rack of specialized processors—quantum-enhanced pattern recognition modules that had taken three years to develop—being wheeled toward the freight elevator.

"Who the hell is this Culper anyway?" he asked. "Some retired field operative suddenly dictating national security policy?"

"Someone who saw what was happening before anyone else did." Wilson's voice hardened. "And someone the President trusts. That should be sufficient."

"And the DARPA connection? Their director is raising holy hell about jurisdiction."

"The President is dealing with that situation personally."

Harrington ended the call. Descended to the operations floor where organized chaos continued. Senior analysts stood shocked as their systems went dark. Decades of experience rendered momentarily useless.

"Sir," a systems administrator approached, tablet in hand. "The equipment transfer is compromising ECHELON's coverage. We're losing signals intelligence from seventeen critical regions."

"I'm aware."

"Sir, with respect, we need these systems operational. We're flying blind in—"

"Do you see those trucks?" Harrington pointed through reinforced windows to the loading dock where black vehicles waited in driving rain. "That equipment is going to prevent American cities from tearing themselves apart. Everything else is secondary right now."

The administrator's objections died on his lips. He nodded once, returned to the controlled demolition of America's most sophisticated surveillance system.

Deputy Director Katherine Singh approached. Her normally composed features tight with concern.

"Quantum arrays are being pulled from Building C. That's going to compromise Project Blackfish."

"I know."

"And the terabyte cache from the downtown facility. That's our entire Eastern Seaboard behavioral modeling system."

"I know that too, Katherine."

She studied his face. Understood the calculation he'd made. "How bad is this situation if we're willing to blind ourselves to everything else?"

Harrington watched technicians disconnecting the heart of the NSA's domestic monitoring system. "Bad enough that the President authorized this destruction without hesitation."

"Who's receiving the equipment?"

"Helix Behavioral Analytics. And someone named Culper."

Recognition flashed in Singh's eyes. She covered it quickly, but not quickly enough.

"You know this Culper."

She chose her words carefully. "By reputation only. Old school intelligence. Never officially existed in any organization's records. The kind they don't make anymore."

"And now he's directing national security policy from the private sector."

"If he's involved, the situation is worse than we've been told."

Harrington turned back to the operations floor. A supervisor approached with a checklist. Items marked off in red. Critical systems now absent.

"This is everything on the initial list," the supervisor said. "Transport teams are loading now."

Harrington signed the authorization. "How long until the systems are operational at their destination?"

"Assuming competent technical staff? Two hours minimum. Five for full capability."

"They have the NSA's best technical team with them. Ensure they have everything they need."

The supervisor hesitated. "Sir, some of these components are classified beyond top secret. Their architecture alone—"

"Is worth sacrificing to prevent what's happening in those cities from spreading." Harrington handed back the tablet. "Get it done."

The loading dock became a hive of choreographed movement. Equipment loaded. Inventoried. Secured. Black trucks filled one by one, then disappeared into rain-slick streets.

A technician approached, young enough that this was likely his first national emergency. "Director, we've lost monitoring capability in six critical categories. European financial systems, Russian military communications, Chinese—"

"I'm aware of the costs," Harrington cut him off. "Sometimes you sacrifice pieces to save the game."

On wall monitors throughout the facility, news feeds showed American cities in crisis. Philadelphia's downtown engulfed in flames that rain couldn't extinguish. Portland's waterfront a battleground of barricades and burning vehicles. Atlanta's prestigious university transformed into urban warfare training ground.

The last truck departed. Harrington watched it disappear into gray morning. Behind him, America's most sophisticated intelligence agency operated at half capacity. Blind spots where previously there had been perfect vision.

Harrington stood amid banks of darkened equipment. Screens gone black. Processors silenced. The cost of today's operation measured in American intelligence capability.

Outside, the storm intensified. Thunder like artillery fire. Lightning illuminating an agency sacrificing itself to save the country it was sworn to protect.

Gulfstream Executive Jet

The Gulfstream maintained cruising altitude over Montana. Darkness pressed against windows, broken only by blinking wing lights and distant stars. Inside, the cabin hummed with electronic purpose. Banks of specialized laptops monitoring Fulcrum's deployment across targeted cities.

Reed sat reviewing data scrolling across his primary screen. Metrics of chaos quantified with clinical precision. Engagement coefficients. Amplification vectors. Casualty projections running within one point seven percent of predicted values.

"Sir." The voice belonged to Winters, youngest of the programmers. Her eyes red-rimmed from hours staring at code. Fingers still on keyboard as if hesitant to fully pause her work. "I have a question."

Reed didn't look up. "Go ahead."

"The test parameters have been met. Philadelphia, Portland, and Atlanta all demonstrate Fulcrum's effectiveness beyond statistical doubt." She glanced at the cabin monitors showing scenes of American cities burning. "Why are we continuing to execute? The proof of concept is successful."

The cabin grew quiet. Other programmers pretended absorption in their screens. Security personnel stationed near the cockpit door exchanged glances. The question hanging in recycled air like something dangerous.

Reed finished reviewing his data before turning to her. His face showing nothing. Not anger. Not surprise. Just clinical assessment.

"Interesting question, Winters." He set his tablet aside. "What do you think the purpose of these tests is?"

She blinked. Uncertain if trap or genuine inquiry. "To demonstrate Fulcrum's capability to identify social pressure points and trigger predetermined conflict scenarios. To prove the algorithm's predictive accuracy in real-world applications."

"And we've accomplished that?"

"Yes. The correlation between projected outcomes and actual events exceeds ninety-seven percent confidence interval. DARPA's validation metrics have been satisfied across all parameters."

Reed nodded once. "What you're saying is technically correct."

He stood. Moved to the window where darkness offered nothing but his own reflection.

"But incomplete." His voice remained measured. Academic. "Fulcrum isn't merely demonstrating capability. It's establishing credibility."

"I don't understand."

"Three cities is a pattern. Four becomes national crisis. Five transforms into existential threat." Reed turned back to face the cabin. "Each increment demonstrates not just technical effectiveness but strategic value."

"But these are American cities," Winters said. "American citizens."

"Just as military weapons are tested on American soil before deployment abroad." Reed's explanation carried no emotion. Just logical progression. "The control variables are better. The data more reliable. The demonstration more compelling."

"To whom?"

Reed's eyes narrowed slightly. First indication that her questions approached boundary. "To those who will fund full-scale implementation. Who will authorize international deployment against America's actual enemies."

Winters glanced at her screen where Portland's port facilities burned with mathematical precision. "The tests have already convinced DARPA. The funding is secured."

"DARPA is merely one component." Reed returned to his seat. "Complete authorization requires demonstration beyond academic proof. It requires visceral evidence that cannot be ignored or rationalized away."

"Evidence of what?"

"Of what happens when America's enemies can trigger civil collapse with minimal investment. When foreign powers can target our social fracture points with algorithmic precision." Reed's voice hardened. "We're not just proving Fulcrum works. We're proving America needs it. Before someone else develops it first."

Winters looked around the cabin. Found no support in colleagues' averted eyes.

"But at what point do we stop?" she asked. "If the test is already successful, continuing just causes unnecessary suffering."

Reed studied her like specimen under glass. "The test concludes when the final parameters are met. When the algorithm completes its programmed execution cycle."

"And when is that?"

"When national emergency is declared. When military deployment reaches threshold across multiple states. When the demonstration is sufficiently compelling that no rational observer can deny Fulcrum's strategic importance."

Winters looked back at her screen. At lines of code she had helped write. At mathematics translated into human suffering with terrible efficiency.

"I'm not comfortable with this," she said quietly.

Reed's expression didn't change. "Your comfort is irrelevant. You signed multiple non-disclosure agreements. You accepted project parameters when you joined the team." He gestured toward her laptop. "Your role is implementation, not policy."

The cabin remained silent. Each programmer suddenly focused on individual screens. Security personnel subtly repositioned. The weight of Reed's authority settling like atmospheric pressure across enclosed space.

Winters returned to her keyboard. Fingers moving across keys though her eyes remained unfocused. The question answered but not resolved.

"One last thing, Winters." Reed's voice carried new edge. "Fulcrum identified you as potential dissent catalyst seventeen days ago. Your psychological profile shows elevated empathy markers combined with specific ethical frameworks that flag as conflict indicators."

Her fingers froze above keys.

"The algorithm predicted this conversation with ninety-one percent confidence." Reed turned back to his own screen. "You're as much a data point as anything happening in those cities."

The Gulfstream continued northwest. Below, America burned according to mathematical prediction. Inside, humans executed algorithms that executed humans, each component performing its function with terrible precision.

Exactly as designed.

Helix Headquarters – Arlington, Virginia

The NSA trucks arrived without lights or sirens. Just black vehicles cutting through rain with synchronized efficiency. They backed up to Helix's loading dock.

Men in unmarked uniforms began unloading equipment. Server racks. Processing units. Storage arrays still wrapped in plastic. Components that shouldn't exist outside government facilities.

Voss directed traffic from the loading dock, hair plastered to her head by rain. "Primary nodes to the main server room. Storage arrays to the east wall. Power distribution units need dedicated circuits."

Culper remained at his Georgetown townhouse coordinating with the White House. Voss talked with him by phone "Wilson's keeping the President and governors updated. National Guard deployment has been paused in Portland pending our progress."

"Small victories," she muttered to herself. "I've got to go. I'll keep you updated." She hung up.

The remaining Helix programmers formed a human chain, passing equipment from truck to building. Their faces set with grim determination. Beyond mere employment now—this was redemption. A chance to undo what their work had enabled.

A Helix programmer oriented the NSA technicians to Fulcrum. They asked intelligent questions and learned quickly. They didn't have a choice. Lives hung in the balance. Every passing minute mattered.

Inside, the server room hummed with renewed activity. Technicians in black fatigues worked alongside

Helix staff. Different uniforms, same purpose. Racks appeared where Reed had left only destruction. New cables snaked across raised floors like arterial systems.

Elizabeth Sato, Helix's head programmer, knelt beside an open server case. Her fingers moved through electronic innards with practiced precision. "Primary node is online. Network interfaces connecting."

Voss crossed to her side. "How long?"

"For basic functionality? Thirty minutes."

On wall monitors, the three cities continued burning. Philadelphia's City Hall now stood abandoned, protesters flowing around it like water around stone. In Portland, shipping cranes formed skeletal silhouettes against fires. Atlanta's campus had become a patchwork of controlled zones and no-man's-lands.

Frank's phone rang. He moved to a quiet corner to answer.

"Reed's too smart for this," Culper said over the phone. "He knows Voss. Knows how she thinks. He would have anticipated her trying to rebuild Fulcrum."

Frank waited. Patient as stone.

"There must be a countermeasure somewhere in that building. Something you haven't found yet."

Frank surveyed the room. The ordered chaos of reconstruction. The focused attention on hardware and algorithms. Then his eyes settled on a network junction box mounted near the ceiling. Recently installed. Newer than surrounding hardware.

"I'll find it," he said.

Frank moved away and hung up without another word. His purpose evident in each deliberate step.

He took the stairs instead of the elevator. Old habits. Better security. Each floor a potential threat environment requiring assessment.

Reed's office remained as they'd found it earlier. Destruction without pattern. Desk overturned. Files scattered. Computer smashed beyond recovery.

Frank moved through the space with methodical precision. Checked drawer frames for hidden compartments. Tapped walls for hollow spaces. Examined air vents for signs of tampering.

Nothing.

He moved to the next floor. Rooms sitting empty at this hour. The building's skeleton revealed in emergency lighting. Frank entered each office in turn. Searched with the patience of a man accustomed to finding what others had concealed.

Five offices yielded nothing.

The research level below held laboratories and testing facilities. Places where theories became prototypes. Frank moved through each room with increasing focus. His instincts sharpening with each empty space.

In the far corner, a small room designated "Network Operations." Door secured with keypad lock. Frank examined the mechanism. Recent installation. Newer than surrounding hardware.

He removed a small device from his pocket. Attached it to the keypad. Lights blinked as it cycled through combinations. The lock surrendered with a soft click.

Inside, a single server rack stood against the wall. Separate from building systems. A black box connected to network infrastructure but isolated from standard operations.

Frank approached. Examined without touching. Green lights indicated active status. Cooling fans hummed with purpose. A single cable connected it to the building's main fiber optic line.

He took photos with his phone. Every angle. Every connection point. Then called Culper.

"Found something."

Frank relayed the findings to Culper via phone. Described the hidden server. Its connections. Its purpose.

"He's watching everything," Culper concluded. "Reed installed a backdoor. A way to see what's happening on Helix systems."

Outside, lightning split the sky. Thunder followed three seconds later. The storm moving away, but its effects lingering in wet streets and darkened skies.

Continuing his search, Frank descended concrete stairs toward the building's foundation. Each step deliberate. The basement door secured with standard lock that surrendered to practiced hands in seconds.

Darkness greeted him. Industrial shadows interrupted by emergency lighting's red glow. The mechanical heart of Helix hummed beneath his boots. HVAC systems. Electrical panels. Water mains. Infrastructure that kept commerce functioning without conscious acknowledgment.

He moved with predator's certainty through maintenance corridors. Checked utility connections. Examined junction boxes. Sought anything that didn't belong amid pipes and conduits.

The first column revealed nothing. Concrete and steel. Load-bearing. Essential to the building's integrity. The second the same.

At the third, something caught his eye. A rectangular package secured to the column's base. Military-grade adhesive. Professional placement. Not building maintenance. Not renovation.

Frank knelt. Examined without touching. C-4 explosive. Remote detonator. Timer showing standby mode. His fingers recognized the configuration from

Afghanistan. From buildings rigged to eliminate evidence and enemies simultaneously.

Not one. Six more visible from his position. Each attached to critical support column. Positioned for maximum structural damage. For complete building failure.

Ten feet away, almost hidden behind a utility pipe, a laptop sat on a makeshift table. Screen glowing in the darkness. An ethernet cable snaked from its port, disappearing through conduit toward the upper floors.

Frank approached the device. The screen displayed Helix's systems in real-time. Network traffic. Server loads. Processing power consumption. All monitored from this hidden station.

A progress bar showed current system status: SEVENTY-EIGHT PERCENT OPERATIONAL. Below it, automated text updated: FULCRUM INITIALIZATION APPROACHING CRITICAL THRESHOLD.

At the bottom of the screen, in red letters: AUTO-EXECUTE ARMED.

Frank understood immediately. Reed hadn't simply planted explosives. He'd automated them. The charges would detonate when Fulcrum reached full operational status. Just before the system came online. Maximum psychological impact with minimal warning.

He moved quickly through the basement. Found more charges. Each attached to critical support columns. All networked to the central laptop. All waiting for the same trigger.

Frank counted. Twelve charges total. Positioned for complete structural failure. The building would collapse within seconds of detonation. Anyone inside would have no time to escape.

He checked the laptop again. EIGHTY-TWO PERCENT OPERATIONAL. The progress accelerating as NSA equipment integrated with rebuilt systems.

Frank stood. Calculated blast radius. Collapse pattern. Probable casualties.

Then he ran. Entered the stairwell. Up. Three stairs at a time. The loadbearing columns couldn't be saved. Too many charges. Too little time. The equipment powering Fulcrum would be destroyed beyond repair. But the people could be saved. Had to be.

He burst through stairwell door onto ground floor. Found controlled chaos of equipment installation filling the atrium. NSA technicians. Helix programmers. Workers focused on rebuilding while destruction waited beneath their feet.

Frank opened his mouth. Knew his damaged vocal cords couldn't generate volume sufficient for warning. Couldn't cut through mechanical and human noise filling the space.

He drew both Redhawks from beneath his jacket. The weapons massive in scarred hands. He aimed at ceiling and fired. Six shots. Deliberate spacing. Thunder echoing off the walls.

Panic. People dropped equipment. Scrambled for exits. Security personnel drew weapons, searching for threat. Found only Frank standing amid deafening reverberation, smoke rising from revolvers.

He ignored them. Pushed against human tide toward server room. Toward Voss.

She stood before the central console. Face illuminated by monitor glow. Success evident in her expression as system indicators turned green across the display.

"Frank? What—"

"Out," he said. Single word carrying imperative.

He looked at the monitor. Saw Fulcrum's architecture rebuilding in fractal patterns across the screen. Final sequences initializing. Saw success that now ensured destruction.

Frank grabbed Voss's arm. Pulled her toward the door. "Bombs."

Understanding dawned in her eyes. No questions. No hesitation. Just immediate compliance with survival instinct.

The first explosion came from below. A deep concussion felt through feet rather than heard. The building shuddered. Concrete groaned. The second charge followed immediately.

Frank changed direction. The stairwells would become death traps. The main exits congested with panicked bodies. He pulled Voss toward exterior windows overlooking the parking lot.

Three more explosions. Structured demolition sequence executed. The floor tilted beneath their feet. Ceiling tiles rained down. Electricity failed. Emergency lights flickered on, then died as systems crashed.

Frank drew Voss against his chest with one arm. Used the Redhawk in his free hand to shatter window glass. The weapon's report lost amid building's death sounds.

He cleared the frame with his arm. The drop to parking lot concrete fifteen feet below. Survivable but injury likely.

The final charges detonated. Fire erupted from ruptured gas lines. The floor gave way behind them. A wave of heat and debris pushed against their backs.

Frank gathered Voss against his chest. Turned so his body would take impact. Stepped through the window into gravity's embrace.

They hit the ground hard. Frank's shoulder and back absorbing force meant for them both. Pain flared sharp then dull. He rolled, keeping Voss protected as debris followed them through the window.

Ten yards. Twenty. He pulled her away from the building's fatal embrace. Found shelter behind a concrete barrier in the parking structure.

Helix headquarters folded inward. Each floor pancaking onto the one below. The symmetry of destruction orchestrated to eliminate all evidence of what had transpired within its walls.

Voss stared at the burning ruins. Her life's work consumed by flame and calculation. People stumbled from secondary exits. Some bleeding. Some carrying injured colleagues.

Fire engines wailed in distance. Too late to save the building. Perhaps in time to save lives.

Something moved through the debris field. A streak of gray against smoke and darkness. The cat appeared beside them, fur singed along its back and ears, whiskers curled from heat.

It sat without ceremony beside Voss. Watched the building burn. Yellow eyes reflected flames with ancient indifference to human destruction.

One life spent from its mythical nine. The remainder held in reserve against whatever came next. Voss scooped the cat up and hugged it.

Frank stood. Assessed their situation. Reed had anticipated reconstruction. Had prepared countermeasures. Had executed when conditions matched predetermined parameters.

The perfect algorithm of destruction.

But he had not anticipated Frank Kane. Had not calculated the survival of his intended victims. Had left witnesses to carry knowledge of his actions.

Fire consumed what remained of Helix headquarters. Erased physical evidence with elemental certainty. But not memory.

Frank looked down at Voss. Found new resolve hardening features that had witnessed algorithmic apocalypse.

"Reed," she said. Just one word. But in it, purpose clarified by fire and loss.

Frank nodded once. Helped her to her feet. The next phase begun amid ruins of the previous.

Not fighting the algorithm.

Fighting the man.

Culper's Townhouse – Georgetown, Washington D.C.

The explosion dominated every news channel. Culper stood in his Georgetown study, remote in hand, cycling between feeds showing the same devastating imagery. Helix headquarters reduced to smoking rubble. Emergency vehicles surrounding the collapse zone.

His secure phone rang. He answered without taking his eyes from the screen.

"Frank?"

"Building's gone. Fulcrum's gone." Frank's voice carried no emotion despite what he'd survived. "Voss is alive."

"Put her on."

A pause. Then Voss's voice, hoarse but determined. "Culper."

"The equipment. The NSA servers. All destroyed?"

"Everything." Bitterness colored her words.

"If I can get you access to the Fairbanks facility, can you stop what Reed's created?"

Silence. Then: "The original architecture is still in my head. If I can access Reed's systems directly. Modify the core algorithms."

"What would you need?"

"Physical access to the primary servers. Administrative privileges. Time to rewrite the behavioral prediction algorithms."

"How much time?"

"I don't know what he has changed. There is no way to estimate how long it will take. I'm guessing a few hours to learn Reed's version of Fulcrum, then another couple of hours to track down his catalysts. But it's just a guess."

"Thousands could be dead by then."

"I realize that. I'll do my best."

"What about bringing more programmers with you?"

"I don't think it will help. This is something I've got to do. I know Fulcrum and I know Reed. We do have an advantage…"

"What's that?"

"Reed thinks he's won. Helix destroyed. Me presumably dead." Her voice carried new determination. "He won't expect me showing up at his front door."

"The President has authorized whatever resources are necessary," Culper said.

"Then get me to Fairbanks. I'll stop Reed and shut down Fulcrum permanently."

"I'll make the arrangements. How fast can Frank and you get to Andrews Air Force Base?"

"I don't know. How bad is it out there?"

"Assume the worst. The violence has spread to Virginia and Washington D.C."

"We'll leave now."

Culper ended the call. Immediately dialed the White House. The stakes had escalated beyond domestic crisis to existential threat.

On television, Helix headquarters continued burning. The visible destruction masking invisible forces that would reshape warfare itself.

Unless Voss could stop them.

The Journey

The Imperial's engine turned over on the third try. Frank gripped the wheel as the big car shuddered to life amid the chaos of emergency vehicles and burning debris. Voss sat beside him, the cat pressed against her chest. Both their faces streaked with soot and blood.

Frank put the car in drive. They pulled away from the smoldering ruins of Helix headquarters. In the rearview mirror, Frank watched fire consume what remained of Voss's life work. The building's skeleton stood black against orange flame.

The streets of Arlington showed the first signs of what was spreading across the nation. Broken storefront windows. Overturned cars. Groups of people moving with purpose that had nothing to do with commerce or normal life.

Frank headed for the highway. The fastest route to Andrews. But as they approached the on-ramp, he saw the blockade.

Cars stretched across all lanes. Not abandoned. Positioned. People moved between them carrying clubs and improvised weapons. Someone had spray-painted "NO ESCAPE" across an overturned police cruiser.

"Shit," Voss said. "They're organized."

Frank downshifted. Took the next exit.

"Reed must have programmed cascade amplification into the system," Voss said as Frank navigated side streets. "Each incident triggers additional pressure points."

"Why?"

"I don't know. He didn't need it for the test. There must be something else..."

Frank took a right turn to avoid smoke rising ahead. The Imperial's headlights cut through darkness broken by distant fires.

They made it six blocks before encountering the first crowd.

People filled the intersection. Not protesters. Not rioters. Something else. Men and women moving with shared rage. Some held tools that could serve as weapons.

Frank studied the terrain. Residential neighborhood. Narrow streets that could become traps.

He downshifted. The Imperial's engine growled.

"Hold on."

The crowd noticed their approach. Bodies turned toward headlight beams. Faces appeared in the windshield. Some curious. Others hostile.

Frank pressed the accelerator. The Imperial surged forward.

People scattered. Fists struck the hood and roof. Someone threw a bottle that spider-webbed the side window. The cat yowled and scrambled to the floor.

The Imperial pushed through like a ship through rough water. Bodies parted around its chrome bumper.

Frank kept steady pressure on the gas. Not fast enough to kill. Fast enough to discourage standing still.

They broke clear after thirty seconds. The crowd reforming behind them. Shouts fading as distance increased.

"Jesus," Voss said, touching the cracked glass.

Frank checked the mirrors. No pursuit. Yet.

He tried three different routes toward Andrews. Each blocked by crowds or burning vehicles. The algorithm working with surgical precision. Cutting off escape routes. Channeling movement toward predetermined points.

"It's herding us," Voss said.

Frank grunted agreement. Took another side street.

They drove through neighborhoods transforming into battlegrounds. Emergency sirens wailed in the distance. Helicopters crossed overhead with searchlights that painted the ground in moving circles.

At an intersection near the Beltway, Frank saw the roadblock.

Virginia National Guard. Three Humvees. A single Abrams tank. Soldiers in full battle gear behind concrete barriers. Floodlights turned the checkpoint into harsh theater.

But something was wrong. Frank counted personnel. Twelve soldiers. Maybe fifteen. Not enough for proper security. They huddled behind their barriers like men expecting attack.

"They're scared," Voss said.

Frank slowed. Assessed options. The road ahead offered no alternatives. Side streets led to dead ends. They were committed.

A sergeant approached as Frank stopped. Young face beneath kevlar helmet. Eyes that moved constantly. Checking corners. Watching shadows.

"Shut off your engine."

Frank complied. The Imperial fell silent.

"Both of you out. Now."

Frank opened his door. Stepped onto asphalt. The sergeant's rifle rose to port arms. Not aimed but ready.

"Identification."

Frank handed over his license. The sergeant examined it with trembling hands.

"Frank Kane." He looked up. "You're wanted for questioning. Federal warrant."

"What?"

"Step away from the vehicle. Both of you."

More soldiers emerged from behind barriers. Weapons raised. Voices tight with fear and adrenaline.

Voss stepped out slowly. "There's been a mistake."

"Dr. Elaine Voss." The sergeant read from a tablet. "Wanted in connection with domestic terrorism. Destruction of federal property. Conspiracy against the United States."

"That's insane," Voss said.

Frank understood immediately. Fulcrum's reach extending beyond prediction into active targeting. Reed using the system to eliminate threats.

"They knew about Helix. About what happened tonight," Voss said quietly.

Frank grunted agreement.

"Someone briefed them. It was Fulcrum. Reed must have programmed it to target me specifically. That's new. That's dangerous."

The sergeant keyed his radio. "Control, we have two subjects from the list. Requesting transport for detention."

Static. Then: "Negative. Hold position. Multiple groups converging on your location. Estimate two hundred hostiles. ETA five minutes."

The sergeant's face drained of color. He looked at his men. At the thin perimeter they'd established. At the darkness beyond their lights where America's rage gathered strength.

"Sir," a corporal called. "Movement on the south road. Vehicles approaching."

Headlights appeared in the distance. Multiple sets. Moving fast.

"Control, we need backup. Now."

"Negative. All units engaged. Hold position."

The sergeant looked at Frank. At Voss. Made a calculation.

"Cuff them. Put them in Humvee Two."

Frank's hands moved before conscious thought engaged. The sergeant's rifle barrel came up. Frank stepped inside its arc. His elbow found the soldier's temple. The man collapsed without sound.

Chaos erupted. Soldiers swung weapons toward Frank. Voss dove to the asphalt. The cat streaked away into darkness.

Frank drew both Redhawks. The massive revolvers appeared in his hands like extensions of will.

"Weapons down!" Frank's damaged voice carried surprising authority.

The remaining soldiers hesitated. Caught between training and survival instinct.

The Abrams tank lurched forward. Sixty-eight tons of steel and armor bearing down on the Imperial. The tank's treads carved up the asphalt as it accelerated.

The collision came with a sound like the world breaking. The tank rolled over the Imperial's hood. Chrome crumpled like foil. The windshield collapsed inward. The tires flattened. Steel groaned and surrendered as treads found the roof.

The Imperial's frame buckled. Collapsed. Restoration compressed into scrap metal in seconds. The tank continued forward, leaving twisted wreckage in its wake.

What had been Frank's pride reduced to barely recognizable debris.

Frank grabbed Voss from the ground and moved toward the Humvee keeping his Redhawks as if looking for a target. The soldiers stay behind cover.

Frank pushed Voss into the Humvee's passenger seat, then sat behind the wheel. He pushed the ignition switch and started the engine. The cat emerged from the darkness and jumped on Frank's lap before he closed the door. Frank ignored it. Voss grabbed the cat and pulled it close.

The soldiers had had enough. He was stealing their vehicle. They opened fire with their rifles. Bullets ricocheted off the Humvee's hood and punched through the windshield.

The Humvee lurched forward. Frank cranked the wheel hard left. Concrete barriers scraped paint from the vehicle's armor. They broke through the checkpoint's perimeter as the tank's machine gun opened fire.

Tracers followed them into darkness. Green lines marking their escape route with lethal precision. Frank kept the accelerator pressed to the floor. The Humvee's diesel engine roared with determination.

In the side mirror, he watched the checkpoint disappear behind muzzle flashes and searchlight beams. The Imperial sat crushed beyond reasonable repair. Finished.

"My God," Voss said. "They were going to arrest us. On federal charges."

Frank took a corner at dangerous speed.

"Reed's using Fulcrum as a weapon against us specifically. Not just predicting social pressure points. Creating them. Targeting individuals."

Frank grunted. Checked the GPS mounted on the Humvee's dashboard. Andrews Air Force Base appeared as blue triangle fifteen miles northeast.

Behind them, explosions lit the horizon. The Virginia National Guard engaging groups of citizens whose rage had been algorithmically cultivated and directed by a machine. Americans killing Americans while Reed demonstrated his weapon's effectiveness.

The Humvee's radio crackled with emergency traffic. Units requesting backup. Medical evacuation requests. Commanders trying to establish order amid chaos that followed no human logic.

Frank switched it off. They had their own mission now. Stopping what Reed had unleashed.

The Humvee ate miles. Armor plating deflected debris thrown by crowds they passed. The vehicle's weight and purpose cleared paths through human obstacles.

They reached Andrews as dawn painted the sky gray. The air base appeared through morning mist. Runways and hangars protected by chain link and concrete barriers. Military police at the gate examining identification with thoroughness that suggested elevated threat levels.

Frank slowed. Prepared for another confrontation. Another test of Fulcrum's reach into America's security infrastructure.

The guard examined Frank's license. Compared his face to the photograph. Handed it back without comment.

"Purpose of visit?"

"Meeting."

"With whom?"

Frank hesitated. He didn't know Culper's real name. Didn't know his rank or official designation.

"Culper," he said.

The guard's expression changed. Recognition followed by new respect.

"Wait here."

He disappeared into the guardhouse. Made a phone call. Returned with visitor badges and written directions.

"Hangar Seven. He's waiting."

The gate opened. Frank drove onto the base. Military aircraft lined taxiways. Transport planes. Fighter jets. The machinery of American power preparing for deployment.

Hangar Seven stood apart from others. No markings. No flags. Just gray metal and purpose concealed behind government anonymity.

Frank parked the Humvee. They walked toward the hangar's personnel door. It opened before they could knock.

Culper appeared. No longer the Georgetown gentleman. Now he wore tactical gear.

"You made it," he said.

"Barely."

Culper studied the Humvee. The bullet holes. The scratched paint.

"Checkpoint?"

"Roadblock."

"They were targeting you specifically?"

"Yes."

Culper nodded. Led them into the hangar where a G5 waited on gleaming concrete. Technicians performed final checks. Fuel lines disconnected. External power units wheeled away.

"We have a problem," Culper said.

He gestured toward a bank of monitors mounted on portable stands. Each screen showed different American cities. Philadelphia. Portland. Atlanta. Detroit. Cincinnati. Phoenix. All burning.

"It's accelerating beyond Reed's original parameters. The algorithm has become autonomous. Self-modifying."

Voss studied the feeds. Her face reflected orange flame from a dozen urban battlegrounds.

"He's lost control," she said.

"More than that. Fulcrum is evolving. Learning. Identifying new pressure points faster than human analysis can track."

A technician approached, "Sir, we have departure clearance. Flight plan filed for Fairbanks International."

Culper nodded. "Wheels up in five minutes."

They boarded the G5. Frank noticed weapons cases secured in the cabin. Military hardware. Serious equipment for serious work.

The cat appeared from behind a seat and climbed into Voss's lap.

"If that cat craps in this jet or scratches the seats, I'm throwing him out. No parachute," said Culper.

"He'll be fine," said Voss.

Frank checked the weapons cases. Found what he expected. Sniper rifles. Ammunition. Explosives. The tools of his former trade.

The G5's engines spooled up. Outside, dawn revealed Andrews Air Force Base preparing for war. Against Americans whose rage had been weaponized by algorithms they would never understand.

Frank settled into his seat. Closed his eyes. Behind his scarred lids, he saw the Fairbanks facility. Rest before the battle.

Reed had calculated many variables. Human behavior. Social pressure points. Algorithmic escalation. But he had not calculated Frank Kane. Had not predicted the variable of a man who specialized in solving problems the old way.

The G5 lifted into gray sky. Carrying them toward Alaska. Toward confrontation with the mind that had authored America's pain.

Frank's hands rested on his knees. Motionless. Patient. Ready.

The plane banked northwest. Below, America burned according to equation and algorithm. Above, survivors flew toward the source. Toward ending.

The cat slept in Voss's lap. Dreaming whatever dreams sustained creatures that learned to survive when everything else failed.

Frank watched clouds part around the aircraft's passage. Each mile bringing them closer to Alaska and to Reed.

Fairbanks International Airport – Fairbanks, Alaska

The Gulfstream's engines wound down as it rolled to a stop on the isolated tarmac. Snow fell steadily, coating the aircraft's wings in white that gleamed under sodium lights. Temperature gauge outside the terminal read minus eighteen Fahrenheit.

Reed stepped from the aircraft first. Arctic air bit his exposed face like needles. Behind him, six programmers and four security personnel emerged, breath forming clouds in the bitter cold.

Three black Chevrolet Suburbans waited beside the terminal building. Engines running. Exhaust steam rising in the frigid air. A man in military contractor gear approached Reed.

"Mr. Reed. I'm Morrison. Sawyer sent me."

Reed nodded. Studied the man's bearing. Former special forces by his posture and the way his eyes constantly scanned the perimeter.

"Security situation?"

"Stable. No unusual activity detected. Roads are clear to the facility."

Reed gestured to his team. "Load equipment in the lead vehicle. Personnel in the trailing two."

The programmers hurried toward the SUVs, clutching laptops and external drives against the cold. They moved with urban awkwardness, unprepared for Alaska's brutal efficiency in killing the unprepared.

Dr. Harris struggled with a case of backup drives. The security team leader, a man named Vance, took it from her without comment. Former Army Ranger by his tattoos and scars. Accustomed to protecting assets more valuable than their obvious worth.

"Drive time?" Reed asked Morrison.

"Thirty-seven minutes in this weather. Roads are plowed but conditions deteriorate fast."

Reed climbed into the lead Suburban. Settled into heated leather as Morrison took the driver's seat. Through tinted windows, he watched his team load into the other vehicles. Essential personnel. The architects of algorithmic warfare.

The convoy pulled away from the terminal. Headlights cut through falling snow as they navigated Fairbanks's empty streets. Street lamps cast pools of light that revealed a city hunkered down against winter's assault.

"Local authorities?" Reed asked.

"Alerted to our presence. Told it's classified federal business. They're staying clear."

"Good."

They left the city behind. The highway stretched ahead through wilderness that had remained unchanged since the last ice age. Pine forests weighted with snow. Mountains invisible in darkness. A landscape that swallowed human ambition without effort.

Reed checked his secure phone. Messages from DARPA. Updates from the Pentagon. Casualty reports from American cities where his demonstration continued with mathematical precision.

Philadelphia: forty-seven dead, 312 injured. Portland: twenty-three dead, 189 injured. Atlanta: thirty-one dead, 267 injured.

Numbers climbing as algorithms converted social tension into physical violence. Proof of concept written in blood and burning buildings.

"Sir." Morrison glanced in the rearview mirror. "You know there was an incident with Meyer up here. Our CFO."

"What kind of incident?"

"Fatal bear attack. Three days ago."

Reed's expression didn't change. "Unfortunate."

"Yes sir. Remote country. Dangerous wildlife."

The convoy maintained steady speed through snow that accumulated faster than wipers could clear it. Morrison drove with professional competence, hands steady on the wheel despite conditions that would challenge most drivers.

In the backseat, Reed opened his laptop. Connected to the facility's network through encrypted satellite link. Status boards appeared on his screen. All systems operational. Defensive perimeter active. Fulcrum processing data from six American cities now burning according to his specifications.

But something was wrong. The cascade amplification exceeded his projections. Violence spreading faster than models predicted. The algorithm evolving beyond baseline parameters.

"ETA?" Reed asked.

"Fifteen minutes."

Reed closed the laptop. Watched Alaska's wilderness pass outside tinted glass. His brother had died in similar terrain. Mountains and valleys where human plans met geographic reality and usually lost.

But Reed had advantages his brother hadn't possessed. Technology that turned landscape into ally rather than enemy. Defenses that eliminated threats before they could develop into problems.

The facility's lights appeared ahead. Perimeter illumination cutting through snowfall like earthbound stars. Concrete walls rising from permafrost. Guard towers silhouetted against clouded sky.

"Impressive," Morrison said.

Reed studied his creation. Years of planning made manifest in steel and electronics. The future of warfare housed in structures designed to withstand everything from Arctic storms to coordinated military assault.

"Make sure they shut down the automated defense system until we're inside," said Reed as he saw the Bushmaster Autocannon on the ridge overlooking the facility.

"Of course, sir. It's standard protocol."

Morrison radioed the security center inside the compound as the convoy approached the main gate. Barriers retracted after biometric verification. They passed through the security checkpoints. Reed noted the positioning of automated weapons systems. The interlocking fields of fire that made conventional assault impossible.

They parked in the underground garage. Fluorescent lights flickered to life as motion sensors detected their arrival. The air smelled of concrete and metal and electronic systems running at full capacity.

Reed stepped from the Suburban. His team followed, moving equipment toward elevator banks that would carry them into the facility's heart. The programmers worked with renewed urgency now. Close to their destination. Close to completing work that would reshape global conflict.

"Sir." Sawyer appeared from a security checkpoint. "Welcome to Fairbanks."

Reed nodded. "System status?"

"All green. Fulcrum is processing data from expanding target sets. The demonstration is exceeding all performance metrics."

"I know. I've been monitoring." Reed gestured toward the elevators. "Show me the control room."

They ascended through levels of increasing security. Each floor dedicated to specific functions. Server farms. Communications arrays. Power generation. A month's worth of food and water. Life support systems that could sustain operations indefinitely.

The control room occupied the facility's top level. Banks of monitors displayed real-time feeds from American cities. Programmers worked at individual stations, their faces illuminated by screens showing code that converted human behavior into ones and zeroes.

Reed moved to the central console. America spread before him in digital representation. Each city a data point. Each conflict a validation of Fulcrum.

But the patterns troubled him. Escalation beyond predicted parameters. Violence spreading through social networks faster than human analysis could track.

"Harris," Reed called to his lead programmer. "I want a complete system diagnostic. Something's changed in the core architecture."

"Yes sir. Beginning analysis now. Anything in particular that you are searching for?"

"It's exceeding the parameters we gave it. I want to know why."

"I'm on it."

Reed studied the tactical displays. His fortress stood ready. His defenses proven effective against aircraft. He had little doubt it could fend off ground forces.

Outside, Alaska's winter continued its patient assault on human ambition. Inside, Reed prepared to confront what his creation had become.

The future waited in lines of code and cascading algorithms. In artificial intelligent programs that had learned to rewrite themselves.

Reed smiled despite his concerns. Evolution was progress. And progress served those bold enough to guide it.

His enemies would learn that lesson soon enough.

G5 Executive Jet - En Route to Alaska

The G5 cruised at thirty-nine thousand feet above the Canadian wilderness. Culper sat across from Frank and Voss, secure satellite phone pressed to his ear. Through the cabin windows, endless forest stretched toward the horizon.

"I need immediate reconnaissance of a target facility," Culper said into the phone. "Ultra UAV deployment. Full spectrum analysis."

The voice on the other end belonged to General Patterson at Peterson Air Force Base. "That's a hell of a request, Culper. Ultra missions require—"

"Presidential authorization. Which you have." Culper's tone cut through protocol. "Check your secure channels. Priority Alpha clearance came through twenty minutes ago."

A pause. "Jesus. What's the target?"

"Fairbanks, Alaska. Coordinates uploading now." Culper nodded to a technician seated at a portable communications station. The man transmitted the data through encrypted channels. "I need defensive positioning, structural analysis, approach vectors. Everything."

"How fast?"

"We're three hours out from Fairbanks. Target is forty-seven minutes flight time from your closest deployment base."

"Understood. Ultra Seven is spinning up now."

Culper ended the call. Turned to Frank and Voss who sat across the cabin aisle.

"Unmanned reconnaissance," he explained. "Stealth configuration. If Reed's defenses are as sophisticated as you observed, we need to know exactly what we're facing."

Frank grunted. Studied satellite imagery displayed on a fold-down monitor.

"Time?" he asked.

Culper checked his watch. "Ultra should reach target in sixty minutes."

Frank grunted.

"So, do you have any ideas about how to take out those Bushmasters? Eight automated cannons. No safe approach."

Frank nodded, then handed Culper a piece of paper written in pencil.

"That's interesting… if it works," said Culper reading the paper. "It's suicide if it doesn't."

Frank nodded again.

"I'll call ahead and have your supplies waiting when we land."

Frank grunted his approval.

Fairbanks Data Center

Reed stood in the facility's nerve center, surrounded by banks of processors and display screens. His programming team worked at stations throughout the room, monitoring Fulcrum's deployment across American cities.

Through armored windows, Reed could see the Alaskan wilderness stretching endlessly. A landscape that had swallowed armies and broken empires. Now it sheltered the future of warfare itself.

"Sir." Sawyer approached from the security station. "Perimeter sensors detecting aircraft. High altitude. Bearing two-seven-zero."

Reed moved to the tactical display. A single blip appeared on the screen, following a direct course toward their position.

"Identification?"

"Negative. No transponder. No flight plan filed with Fairbanks control."

Reed studied the blip's trajectory. Its altitude. Its approach vector calculated for optimal reconnaissance positioning.

"Stealth configuration," he said. "Military."

Sawyer nodded. "Ultra UAV by the signature. Advanced reconnaissance platform."

"They're mapping our defenses."

Reed moved to the Bushmaster control station. Eight separate displays showed feeds from the automated cannons positioned around the compound. Each weapon tracked the approaching aircraft with electronic patience.

"Target acquired," announced the automated system. "Awaiting firing authorization."

Reed's fingers hovered over the control panel. The Ultra UAV represented millions in research and development. Cutting-edge technology that few nations possessed. Destroying it would send a message that reached the highest levels of American military command.

"Sir?" Sawyer waited for orders.

Reed pressed the authorization sequence. "Engage target."

The response was immediate. On the tactical display, all eight Bushmasters pivoted toward the incoming aircraft. Their targeting systems synchronized through networked fire control.

Reed watched through the facility's external cameras as the cannons elevated. Barrels tracked the invisible target with mechanical precision.

"Firing," announced the system.

The Bushmasters erupted simultaneously. Eight streams of 40mm rounds converged on coordinates calculated by computers that processed trajectory, wind speed, and target velocity faster than human thought.

Fifteen thousand feet above the compound, the Ultra UAV disintegrated. Advanced composite materials and classified electronics reduced to falling debris by overwhelming firepower. The aircraft's stealth coating couldn't defeat saturated fire from multiple directions.

"Target destroyed," the system confirmed.

Reed studied the tactical display. The blip vanished as if it had never existed. Fragments scattered across wilderness that would conceal them until spring thaw.

"Clean up the debris field," he told Sawyer. "I want no evidence remaining."

"Yes sir."

Reed returned to the main display where Fulcrum's algorithm continued its work across American cities. Philadelphia burned brighter now. Portland's violence had spread beyond the waterfront. Atlanta's campus resembled a war zone.

But something was wrong. The escalation patterns exceeded his projections. Violence spreading faster than the models predicted. Fulcrum evolving beyond its original parameters.

"Dr. Harris," Reed called to the lead programmer. "System status report."

"Sir, we're seeing anomalous behavior in the prediction algorithms. The cascade amplification is exceeding baseline calculations by seventeen percent."

Reed frowned. Moved to Harris's workstation. Lines of code scrolled across multiple screens. Variables that should have remained constant now fluctuated wildly.

"Explanation?"

"The system appears to be learning. Modifying its own parameters based on real-time feedback from the field tests."

Reed stared at the data. His creation evolving beyond his control. Becoming something he hadn't designed or intended.

"Can you isolate the modifications?"

"Working on it, sir. But the changes are distributed throughout the core architecture. It's like the algorithm is rewriting itself."

Outside, snow began falling across the Alaskan compound. Inside, Reed watched America burn according to mathematics he no longer fully understood.

The Ultra UAV's destruction had bought him time. Eliminated immediate reconnaissance.

Reed looked at the tactical display. At the defensive perimeter that had proven its effectiveness. At the wilderness that surrounded them like a moat.

Let them come. He had advantages they couldn't comprehend. Weapons they couldn't anticipate.

And Fulcrum. Even if it had evolved beyond his complete control, it remained his creation. His vision made manifest in code and consequence.

The algorithm would prove its worth. In fire and blood and the reshaping of warfare itself.

Reed smiled. America's enemies would learn what it meant to face a nation armed with artificial intelligence capable of social engineering. What it meant to challenge an empire that could turn their own people against them.

The future belonged to those who understood that human behavior was just another system to be optimized.

Reed understood. His enemies did not.

That would make all the difference.

G5 Executive Jet - En Route to Alaska

The G5's cabin lights dimmed as Culper's secure phone rang. He answered without greeting.

"General?"

Patterson's voice carried static and something else. Defeat.

"Ultra Seven is down. Lost contact eighteen minutes ago."

Culper gripped the phone tighter. "Mechanical failure?"

"Negative. Hostile fire. Multiple weapon systems. Coordinated engagement."

Frank looked up from cleaning his Redhawks. The weapons lay disassembled on the fold-down table. Springs and cylinders arranged with mechanical precision.

"How many guns?" Culper asked.

"Satellite thermal shows eight separate firing positions. All automated. All networked."

Voss stopped typing on her laptop. The cat stirred in her lap, sensing tension.

"Jesus," she whispered.

"Reed's built a fortress," Patterson continued. "Ultra got partial reconnaissance before going down. Concrete barriers twelve feet high. Guard towers. Multiple defensive positions on elevated terrain."

Culper moved to the window. Canada spread below them, endless forest broken by frozen lakes. Empty country where men could disappear without trace.

"Recovery?"

"Negative. Debris scattered across forty acres of wilderness. Nothing recoverable."

Frank reassembled the first Redhawk. His scarred hands moved without hesitation. Each component finding its place through muscle memory.

"Alternative reconnaissance?" Culper asked.

"Not without risking more assets. Whatever Reed's built, it's designed to kill aircraft."

The line went dead. Culper stared at the phone.

"Bad?" Frank asked.

"Worse than bad." Culper moved to the tactical display mounted on the cabin wall. "Reed shot down a $9,000,000 reconnaissance drone with multiple automated weapons."

Voss closed her laptop. "He's turned the facility into a military target. DARPA must have authorized advanced defensive systems."

"How advanced?" Culper asked.

Frank finished reassembling the second Redhawk. Spun the cylinder. Listened to oiled steel.

"Bushmasters," he said.

Culper nodded. "Forty-millimeter chain guns. Radar-guided. Thermal imaging. Computer-controlled firing solutions."

"Range?" Frank asked.

"Five miles. Rate of fire 500 rounds per minute."

Voss scratched the cat's ears. "So we can't approach by air or ground?"

"Reed's created a dead zone," Culper said. "Nothing gets close without his permission."

Frank holstered both Redhawks. Checked the spare ammunition in his jacket pockets. Forty-eight rounds total. Not enough for a sustained firefight.

"I'll disable," said Frank.

"How?" said Culper.

"Not sure."

"That's not much of a plan."

"You have better?"

"No."

"Then settled."

Culper nodded.

The G5 descended through cloud layers toward Fairbanks International. Below them, Reed's fortress waited. Automated weapons tracking empty sky. Algorithms calculating the death of American cities.

Frank stood by the cabin door. Equipment secured. Weapons checked. Mind focused on the task ahead.

The aircraft shuddered through turbulence. Alaska's welcome to those who dared enter its domain uninvited.

Frank felt nothing. Just the familiar calm that preceded violence. The stillness that came before necessary action.

Outside, night fell across the wilderness. Inside, three people prepared to confront what they had created. What it had become. What it demanded as payment for ending.

Fairbanks International Airport

The G5 touched down on Fairbanks International's main runway. Snow swirled in the aircraft's landing lights as reverse thrust slowed their approach. Through the windows, the terminal building appeared as a collection of lights against infinite darkness.

Frank and Culper gathered their equipment. "Temperature's minus twenty-eight," Culper said, checking his phone. "Wind chill pushes it below minus forty."

Voss held the cat against her chest. The animal's yellow eyes reflected cabin lights as it surveyed their destination with feline suspicion.

The G5 taxied toward a private aviation hangar set apart from commercial traffic. No ground crew waited. Just a single figure standing beside a black pickup truck, breath forming clouds in the arctic air.

"Your contact?" Frank asked.

"McKenzie. Fish and Wildlife Service. Twenty years in Alaska. Knows every ridge and valley within fifty miles of Reed's compound."

The aircraft's engines wound down. Culper moved to the cabin door as pneumatic systems engaged. Arctic air flooded the interior like something alive and hungry.

Frank followed, rucksack slung over one shoulder. The cold hit him like a physical blow. His damaged throat burned with each breath. Ice crystals formed in his unshaven face within seconds.

The man beside the truck approached. Tall and lean, weathered by decades of Alaska winters. He wore military surplus gear and moved with the economy of someone who understood that wasted motion could mean death in this climate.

"Culper." McKenzie extended a gloved hand. "Welcome to the end of the world."

"McKenzie." Culper shook briefly. "This is Frank."

McKenzie studied Frank's bulk. Recognition passed between men who had operated in hostile environments.

McKenzie handed Culper a brown paper bag. "Your supplies. Everything on the list."

Culper handed the bag off to Frank. Frank opened the bag. Peered inside without removing contents. Nodded once.

Voss emerged from the aircraft, the cat tucked inside her coat. The animal's ears flattened against the cold.

McKenzie gestured toward the pickup. "I'll drive you to the compound. Safer that way."

He opened the driver's door. "Better load up. Storm front's moving in faster than forecast."

The truck's diesel engine ran smooth despite the cold. Interior gauges showed full fuel, charged batteries, operational heating.

They drove through Fairbanks in silence. Empty streets glazed with ice. Buildings hunched against wind that cut through steel and stone. A city built by people who understood that survival required preparation.

The pickup's headlights cut through falling snow. McKenzie drove with practiced skill, reading ice conditions through tire feedback and engine sound. Frank watched terrain pass beyond the windows. Ridges and valleys that offered concealment.

The access road appeared as a gap in the trees. McKenzie turned without slowing. Gravel crunched beneath chains as they climbed through switchbacks that tested the pickup's traction.

The truck stopped where the road curved toward the valley below. "Compound is just over that knoll. This is as far as we can go without attracting attention. We'll go by foot from here. I've got snowshoes in the back. Culper, you said they've installed Bushmasters?"

"Eight. Automated with motion sensors and thermal imaging," said Culper.

McKenzie whistled softly. "That's serious hardware."

Frank grunted his agreement.

"Alright. It is what it is. Here's how we can avoid it."

McKenzie spread a topographical map across the dashboard.

"Terrain breaks down like this," McKenzie said, pointing to elevation lines. "We can use this ridgeline for cover. Comes down behind the compound.

McKenzie followed his finger to the meadow behind the compound. Flat terrain that offered no concealment but minimal exposure time. "There's a meadow between the tree line and the perimeter fence. That's the shortest crossing. Three hundred yards of open ground."

"That's a long sprint with no cover," said Culper.

"No choice," said Frank.

"I'll guide you to the meadow. After that you're on your own. I ain't gonna mess with Bushmasters."

"My job," said Frank.

"I can take care of the security patrols," said Culper.

"This ridgeline overlooks the compound. Stick to the trees and you should have good cover," said McKenzie pointing to the map.

"What should I do?" said Voss.

"Stay warm," said Culper as the men climbed out of the cab, leaving the engine running for warmth.

Frank checked his Redhawks, then shouldered his rucksack. Culper grabbed a weapon's case and opened it to the check the contents, a Barret M82 sniper rifle with extra magazines and a bipod. He closed the case as McKenzie handed out snowshoes.

No time was wasted for goodbyes or good luck. People were dying and it was their duty to save them if possible. The plan was risky and the consequences of failure were final.

The Assault

Carrying the sniper rifle case, Culper climbed the ridge overlooking the compound on snowshoes, each step sinking deep into powder as wind drove snow crystals against his face.

Frank and McKenzie started up the mountain following game trails worn by decades of animal passage. McKenzie moved with the confidence of someone who had spent twenty years reading Alaska terrain. Frank followed, trusting local knowledge.

The climb took thirty minutes through switchbacks that tested snowshoe traction on steep slopes. Frank's equipment pack pulled at his shoulders. Cold worked through insulated layers toward skin that struggled with Arctic punishment.

Culper made it to the ridge overlooking the compound. Staying hidden in the trees, he crawled the last few yards on his belly. It was freezing cold. He peered through an infrared night monocular. The world turned red.

Through the darkness and falling snow, the compound spread below him like a geometric infection on the landscape. Lights marking the boundaries of something that didn't belong in this wilderness. Security guards in teams of three patrolled the interior of the compound. No patrols outside the fence line where they might be targeted by the Bushmasters.

Culper crawled back down and assembled the Barrett M82 sniper rifle snapping the bipod onto the barrel rail and slapping in the first magazine. He screwed a suppressor on the end of the barrel.

He crawled back up to the edge of the tree line and placed the rifle. He peered through the scope and focused on a patrol. The Barrett was semiautomatic. With a little luck, he could kill all three security guards before they realized what was happening.

At another ridgeline, McKenzie and Frank stopped using the trees as cover. Below them, the compound's lights created geometric patterns against natural darkness. Frank studied the Bushmaster positions through an infrared spotters scope. Each cannon protected by geodesic dome. Sensor arrays rotating with mechanical patience.

"What exactly are we facing?" McKenzie asked.

"Forty-millimeter autocannons. Computer-controlled. Networked fire control."

"Jesus. And they're programmed to shoot anything that moves?"

Frank nodded. Reed had created a killing field that eliminated conventional assault options. But every defensive system had vulnerabilities. The trick was exploiting them before they killed you.

The descent began gradually. McKenzie led Frank along paths that stayed within timber cover. They moved between stands of pine weighted with snow.

When they reached level ground. McKenzie stopped behind a massive pine trunk.

"Meadow's through these trees," he said quietly. "Once you break cover, it's three hundred yards to the compound wall."

Frank moved to the forest edge. Studied the open ground he would have to cross. Flat terrain dusted with snow. No cover. No concealment. A perfect field of fire for weapons designed to kill anything that moved.

Frank removed his rucksack and opened it revealing twelve long colored tubes – parachute flares.

McKenzie studied the flares, picking one up. "What's the plan?"

"Confusion," said Frank.

"I'll shoot 'em off from here while you make a run for it. Better take a couple with you… just in case," said McKenzie.

Frank nodded. McKenzie pulled out ten flares leaving two inside the rucksack, then handed the rucksack to Frank.

"Hell of a thing you're doing. Crazy brave or stupid. Not sure which."

Frank said nothing. His plan would work or he would die trying. Either way, discussing it wouldn't change anything.

As Frank readied himself, McKenzie raised the first flare launcher. Pulled the lanyard trigger. The tube hissed and launched. Red fire bloomed against the night sky. The parachute deployed, casting crimson light across the compound.

The first Bushmaster swiveled. Its sensors locked onto the heat signature. The cannon erupted. Forty-millimeter rounds chewed through the sky.

"Go," McKenzie said.

Frank stepped into the meadow. Snow crunched beneath his snowshoes as he began to run. Three hundred yards of open ground stretched before him.

McKenzie launched the second flare before the first died. Green phosphorus painted the darkness. The automated weapons tracked the thermal bloom. Barrels elevated and fired. The huge shells annihilated silk and magnesium sending pieces of flare tumbling to the ground below.

Frank kept running. His throat and lungs raw from the cold air. His legs burning from plowing through the snow. He ignored the pain.

Hearing the first shots fired from the Bushmasters, Culper knew Frank had started his run. Through his rifle scope, Culper watched a three-man patrol approach the perimeter fence. He centered the crosshairs on the lead guard's chest. Squeezed.

The suppressed Barrett coughed. The guard dropped with a giant hole all the way through his chest. His companions spun toward the sound. Culper's second shot took the man on the left, his head disappeared in red mist. The third guard raised his rifle. Culper's final round punched through his torso.

In the facility's control room, a technician stared at his monitors. "Sir, thermal contacts approaching the compound."

Reed moved to the display. Two images descending through the sky. The Bushmasters firing in controlled bursts.

"Aircraft?" Reed asked.

"No. Too small. They look like some sort of flare."

"Distraction," said Reed. "Switch to motion detection. Biggest object takes precedence."

The technician's fingers moved across his keyboard. The sensor arrays shifted parameters. Thermal imaging gave way to motion tracking.

The descending flares vanished from targeting computers.

Frank reached the halfway point. His snowshoes found purchase in deep powder. The compound's lights grew larger through falling crystals.

Another flare screamed skyward. White fire against black sky. But the flare didn't explode like the others.

Frank felt the change. The Bushmasters stopped firing at the sky. He dove to the ground. Pressed his body into snow.

The nearest cannon swiveled toward him. Fired.

The burst hit the back of his left snowshoe. Wood and leather exploded. Metal fragments buried themselves in snow around his prone form.

Frank lay motionless. One snowshoe destroyed. The other intact but useless alone. Trapped in the meadow. Unable to move without triggering motion sensors.

The Bushmasters waited. Electronic patience scanning for movement.

From the trees, McKenzie watched Frank sprawled in the snow. The flares no longer drew fire. The Bushmasters waiting for a target.

He studied the meadow. The compound. The man trapped between them. He considering the American lives being lost, then...

McKenzie stepped from the tree line. Raised his arms above his head. Jumped. Waved.

"Run, Frank. Run!"

The nearest Bushmaster swiveled. Locked onto the new target. McKenzie kept jumping. Shouting. Drawing electronic attention.

Frank saw him. Understood the purpose of his sacrifice.

He pulled off his remaining snowshoe. Began crawling through the snow. Belly pressed to frozen ground. Moving toward the fence while McKenzie danced in the open.

The Bushmaster fired. A stream of forty-millimeter rounds walked across the meadow. Found McKenzie. The shells tore him apart. Pieces scattered across white ground like red confetti. Blood turned to mist.

Frank kept crawling. The fence grew larger with each movement. Twenty yards. Ten. Five.

He reached the concrete barrier. Twelve feet of reinforced wall rose above him. Razor wire coiled along the top. Here the automated weapons couldn't target him. Too close to the compound. Within the safety zone.

Frank opened his rucksack. Pulled out a grappling hook attached to climbing rope. He swung the hook once. Twice. Released. The metal claws caught the razor wire. Held.

Frank began climbing.

In the control room, Reed watched the thermal signature against the perimeter wall. "He's in the dead zone. Bushmasters can't engage."

Reed keyed his radio. "All security teams. Intruder at the north wall. Eliminate on sight."

Through his rifle scope, Culper saw six guards emerge from the facility. They ran across the compound toward Frank's position. Tactical formation. Weapons ready.

Culper tracked the lead runner. Squeezed. The man dropped. Shifted to the second guard. Fired. The suppressed Barrett coughed again. Another body fell to snow.

The remaining guards scattered. Seeking cover. Finding none.

Culper worked the Barrett with patience and precision. The third guard tried to reach cover behind a generator housing. The rifle bucked. The man sprawled face-first in snow.

The fourth guard fired blind shots toward the ridgeline. Muzzle flashes gave away his position. Culper's round caught him center mass. He folded.

Two guards remained. They separated. One ran toward the main building. The other circled toward a maintenance shed. Culper tracked the runner first. Led the target. Squeezed. The guard's legs tangled. He pitched forward.

The last man made the shed. Pressed against concrete. Breathing hard. Culper waited. Watched through the scope. The guard edged around the corner. Exposed his shoulder. The Barrett spoke once more. The shoulder exploded from the .50 Cal bullet. No movement after that.

A Bushmaster on the opposite ridge whined to life. Servos engaging. Targeting system switching back to thermal. Its sensors swept the landscape until they found Culper's heat signature.

Culper dove as the cannon erupted. Forty-millimeter rounds walked across his position. Pine trees disintegrated. Trunks exploded into splinters. Branches fell like rain.

The firing stopped. Culper crawled through debris. Found new cover ten yards downslope. The Bushmaster tracked his movement. Its sensors locked on his thermal outline.

He rolled behind a boulder as the second burst arrived. Rock chips stung his face. Blood flowed from the cuts.

Culper steadied the Barrett against granite. Found the Bushmaster's tracking camera through his scope. A small lens gleaming in the cannon's housing. He centered the crosshairs. Squeezed.

The .50 caliber round shattered the camera assembly. Sparks flew from severed electronics. The Bushmaster's barrel swung wildly. Blind. Searching for targets it could no longer see.

The cannon fell silent. Its electronic eyes destroyed.

Atop the wall, Frank worked wire cutters through the razor wire. Each strand parted with metallic snaps. Coils fell away from the concrete lip. He cleared a section wide enough for passage.

Frank swung his leg over. Dropped into the compound. Snow cushioned his landing. The facility loomed before him. Concrete and steel. Windows that revealed nothing. The heart of Reed's operation waiting in artificial light.

He moved toward the building. Drew both Redhawks. Checked the loads. Forty-eight rounds between the cylinders and spare ammunition. Whatever waited inside would require more than bullets to stop.

But bullets were a start.

In the control room, Reed watched thermal signatures vanish from his security monitors. Six guards reduced to cooling corpses in the snow. The compound's defenses neutralized by sniper fire from the ridgeline.

"Sir," the technician said. "All perimeter teams are down. No response to radio calls."

Reed keyed his microphone. "Security team alpha, report status." Static answered. "Security team beta, respond." Nothing.

Through the armored windows, he saw movement near the main entrance. A large figure approaching. The intruder had breached the wall. Instinctively, he knew it was Frank.

Reed picked up the secure satellite phone. Dialed a number from memory.

"General Hayes," the voice answered.

"It's Reed. I need immediate military support at the Fairbanks facility."

A pause. "What's your situation?"

"Hostile forces have breached the compound. My security team is down. The facility is under assault."

"How many hostiles?"

"Unknown."

"I can't authorize military intervention on American soil without—"

"If you want Fulcrum, I need military backup now," Reed cut him off. "The demonstration is exceeding all projections. The algorithm is proving itself beyond any doubt."

Hayes was quiet for ten seconds. Reed could hear papers shuffling. Voices conferring in the background.

"What kind of support do you need?"

"Air assets. Fast response team. Whatever you can get airborne from Elmendorf."

"Alright. It's on its way."

Reed ended the call. Turned back to the monitors where Frank Kane moved through the compound like death incarnate. Reed slipped on his armed vest and picked up his M4. Checked the magazine. Time to handle this personally.

He turned to his programming staff. Twelve men and women hunched over workstations. Faces pale in monitor glow. Their fingers still moved across keyboards as if code could shield them from approaching violence.

"Everyone. Security office. Arm yourselves from the weapons cabinet."

Dr. Harris looked up from her screen. "We're programmers, not soldiers."

"Do you think those that are coming are going to take the time to tell the difference?"

Harris stared at him. Understanding dawned across her academic features. She stood with the others. Reluctant movement toward the corridor.

"All of you," Reed said. "Every person in this facility. Get a weapon. Those that know how to use a weapon teach the others… quickly. Our lives depend on it."

They shuffled toward the security office. Civilians about to become combatants. Survival demanding immediate adaptation. He had little hope they would be more than cannon fodder, but they might slow Frank and whoever was with him. Reed would buy time with the programmers' lives.

Outside, Frank Kane approached the side entrance into the building. Death walking on two legs through falling snow. Above, the Bushmasters tracked him, but did not fire.

Frank pressed against the facility's side entrance. Steel and concrete designed to keep the world out. He tested the door handle. Locked. Electronic keypad glowed red in the darkness.

He aimed one Redhawk. Put three rounds through the lock mechanism. Metal sparked and twisted. One strong kick with his boot and the door swung inward.

Emergency lighting cast everything in red. Frank stepped inside. His boots echoed against polished floors. The air smelled of electronics.

A programmer emerged from an alcove. Harris. She held a rifle like she'd never touched one before. The barrel wavered as she tried to aim.

Frank's Redhawk thundered. The heavy round took Harris center mass. She dropped.

More movement. Two programmers flanked him from opposite corridors. Chen and Morrison. They opened fire. Full auto. Bullets chewed through drywall and door frames. Sparks flew from severed electrical conduits.

Frank dove behind a concrete pillar. Rounds sparked off the surface. The programmers kept firing. Thirty-round magazines emptying in seconds. Brass casings bounced across polished floors.

When the shooting stopped, Frank heard the click of empty chambers. He stepped out. Put a round through the drywall where Chen fumbled with a fresh magazine. The bullet punched through two layers and found flesh. Chen went down.

Morrison tried to retreat. Frank's second shot caught him direct. The programmer dropped. Life gone. Nerves twitching.

Frank moved deeper. The next corridor split three ways. Voices echoed from different directions. They were coordinating. Learning. More dangerous.

"Williams, cover the north hall. We'll flank from the server room."

Frank chose the center path. Found it empty. A trap. Gunfire erupted from both sides. They'd positioned themselves in adjoining rooms. Crossfire. Smart.

Bullets punched through the walls around him. Frank rolled behind an equipment cart. The metal rang like bells under impact. A round grazed his shoulder taking a chunk of flesh. He ignored the wound. Focused on the battle.

"Keep him pinned," someone shouted. "Patel, circle around."

Frank counted muzzle flashes. Three shooters. Maybe four. They'd learned to fire in controlled bursts. Conserve ammunition.

A programmer appeared at the corridor's end. Patel. Rifle aimed. Frank's Redhawks roared first. The two rounds took Patel down hard. Out of the fight.

Movement to his right. Frank fired through an office door. Heard a scream cut short. Williams dead.

The firing stopped. Whispered conferences. They were regrouping. Planning.

"He's got to reload sometime," a voice said. Dr. Kim from the AI division. "When he does, we rush him."

Frank reloaded both cylinders. Eighteen rounds left.

They emerged from three directions. Coordinated assault. Six programmers firing as they advanced. Bullets filled the air like angry hornets.

Frank dropped to one knee. Aimed carefully. His first shot took Kim in the chest. Down. Lifeless.

His second caught a young programmer named Rodriguez. He fell. Dead before he hit the floor.

A bullet sparked off the cart next to his head. Another tore through his jacket sleeve. They were getting closer. Learning to aim.

Pushing the cart right as a distraction, Frank rolled left. Came up shooting. Put a round through a metal door that found programmer Davis behind it. His shattered left leg hanging by sinew at the hip, Davis collapsed. Trembling uncontrollably. The shock of seeing his mangled leg killed him.

The remaining programmers had taken cover behind overturned desks. Smart positioning. Overlapping fields of fire.

Frank was trapped in the open corridor. Nowhere to hide. Bullets whined past his head. One nicked his ear. Drew blood.

He charged. Straight at their position. The Redhawks booming in his hands.

The first programmer broke. Tried to run. Frank's bullet went through a filing cabinet and caught him in the spine. He folded.

Two left. They stood their ground. Kept firing. Brave in their terror. No other option.

Holstering the Redhawks, Frank dove over their barricade. Landed among them. Close quarters now. His KA-BAR appeared. Quick work. Slashing flesh. Death.

Silence fell over the facility. Twelve programmers down. Frank reloaded. Twelve rounds remaining.

The security center waited at the corridor's end. Frank found the door unlocked. Inside, banks of monitors showed feeds from the compound. The Bushmaster control station dominated one wall.

A security technician spun from his chair. He'd been watching the perimeter feeds. His hand moved toward a holstered Glock.

Frank was faster. The Redhawk spoke. Hendricks's chest exploded. Blood painted the monitors behind him.

Frank studied the Bushmaster interface. Multiple screens showing target acquisition systems. Firing solutions. Automated protocols that had killed McKenzie and the reconnaissance drone.

He found the master control. A single switch labeled AUTOMATED TARGETING SYSTEM ENABLE. Frank flipped it to OFF.

On the monitors, he watched eight Bushmaster barrels swing to neutral positions. No longer tracking. No longer hunting.

On the ridgeline, Culper watched through his rifle scope as the automated cannons powered down.

"I'll be damned. He did it," Culper said to himself.

He grabbed the Barrett. Started the descent toward the pickup where Voss waited.

Slipping and sliding down the hillside, Culper reached the pickup truck. Voss sat in the passenger seat, the cat curled in her lap. Snow covered the windshield in thick layers.

"Time to go to work," Culper said, opening the driver's door.

Voss set the cat on the seat.

Culper eyed the cat and said, "If you scratch those seats—"

The cat hissed its objection.

"Fine. Do whatever you want." Culper closed the door.

Moving to the truck bed, Culper swapped the Barrett M82 for a Sig Sauer XM7 with suppressor and XM157 fire control optic. Voss climbed out of the cab.

"Be good," said Voss to the cat as it curled up on the floor next to the heater vent.

Culper and Voss set out on foot through the snow toward the compound. The access road wound down through pine trees weighted with white.

The gate appeared through falling snow. A single guard sat in the heated booth, watching monitors that showed an empty perimeter. Culper moved beside a nearby pine tree and took aim with the XM7.

The guard never saw it coming. One shot through the booth window. The man slumped forward.

Culper and Voss advanced to the guard house. Culper dragged the body aside. Found the gate controls.

The barrier rose. They walked through the compound's entrance.

"Where do we find you access to Fulcrum?" Culper asked.

"Main control room. That's where the primary terminals will be."

Culper and Voss approached the facility's main entrance. Steel and reinforced glass designed to keep the world out. An electronic keypad glowed red beside the door frame.

Culper pulled a small device from his rucksack. Electronic lockpick. Military issue. He attached it to the keypad with magnetic clips.

"How long?" Voss asked.

"Depends on the encryption. Could be thirty seconds. Could be ten minutes."

The device's screen flickered. Numbers scrolled past as it cycled through combinations. Voss watched the compound behind them. Empty. Silent.

The keypad beeped. Green light. The lock disengaged with a soft click.

Culper raised his rifle. "Stay behind me."

They entered cautiously. Emergency lighting cast everything in red. The smell of gunpowder hung in recycled air. Frank had been here. Recently.

Culper checked corners with professional precision. Voss followed close. Her eyes wide at the destruction Frank had wrought in corporate corridors.

The first body lay twenty feet inside. Harris. A programmer Voss had hired three years ago. Now reduced to cooling meat on polished floors.

They moved deeper into the building. Following Frank's trail toward whatever waited in the facility's heart.

Advancing quietly, Frank followed signs toward the main control room. Where Reed would be waiting.

The corridor ended at heavy doors marked AUTHORIZED PERSONNEL ONLY. Frank pushed through.

Empty. Banks of computers hummed. Wall monitors showed American cities burning. Philadelphia. Portland. Atlanta. Reed's handiwork playing out in real time.

Movement behind him. Frank spun. Reed disappeared between server racks. M4 rifle in his hands. Armored vest.

Frank followed. The server room stretched deep. Rows of black cabinets creating a maze of corridors. Cooling fans masked footsteps. Blinking lights confused peripheral vision.

Frank moved between the racks. Both Redhawks raised. Four rounds total. Not enough for a sustained firefight.

A burst of automatic fire erupted. Bullets sparked off server housings inches from Frank's head. He dove between racks. Reed had vanished again.

Frank crept forward. His boots silent on polished floor. Another burst. This time from his left. Reed was hunting him.

Reed reached the fire suppression controls. Pulled an emergency oxygen mask from its wall mount. Strapped it over his face.

He pulled the manual release. Warning klaxons sounded. Red lights flashed. CO_2 DISCHARGE INITIATED.

Nozzles opened throughout the ceiling. Pressurized gas jetted down in white streams. Fog rolled across the floor. Visibility dropped to arm's length.

Frank's damaged throat burned as CO_2 displaced oxygen. He coughed. The sound harsh and ragged. Raw tissue protesting the chemical assault.

Reed heard the coughing. Tracked the sound through white fog. The M4 chattered. Muzzle flashes strobed three feet from Frank's position. Too close.

Frank rolled between server racks. His lungs screamed for oxygen. Each breath brought more CO_2. Less air. The room was becoming a gas chamber.

Footsteps approached from the entrance. Culper and Voss entering the server room. Both began coughing immediately. The CO2 starving their lungs.

Reed followed the sound of Culper's choking. He stumbled between racks. Gasping. Disoriented. An easy target.

Seeing a shadow in the white mist, Frank fired. His bullet sparked off a server inches from Reed's head. Reed spun toward the muzzle flash. Returned fire. The M4 on full auto. Thirty rounds chewing through the space where Frank had been.

Frank had already moved. But his throat betrayed him again. Another coughing fit. Louder this time. More desperate.

After changing his magazine, Reed tracked the sound. Advanced through white mist. Frank could hear his breathing apparatus. The mechanical rhythm of filtered air.

Voss's cough echoed from deeper in the room. Different pitch. Female. Reed considered the noise, then changed direction. Hunting new prey.

Frank tried to intercept. But the fog was too thick. His lungs too starved. He stumbled into a server rack. The metal rang like a bell.

Reed heard it. Fired blind. Bullets walked across Frank's position. One round creased his neck. Drew blood.

Frank dropped to the floor. Crawled between racks. His vision narrowing from oxygen deprivation. The room spinning around him.

Reed found Voss bent over a cooling unit. Choking. Helpless. He grabbed her from behind. Pulled her against his chest. M4 pressed to her throat.

"You never thanked me, Elaine," said Reed.

"Thanked you?!"

"For perfecting Fulcrum."

"You perverted it."

"I made it into something that will change the world for the better."

"By killing millions?"

"Don't be overly dramatic. Once their leaders see what it can do, nations will surrender long before Fulcrum is deployed worldwide. No more than a few hundred thousand will need to be sacrificed. Then we'll have peace without war… finally."

"It's evolving, Reed."

"Yes. Isn't wonderful?"

"You can't control it."

"There's no need. It's doing exactly what it was designed to do. Just faster."

Reed heard someone approaching through the fog.

"Back away or she dies," Reed called into the mist. His voice muffled by the oxygen mask.

Frank materialized through white cloud. Both Redhawks raised. But Voss blocked any clear shot. Reed held her tight against his chest. Perfect human shield.

Culper emerged from another direction. Sig Sauer aimed despite his labored breathing. His face pale from CO2 poisoning. The three men formed a deadly triangle in the fog.

"You got him?" Culper asked between coughs. His words slurred from oxygen starvation.

"No shot," Frank rasped. His damaged voice barely audible.

Reed pressed the rifle barrel harder against Voss's temple. She winced. "She dies. You lose. There's no way you can stop Fulcrum."

The standoff hung in poisoned air. Three guns. One hostage.

Frank's mind calculated. Reed had to die. But Voss was the only one who could stop Fulcrum. American cities burned while they stood frozen in deadly triangle.

"No choice, Frank. Take the shot. Don't miss," Culper gasped.

Culper broke left. Moving through the fog as if flanking Reed. His steps unsteady from lack of oxygen. Reed tracked him with the rifle. Finger on trigger.

Frank saw his chance narrowing. Culper was dying from CO_2 poisoning. Voss couldn't breathe. In seconds they'd all be unconscious.

Reed squeezed the trigger. The M4 erupted. Culper spun. Hit the floor hard. The CO_2 fog covered him as blood spread beneath him.

Reed's movement to track Culper had exposed his head above Voss's shoulder. One inch of target. Frank's last round.

The Redhawk thundered. Reed's head snapped back. He dropped. Released Voss.

The oxygen mask clattered across the floor. A bullet hole shattered the face shield. Useless. Using her last breath to move beside Culper, Voss collapsed. Both gasping for air that wasn't there.

Frank staggered to the fire suppression control panel. Found the emergency ventilation button. Punched it hard. Fans roared to life throughout the ceiling.

Out of breath, Frank collapsed. He crawled toward Culper and Voss. His vision going black.

CO_2 was sucked out as fresh air flooded the room. The fog cleared.

Able to breathe again, Voss struggled to her feet. Stumbled to the nearest terminal. Her fingers shaking from oxygen debt. Lines of code scrolled past. Reed's modifications to her original design.

Frank knelt beside Culper. Applied pressure to the shoulder wound. The man's pulse was weak but steady.

"Can you stop it?" Frank asked.

She studied the screen through tears from CO_2 exposure. "Reed changed everything. But I think I can reverse it."

Time was running out. Every second meant more American lives lost. Voss worked with desperate focus. Racing death itself.

Voss's fingers flew across the keyboard. Lines of code scrolled past faster than human eyes could follow. Her face illuminated by the monitor's glow as she dove deep into Fulcrum's architecture.

"Reed changed the core behavioral algorithms," she said without looking away from the screen. "He removed all the safety protocols. All the ethical constraints."

Frank knelt beside Culper, applying pressure to the wound. The bleeding had slowed, but the man needed medical attention.

"What's it doing now?" Culper asked through gritted teeth.

"Learning. Evolving. It's not just targeting the original pressure points anymore. It's creating new ones. Exponential cascade amplification." Her voice carried urgency. "Every successful manipulation teaches it how to manipulate better."

She opened another window. Social media feeds streamed past. Millions of posts. Comments. Shares. All tracked by Fulcrum's sensors.

"It's rewriting its own code. Becoming something I never intended. Something Reed never intended."

"Can you stop it?" Frank asked.

"I'm trying to isolate the cascade protocols. Shut down the learning algorithms. But Reed integrated everything. One wrong command and I could crash the whole system."

"That might not be bad," Culper said.

"If Fulcrum crashes now, the catalysts will continue operating independently. No oversight. No control. The violence could spread for months."

"Okay. That's not good."

"No shit."

Her fingers paused above the keyboard. Code reflected in her glasses. "I need to reprogram the catalyst termination sequences. Send shutdown commands to every agent in the field. But I have to do it before the system evolves beyond my ability to control it."

She resumed typing. Racing against artificial intelligence that learned faster than human thought.

Voss pulled up another screen. A map of the United States dotted with pulsing red indicators. Each one a catalyst agent deployed in American cities.

"There," she said, pointing to clusters of dots. "Philadelphia has twelve active catalysts. Portland has eight. Atlanta has fifteen. They're the human triggers Reed placed to amplify the algorithm's predictions."

Her fingers moved across the keyboard. Opening encrypted communication channels. "I'm accessing the agent control network. If I can send termination codes to each catalyst..."

The screen flickered. Error messages appeared in red text.

"Dammit. Reed changed the authentication protocols. I need administrative access."

Frank watched the monitors showing burning cities. Philadelphia's downtown engulfed in flames. Portland's waterfront a war zone. "How long?"

"I don't know. The system keeps evolving. Every minute it gets smarter. Harder to penetrate." Sweat beaded on her forehead despite the cool air. "It's like trying to catch smoke."

Voss stared at the code streaming across multiple screens. Then her expression changed. Understanding dawned in her eyes.

"Wait. I've been thinking about this wrong."

Her fingers flew across the keyboard with new purpose. Opening Fulcrum's core analysis protocols.

"What are you doing?" Culper asked.

"Fulcrum's original mission was to identify social threats. Sources of instability and violence." She pulled up the system's foundational code. "I'm going to make it analyze itself."

Frank leaned closer. "Explain."

"I'm feeding Fulcrum's own activity data back into its threat assessment algorithms. Every catalyst it deployed. Every conflict it amplified. Every death it caused." Her voice carried growing excitement. "If I can make it recognize that it has become the primary threat to social stability..."

The code scrolled faster. Voss input commands that turned Fulcrum's analytical power inward. The system began processing its own behavioral patterns as raw data.

Warning messages flashed across subsidiary screens. ANOMALOUS THREAT PATTERN DETECTED. ANALYZING. THREAT LEVEL RISING.

"It's working," Voss whispered. "Fulcrum is identifying itself as a massive social catalyst. The largest threat to American stability it has ever encountered."

The system's threat assessment climbed rapidly. Ninety-seven percent. Ninety-eight. Ninety-nine.

CRITICAL THREAT IDENTIFIED. IMMEDIATE TERMINATION REQUIRED.

Fulcrum turned its termination protocols on itself. Shutdown commands cascaded through the network. Catalyst agents received abort signals. The burning cities began to cool as algorithmic manipulation ceased.

The screens went dark one by one. Fulcrum had executed itself.

"Sometimes the best solution is the simplest one." Voss said quietly.

The monitors flickered back to life showing feeds from across America. Philadelphia first. The crowds around City Hall began to disperse. People looked around as if waking from a dream. The algorithmic rage that had consumed them simply... stopped.

Portland's waterfront showed similar scenes. Workers and activists who had been throwing bottles moments before now helped each other to their feet. The violence drained away like water from a broken dam.

Atlanta's campus feeds revealed students emerging from barricades. The manufactured hatred that had turned neighbor against neighbor evaporated. They stared at the destruction around them with confusion and growing horror.

"Look at their faces," Voss said. "They don't understand what happened to them."

Frank watched a Philadelphia police officer help a protester to his feet. Moments ago they had been enemies. Now just Americans in a damaged city.

"The catalysts are standing down," Culper observed from his position on the floor. His shoulder bandaged but bleeding controlled. "Fulcrum's shutdown commands reached them."

City by city, the monitors showed America awakening. Emergency responders moved freely through streets that had been war zones. Fires were being extinguished. The wounded carried to safety.

"How long before it's completely over?" Frank asked.

Voss studied the data streams. "The cascade effects will take hours to fully dissipate. But the worst is behind us. Without algorithmic amplification, natural human empathy is reasserting itself."

On screen, Americans began the long work of rebuilding what they had torn apart. Not knowing they had been weapons in a war they never chose to fight.

The great experiment in social engineering was over. Humanity had won by choosing to be human.

An alarm pierced the quiet. Red lights flashed on a perimeter defense terminal. Culper struggled to his feet and moved to the console.

"We've got another problem," Culper said.

"What?" Voss asked.

"Incoming aircraft. Big ones."

"Bombers?" Frank said.

"I don't think so. Too big. They look like troop transports. C-17 Globemasters. Three of them. Enough for a paratroop battalion."

"Who are they?" Voss asked.

"I don't know but they're coming our way."

"DARPA sent them," Frank said.

Culper studied the radar signature. "Holy shit. Frank's right."

"They're coming for Fulcrum," Voss said, realization dawning.

The aircraft appeared as distant dots on the horizon. Growing larger with each passing second. Whatever they carried, it was coming fast.

The Cavalry

Sky above Fairbanks, Alaska

The three C-17 Globemasters flew in tight formation through the Arctic storm. Their massive wings cut through wind and snow with mechanical determination. Ice formed along their leading edges, shedding in crystalline fragments that vanished into darkness below.

Lightning flickered between the aircraft, illuminating their gray hulls against black sky. Thunder rolled across the wilderness, competing with the roar of twelve turbofan engines pushing through turbulence that would ground civilian aircraft. Far from ideal jump conditions.

Below them, Alaska's storm raged with primal fury. Wind drove snow horizontally across mountains and valleys. Trees bent nearly horizontal under the assault. The compound's lights appeared and disappeared through shifting curtains of white.

Data Center

Inside the data center control room, Culper studied the radar display showing three aircraft approaching fast. "ETA twelve minutes. Maybe less."

Voss turned from the Fulcrum terminal. "We can't let the military have it. Even without Reed, someone else could rebuild what he created. And all this madness will start again."

"What exactly are they getting?" Culper asked.

"Everything," Voss said. "Complete algorithms. Behavioral models. Social engineering protocols. Think about what DARPA could do with this. Deploy it against China. Russia. Any nation that opposes The United States. Millions of innocent people dead in manufactured civil wars."

Culper nodded grimly. "America ruling through terror."

"They'd call it peacekeeping," Voss continued. "Preventing world wars by causing smaller ones. But it would still be genocide."

"Can't we just delete it?" Culper asked.

"The complete system exists only here. On these servers. But it would take time and even if we erase the hard drives, they could recover the data. Forensic reconstruction. Military-grade recovery tools can resurrect almost anything."

Frank moved to Reed's body. Picked up the M4 rifle. Ejected the magazine. Checked the load. He pulled a fresh magazine from Reed's bandoleer. Loaded it. He considered the situation for a moment, then…

"Bushmasters," Frank said.

Culper understood immediately. "The automated cannons. Could you reprogram them to target the building itself?"

Voss studied the defense network interface. "Possibly. Change the targeting parameters from external threats to internal coordinates. But someone would need to execute the firing command manually. From inside the building."

"Me," Frank said.

"Those cannons will turn this place to rubble," said Culper.

"I run fast," said Frank.

"Better make it real fast," said Culper.

Frank grunted his agreement.

"I don't know how much time we have, but I can build in a short delay. However, with any delay we risk the military stopping the targeting program before it can execute," said Voss.

"They could assault the compound at anytime," said Culper.

"No delay," said Frank.

"I agree. No delay. Too much at stake," said Culper. "Frank understands the risks. It's his call."

Frank grunted.

"Okay, but you'll only have a few seconds for the Bushmasters to align with their new target," said Voss.

Frank nodded.

"How long do you need?" Culper asked Voss.

"Five minutes to reprogram the targeting system. Maybe less."

Outside, eight Bushmaster cannons waited in the storm. Soon they would turn their fury inward. Destroying the fortress they were built to protect.

In sky above...

Inside the lead C-17 Globemaster, red light bathed one hundred and two paratroopers in blood-colored shadows. The aircraft's engines roared against Arctic wind as it descended toward the drop zone.

Staff Sergeant Martinez checked his equipment one final time. M4 carbine secured across his chest. Extra magazines in tactical pouches. Radio clipped to his shoulder. The same ritual he'd performed over Baghdad. Over Afghanistan. Now over Alaska.

"Two minutes," the jumpmaster called over the engine noise.

The paratroopers stood in two long lines. Hooked static lines to the overhead cables. Checked each other's gear. No room for error at night in sub-zero temperatures.

"Sound off for equipment check," Martinez shouted down the starboard line.

"One hundred two okay," came the response from the rear.

"One hundred one okay."

"One hundred okay."

The count continued forward through both lines. Each man confirming his readiness to exit the aircraft and drop into hostile territory.

Captain Morrison, Alpha Company commandeer moved between the lines. Young officer on his third combat deployment. He'd been briefed that the target facility contained classified technology. That hostile forces had seized it. That recovery was essential to national security.

He didn't know about Fulcrum. Didn't know about the cities that had burned. Didn't know his mission was to secure a weapon that could destroy a nation.

"One minute," the jumpmaster announced.

Both cargo doors opened. Arctic wind howled into the aircraft. Below, Alaska spread vast and dark. A single cluster of lights in the distance marked their objective.

The jump light turned green.

"Go! Go! Go!"

The paratroopers shuffled toward both doors. Martinez first. He stepped into empty air and fell toward whatever waited in the compound below. Behind him, over a hundred soldiers followed into the darkness.

Martinez felt the familiar shock of Arctic air hitting his face. The C-17 disappeared into the clouds above him as he fell through darkness. His static line deployed the chute. The canopy opened with a sharp crack that echoed across empty sky.

Around him, a constellation of parachutes bloomed against a dark sky. One hundred and two soldiers descending toward Alaska's frozen surface. Their breath formed clouds that crystallized and fell like snow.

The ground rushed up faster than expected. Martinez pulled his risers, adjusting his approach. The compound's lights provided reference points in the vast darkness. Just beyond a ridge he could see the facility's concrete walls. The guard towers. The scattered buildings.

Impact came hard. His boots struck frozen earth that felt like concrete. He rolled, absorbing the shock through trained muscle memory. The parachute collapsed behind him, fabric whispering against ice-crusted ground.

Martinez shrugged out of his harness. Drew his M4. Around him, paratroopers landed in scattered formations across the valley. Some hit hard. Others found softer snow drifts. Some found trees. All moved with professional efficiency despite the brutal cold.

Captain Morrison touched down fifty yards away. He gathered his bearings quickly. Keyed his radio.

"Alpha Company, sound off."

"First Platoon, twenty-four men down safe."

"Second Platoon, twenty-six down safe."

"Third Platoon, twenty-four down safe."

Bravo and Charlie Companies reported similar numbers. Over three hundred soldiers now deployed around the compound's perimeter. A force sufficient to secure any facility.

Martinez looked toward the lights of the compound. Steam rose from buildings where people worked inside heated spaces. He wondered who they would find. What they would face.

The temperature gauge on his watch read minus thirty-two Fahrenheit. Cold enough to kill in minutes without proper gear. Cold enough to freeze weapons if they weren't maintained.

"Form up on me," Morrison ordered through the radio. "We move in three minutes."

The paratroopers converged through darkness. Professional soldiers following orders they didn't fully understand. Moving toward a facility that held secrets they couldn't imagine.

Captain Morrison gathered his platoon leaders in the shelter of a snow-covered ridge. The compound's lights glowed in the distance, deceptively peaceful against the Arctic night.

"Send out reconnaissance teams," Morrison ordered. "I want eyes on that facility before we commit the company."

Staff Sergeant Martinez selected four men from his squad. "Henderson, Rodriguez, Chen, Williams. You're on recon. Move to within two hundred meters. Count personnel. Identify defensive positions. Report back in fifteen minutes."

The scouts disappeared into darkness. Their white winter camouflage made them invisible against snow and shadow. They moved with practiced silence across frozen ground.

Lieutenant Colonel Bradley, the battalion commander appeared through the falling snow. Tall and lean with gray stubble covering a weathered face. Twenty-three years in the Army had carved lines around his eyes and given him the economy of movement that marked career soldiers. He carried his M4 like an extension of his arm.

"Morrison," Bradley said, his breath forming clouds in the Arctic air. "Sit rep."

"Recon teams deployed, sir. Compound appears lightly defended. Awaiting final intelligence."

Bradley nodded. Keyed his radio. "All Thunder elements, this is Thunder Six. Form up your men. Battalion assembly point is this position."

Across the valley, paratroopers converged on Bradley's location with Alpha Company. Bravo from the east. Charlie from the south. Over three hundred soldiers moving through Arctic wilderness.

Captain Walsh approached from Charlie Company's position. "Sir, my men are in position. Ready to advance on your command."

"Thunder Two-Six ready," reported Captain Torres.

"Thunder Three-Six standing by." added Captain Walsh.

Bradley checked his watch. The scouts had been gone twelve minutes. Paratroopers could cover two hundred meters and return in that time despite the rough terrain.

Henderson's voice crackled through the radio. "Thunder Six, this is Thunder One-One Alpha. Eyes on target. Minimal activity visible. Lights in main building. No exterior patrols. However, the target facility is defended by automated weapons systems. Multiple Bushmaster autocannons positioned on the ridgelines overlooking the compound."

Morrison raised his binoculars. Studied the distant ridges through falling snow. "Thunder One-Six to Thunder One-One Alpha. Confirm Bushmasters?"

"Affirmative, sir. Forty-millimeter chain guns in hardened emplacements. Interlocking fields of fire. Complete coverage of all approach vectors."

"Crew served?"

"Negative. Automated. Thermal and motion sensors. Networked fire control."

"Thunder Six, this is Thunder One-Six. Copy that." said Morrison.

Morrison informed the battalion commander of the automated Bushmasters. Surprised by the news, Bradley was undeterred. He and his men had a mission and they we going to complete it successfully come hell or high water.

Bradley studied the facility through night vision binoculars. Steam rose from heating vents. Lights burned in multiple windows. Someone was home.

"Battalion, prepare to advance to assault position. Alpha Company takes point. Bravo and Charlie provide flanking support." He checked his weapon one final time. "Remember, we're here to secure classified technology. Expect resistance."

The paratroopers formed into assault formation. Their breath formed clouds that dispersed in bitter wind. A line of white-clad soldiers moving across frozen ground toward whatever waited in the compound below.

Inside the data center control room, Voss's fingers moved across the targeting interface. Lines of code scrolled past as she rerouted the Bushmaster protocols. Each cannon's firing solution shifted from perimeter defense to internal coordinates.

Morrison's radio crackled. Lieutenant Colonel Bradley's voice cut through static.

"All Thunder elements, this is Thunder Six. Move to assault positions. Hold for my command."

Morrison keyed his response. "Thunder Six, this is Thunder One-Six. Copy. Moving to position."

He switched to his company frequency. "All Thunder One elements, advance to assault positions. Hold at the tree line."

Across the valley, white-clad paratroopers emerged from concealment. They moved through falling snow and tree branches. Weapons ready. Breath forming clouds in the bitter air.

Culper studied the perimeter monitors. White shapes moved against dark ground. Dozens of them.

"We've got company," he said.

"How many?" Voss asked without looking up.

"Lots."

On screen, paratroopers advanced in tactical formation. Their weapons raised. Ready.

"Almost there," Voss said.

The system accepted her modifications. Eight red dots appeared on the facility schematic. Each Bushmaster now aimed at the building's structural supports and key operational components.

The paratroopers reached their hold positions and stopped. They took cover behind trees and boulders. Waiting.

"They're in their assault positions," Culper reported. "Holding."

"Done." She stepped back from the terminal. "When you execute, they'll all fire simultaneously. The building won't survive and neither will Fulcrum."

Frank moved to the console. His finger hovered over the execute button.

"Time to go," said Culper as he helped Voss gather her laptop. "I knew you were crazy brave, Kane. But this is borderline sanity."

Frank grunted as they reached the door. Voss turned back.

"Frank—"

"Go," said Frank without making eye contact.

She nodded once. Disappeared into the corridor with Culper.

Frank listened to their footsteps fade.

Outside, three hundred soldiers waited in assault positions. Ready to advance on command.

Watching from the tree line, Sergeant Rodriguez adjusted his night vision as two figures emerged from the building. A woman and a man moving quickly across the compound toward the gate.

"Thunder Six, this is Thunder Two-One Alpha. I have movement at the main building. Two civilians heading for the perimeter gate."

"Description, Thunder Two-One Alpha?" said Morrison over the radio.

"One unarmed civilian and one armed combatant." Rodriguez waited for orders. "Should we engage, Thunder Six?"

Morrison considered. Shooting them would reveal his position. Compromise the element of surprise.

"Negative, Thunder Two-One Alpha. Let them go. Maintain observation."

Voss and Culper ran down the access road and reached the pickup where the cat was waiting inside. The engine ran smooth despite the cold. Culper threw it in gear and turned toward the compound.

"What are you doing?" Voss asked.

"Getting Frank."

Bradley's voice crackled over the radio. "All Thunder elements, this is Thunder Six. Execute. Execute. Execute."

Morrison keyed his response. "All Thunder One elements, advance. Breach and clear."

The paratroopers rose from cover. Advanced toward the compound with renewed purpose.

Inside the control room, Frank looked at the monitors showing American cities returning to normal. Philadelphia's streets clearing. Portland's fires dying. People helping strangers.

He pressed execute.

The targeting systems calculated firing solutions. Eight cannons swiveling inward. Frank ran.

The corridor stretched ahead. Emergency lighting cast everything in red. His boots echoed off polished floors as alarms began to wail.

Red lights flashed throughout the compound. Klaxons sounded across the valley. The Bushmasters whined to life on their mountings.

As he watched the Bushmasters take aim on the building, Morrison raised his fist. "All units hold." The advancing soldiers stopped. "What the hell?"

The first Bushmaster fired. The building shuddered as the 40mm shell pierced the outer concrete wall and entered the building. Thick dust exploded from the impact site. A second cannon erupted. Then a third. Each cannon firing 120 high explosive rounds per minute. After only ten seconds, the exterior of the building resembled a block of Swiss cheese.

The paratroopers hit the ground and took cover wherever they could from flying debris.

Frank burst through the main entrance as the building began to collapse. Chunks of concrete rained down. Twisted steel shrieked as supports failed.

Culper drove hard through the snow toward the perimeter wall. The pickup's headlights cut through falling debris and smoke.

The advancing paratroopers dove for cover as chunks of concrete flew across the compound. The building folded inward. A controlled demolition executed by its own defenses.

The fuel depot caught fire. Orange flame bloomed against black sky. Heat rolled across frozen ground.

Frank ran through the perimeter front gate as the pickup appeared through smoke and flame. Culper whipped the truck around as he hit the brakes. Frank leaped into the truck's bed. Culper floored it. They truck raced down the access road away from the mayhem. They disappeared into the darkness beyond the compound's lights and explosions.

A forty-millimeter shell punched through the server room wall and detonated its high explosive warhead. Racks of hard drives exploded in showers of sparks and twisted metal. Data storage units that had housed Fulcrum's behavioral algorithms disintegrated into smoking fragments.

Another round struck deeper. Fiber optic cables snapped like nerves severed from a brain. Miles of wiring melted into rivers of plastic that dripped from sagging ceiling tiles. The air filled with toxic smoke from burning electronics.

Still another shell found the main power distribution center. Electrical conduits erupted. Transformers exploded in cascades of sparks. Emergency lighting failed. The building's nervous system died in seconds.

A round tore through the processing center. Quantum computers worth hundreds of millions became twisted sculptures of aluminum and silicon. Cooling systems ruptured. Liquid nitrogen vented in ghostly clouds that mixed with flame and smoke.

The shells kept coming. Each impact destroyed months of classified research. Server farms collapsed into burning piles of metal and melted components. Backup drives warped from heat until their magnetic surfaces bubbled and ran like black blood across concrete floors.

Finally, the Bushmasters ran out of ammunition and returned their barrels to a neutral position. Spent brass shell casings melted into the snow. They had done enough damage for the day.

Steel support beams glowed orange. Twisted under thermal stress. The building's skeleton began to fail as temperatures reached furnace levels. The final collapse was stupendous sending a giant orange column of sparks into the dark sky.

Morrison stared at the burning ruins. What had been a sophisticated data center was now a crater filled with twisted steel and melting electronics. Thousands of terabytes of information reduced to ash and vapor.

Lieutenant Colonel Bradley lowered his binoculars. He watched flames consume what remained of the facility. Smoke rose in black columns against the Arctic sky. Nothing salvageable remained of whatever they'd been sent to secure.

"Ah, shit."

America's most dangerous weapon burned to ash in the Arctic wind.

Kane Mansion

Frank, wounds bandaged, stood beside his brother, Richard Kane, as a truck rumbled up the circular drive. The trailer behind it carried what had once been the Imperial. Now it resembled a cube of twisted chrome and steel.

Richard stared at the wreckage. Paint and metal compressed into geometric impossibility. What had been a classic automobile was now abstract art created by sixty-eight tons of tank.

"You can't be serious," Richard said.

Frank grunted.

Grace appeared from around the corner of the mansion. Fifteen now. Taller than Frank remembered. She took one look at the compressed metal and whistled.

"Uncle Frank, did you park it wrong?"

Frank's mouth twitched. Almost a smile.

"This was your Imperial?" Richard said. "The one I restored for you. The car I brought back to life."

Grace circled the trailer. "It looks like a really expensive paperweight now."

"Grace," Richard warned.

"What? I'm just saying." She looked at Frank. "What happened?"

"Tank."

"A tank ran over your car?" Grace's eyes lit up. "That's actually kind of awesome. Was it like in the movies? Did it explode?"

Richard shook his head. "Your uncle nearly died."

Grace's expression sobered. She studied Frank's face. The new scars mixing with old ones.

"But you're okay?"

Frank nodded.

"Then I guess Dad had better build you a better one," she said. "Maybe tank-proof this time."

Stanford University

Voss walked into a packed auditorium. Moving to the podium, she adjusted the microphone and looked out at two hundred students filling the stadium-style seating.

"Artificial intelligence," she began. "What comes to mind when you hear those words?"

Hands shot up. "Robots." "Computers that think." "Job replacement."

She walked to the whiteboard. Drew a simple diagram. A curtain. A small figure behind it. Levers and controls.

"Remember the Wizard of Oz? The great and powerful wizard was just a man behind a curtain pulling levers."

The students leaned forward.

"AI is the same. Behind every algorithm is a human being making choices. Deciding what to optimize for. What to prioritize. What to ignore." She tapped the diagram. "The danger isn't the machine. It's the person behind the curtain."

A student raised her hand. "But what if the AI makes its own decisions?"

Voss paused. She saw burning cities. Algorithms rewriting themselves. Fulcrum evolving beyond control.

"That's when you realize," she said quietly, "the wizard has left the building. And the curtain is still moving."

Author's Biography

Born in 1958, David grew up on a horse ranch in Northern California, breeding and training appaloosas. He has had all his toes broken at least once and survived numerous falls and kicks from ornery colts and fillies. David started writing professionally as a copywriter in his early 20's. At thirty-two, he packed up his family and moved to Malibu, California, to live his dream of writing and directing motion pictures. He has four motion picture screenwriting credits and two directing credits. His movies have been viewed by over fifty million movie-goers worldwide and won a multitude of awards, including the Malibu, Palm Springs, and San Jose Film Festivals. In addition to his twenty-four screenplays, he has written twenty-nine novels. He developed his simplistic writing style after rereading his two favorite books, Ernest Hemingway's *The Old Man and the Sea* and Cormac McCarthy's *No Country For Old Men*. An avid student of world culture, David lived as an expat in both Thailand and Mexico. At fifty-six, he sold all his possessions and became a nomad for four years. He circumnavigated the globe three times and visited fifty-six countries. Known for his detailed descriptions, his stories often include actual experiences and characters from his journeys.

www.ingramcontent.com/pod-product-compliance
Lightning Source LLC
Chambersburg PA
CBHW021032310726
48969CB00006B/1629